A Trunk, a Canoe, and all the Barbecue

A JESS AND LIBBY PARANORMAL COZY MYSTERY

AFTERLIFE ISSUES
BOOK TWO

A.W. HARTOIN

A Trunk, a Canoe, and all the Barbecue

Afterlife Issues Book Two

Copyright © A.W. Hartoin, 2023

Cover designed by MiblArt

This book is a work of fiction. Names, characters, places and incidents either are products of the author's imagination or are used fictitiously. Any resemblance to actual events or locales or persons, living or dead, is entirely coincidental.

All rights reserved. Except as permitted under the U.S. Copyright Act of 1976, no part of this publication may be reproduced, distributed or transmitted in any form or by any means, or stored in a database or retrieval system, without the prior written permission of the publisher.

Also by A.W. Hartoin

Afterlife Issues

Dead Companions (Afterlife Issues Book One)

A Trunk, a Canoe, and all the Barbecue (Afterlife Issues Book Two)

Old Friends and Fedoras (Afterlife Issues Book Three) coming soon

Mercy Watts Mysteries

<u>Novels</u>

A Good Man Gone (Mercy Watts Mysteries Book One)

Diver Down (A Mercy Watts Mystery Book Two)

Double Black Diamond (Mercy Watts Mysteries Book Three)

Drop Dead Red (Mercy Watts Mysteries Book Four)

In the Worst Way (Mercy Watts Mysteries Book Five)

The Wife of Riley (Mercy Watts Mysteries Book Six)

My Bad Grandad (Mercy Watts Mysteries Book Seven)

Brain Trust (Mercy Watts Mysteries Book Eight)

Down and Dirty (Mercy Watts Mysteries Book Nine)

Small Time Crime (Mercy Watts Mysteries Book Ten)

Bottle Blonde (Mercy Watts Mysteries Book Eleven)

Mean Evergreen (Mercy Watts Mysteries Book Twelve)

Silver Bells at Hotel Hell (Mercy Watts Mysteries Book Thirteen)

<u>Short stories</u>

Coke with a Twist

Touch and Go

Nowhere Fast

Dry Spell

A Sin and a Shame

Stella Bled Historical Thrillers

The Paris Package (Stella Bled Book One)

Strangers in Venice (Stella Bled Book Two)

One Child in Berlin (Stella Bled Book Three)

Dark Victory (Stella Bled Book Four)

A Quiet Little Place on Rue de Lille (Stella Bled Book Five)

Her London Season (Stella Bled Book Six)

Paranormal

It Started with a Whisper

Young Adult fantasy

Flare-up (Away From Whipplethorn Short)

A Fairy's Guide To Disaster (Away From Whipplethorn Book One)

Fierce Creatures (Away From Whipplethorn Book Two)

A Monster's Paradise (Away From Whipplethorn Book Three)

A Wicked Chill (Away From Whipplethorn Book Four)

To the Eternal (Away From Whipplethorn Book Five)

For Maddie
The best daughter and cover consultant

Chapter One

Glum ghosts are the worst. Okay, maybe not the worst in the grand scheme of things. Compared to floods, famine, and various catastrophes, living with a grieving ghost isn't so bad, but for me, in my little corner of the world, #8 Elizabeth Street in St. Sebastian, it was the worst.

I sat at my new desk in my office, working away on my laptop and trying to ignore Leo Pereyra's presence. He tried to be discreet, I'll give him that, but I can always tell. First of all, I was home alone, in a manner of speaking, and our cat, Poptart, wasn't with me. He was a social cat who would normally be curled up in the cushy bed I'd put on the desk for him, but he wasn't.

And then there was the smell. When Leo's upset, he puts off the odor of cigarettes. I have a sensitive sense of smell, and it was there in my office. Just a whiff. Try as he might, Leo couldn't control the smell of his distress.

Smells bother me. I needed to concentrate. I'd landed a temporary job as a claims adjuster at Eric Otto's company, and I needed it. We needed it. My best friend Jess's husband, Hal, died almost four months ago, and his brother held up Hal's insurance money for self-serving reasons and my divorce was going nowhere, so my settlement would not come in anytime soon. If I could prove myself invaluable, maybe, just maybe, Eric would keep me on, but I just couldn't focus. The claim in front of me was important. The report, the numbers, and the people were important. They needed me to be accurate and fair.

I stopped typing. "Can't you just go visit Tank, Eric, or Darren?"

Silence, but the cigarette smell got just a tad stronger.

"Seriously. You're distracting me. The Clancy family needs this money, like yesterday."

Nothing.

"Their house burned down. They lost everything."

More cigarettes.

I closed my laptop and put my head down on it. "Please, Leo."

"I'm not doing anything," he said.

"You're here," I said.

"Oh." His voice reeked of sadness and regret.

"It's not *you* exactly."

"Sounds like it is," said Leo. "You don't want me around anymore."

I sat up and turned around. "You may as well be visible. You're obviously here."

There was a pop and Leo Pereyra, the handsomest man not alive, stood in the far corner of my office. He wore his funeral attire from when he was a living mortician, a black suit, white shirt, and black tie. Since he'd found out that his stepson, Patrick, murdered him, he wore it all the time. That was what he'd been wearing when he died, but ghosts weren't trapped in the place, clothes, or condition that they died in. He could wear anything that he'd worn in life, from

Halloween costumes to swim trunks, anything. Before he'd found out, Leo had worn a lot of different things. My favorite was what he called his tutoring outfit, a grandpa sweater, jeans, and a pair of horn-rimmed glasses. I didn't mind the mortician getup. It was his job, and he was darn good at it, but now he wore it in grief, and that wasn't so great.

"I don't understand how I'm bothering you," he said. "I'm not even close."

"It's the cigarettes," I said.

His broad shoulders slumped. "I only ever smoked when I was stressed or upset. I wish I'd never taken it up."

That makes two of us.

"Nobody else minds," I said.

"Mariah does," he said, with sadness decorating his features.

"She's the only one. Go see Jess at Exclusive Escapes."

"She's busy."

I'm busy.

"You could chat with the fur trappers. They love you," I said.

Leo grimaced, and I didn't blame him. Exclusive Escapes, better known around St. Seb as the Horny Hotel, where Jess taught art classes, was a boutique hotel with a well-heeled clientele and a set of unusual residents that we'd met just before Halloween when we were investigating Leo's death.

Wheeler, Johnny, Jedidiah, and Boy were four fur trappers that had died about two hundred years ago and taken up residence on the hotel grounds long before it was a hotel. They were a pleasant bunch for the most part, but they smelled awful and they liked it. Their favorite thing, other than following around unsuspecting women hoping to get an eyeful, was cooking opossum over a spit. The smell was beyond description. Just the thought made my eyes water. The trappers themselves stank to high heaven, having believed in life that bathing was bad for you.

"Maybe you could talk them into being less smelly?" I asked. "Consider it a public service."

"They love their smell," said Leo. "They think stinking means you're a man. Men smell."

"You don't smell," I said.

Leo eyed me and crossed his arms.

"I mean, you personally. The cigarettes are different from body odor."

"That's what I'm saying. They like body odor."

"Haven't they noticed you don't stink?"

He ran a hand through his thick curly hair and said, "They have, and they don't consider me a man in the strictest sense."

"Oh, come on," I said. "They like you."

"Because I'll talk to them," said Leo.

"It's nice to be acknowledged. You should go see them. Talk them into being ten years old. They couldn't have smelled so bad at that age."

"You're just trying to get rid of me."

Sadly, yes.

"I'm supposed to get this done before my appointment with Betsy's friend," I said. "It's due today."

Leo walked over and said, "I can help."

"With claims adjusting? I don't think so."

"No. With the librarian's friend." He showed me a hint of his old self, a glint in his dark eyes. "I've helped before."

I couldn't deny that. Jess and I had a side hustle going. It happened without us even trying. We could see ghosts with surprising frequency. Seeing individual ghosts in St. Seb isn't all that rare, but being able to see lots of them easily is, so we'd gotten hired to talk to them. Sometimes just to find out information or sometimes to talk them into buzzing off and stop pestering the occupants of their former homes. Leo was great with that. It turns out a lot of ghosts don't realize what they do is distressing, and once we explain it to them, they knock it off and everyone's happy, especially our bank accounts.

"I could use the help," I said. "Definitely, but I have to get this done first."

"You want me to go?" Leo looked at the floor.

"Why do you want to stay?" I opened my laptop. "I'm working. This cannot be entertaining."

"I like you," he said.

I'm a big jerk.

"I like you, too, but you're sad, and the cigarettes just make things hard," I said.

"I can't help it."

"What can we do?" I asked. "How do we help?"

An armchair with thick padding and bright flower-patterned fabric appeared behind Leo, and I knew I was done for. That was Leo's wife's chair, and he loved to sit in it. Once he did, it was over. He wasn't moving.

"Grief takes time," he said, settling in for the long haul. "I can't just get over what happened. I wish I could."

"Won't you at least tell me what he said?" I asked.

Leo shook his head, as I knew he would. When Leo found out his stepson had killed him, he'd summoned him. I guess ghosts can do that if they really try, and Leo pounced on Patrick. We hadn't seen Patrick since. He'd died three years after he killed Leo, and we'd discovered him at the Horny Hotel. Jess kept an eye out and so did the trappers, but Patrick hadn't returned. I kinda hoped he'd moved on to the bad place, but I knew I couldn't say that to Leo.

"Okay. Fine." I turned back to my laptop and started working. It was like swimming through mud. I'd always hated the smell of cigarettes, and having Leo sitting behind me, however patiently, wasn't helping. Why me? It was always me. Eric could see him. Sylvia could see him, and so could their daughter Samantha. Not to mention Jess and her daughter Mariah, and my boys, Max and Henri. Tank Tancredi, the editor of the Sentinel, finally saw Leo, and they'd been friends in life, but I was the one Leo hung out with. He told Jess that I was soothing. I couldn't see how. I was currently gritting my teeth so hard, I'd be surprised if I wasn't damaging the enamel.

"You made a mistake," said Leo.

"Huh?"

"You transposed three and five."

I looked, and he was right. I fixed the error and glanced back. "Thanks."

He gave me a wan smile. "I'm good at math."

"Yes, you are." I turned back and tried to focus as the doorbell rang.

"Is that him?" Leo asked.

"If it is, he's early."

"I'll get it." There was a pop and Leo was gone.

I rolled my eyes. Sometimes our ghost forgot his own ghostly guidelines. To be seen, ghosts have to want to be seen by an individual, but that's not enough. The individual has to want to see them and, this is the important bit, believe in ghosts deep down for real in their very soul. Lots of people think they believe in ghosts, but they don't, not really. So far, out of all the random people who showed up at Number Eight and told me they believe in ghosts, zero had been able to see Leo. He'd wanted them to see him, but no such luck.

I closed my laptop and stood up as Leo popped back in.

"He can't see me," he said with a furrowed brow. "What do you think I'm doing wrong?"

"Nothing."

The doorbell rang again.

"I must be doing something wrong," said Leo. "He has a ghost. He must believe in them."

I left the office and worked my way through our enormous

Victorian that had once housed the Otto Funeral Home. That fact and Leo haunting it was the reason Jess and I could buy it dirt cheap and restart our lives post death and divorce. The ghost that made it possible walked right with me, behaving as though he could bump into walls or me, although he couldn't, and it made me smile. I had the feeling he did that for our benefit because Leo looked solid. He wasn't faded or indistinct. Having a solid person walk through walls is disconcerting. The trappers did it, and I couldn't get used to it.

The doorbell rang a third time just as I reached the foyer. Leo stepped to the side as I swung open one of the oak doors to face a figure that filled the entire space of the doorway. I was nose to pecs. I'm a normal height of five six, and that had never happened before.

I looked up at a man that was absolutely enormous. He was the size and shape of a refrigerator with a head.

"Libby?" he asked with a strong accent I couldn't place.

"Um... yes," I said.

"Hello. I'm Miroslav Blazevic. We have an appointment." The man stuck out a hand that resembled a catcher's mitt, and my hand was completely engulfed.

"You're Betsy's friend?" I asked when he released my hand from his viselike grip.

He chuckled. "Yes. You are surprised?"

I couldn't think of a polite way to sell my reaction, so I went with the truth. "Very. She didn't tell me anything other than the time, and I thought your name was Mika."

"That is what my friends call me," he said. "I hope to count you in that number."

I stepped back and welcomed him into the house, marveling at how thick his chest was. We're talking thick, over a foot, well over a foot. I didn't know they made real people like that. He looked like a character from a superhero movie with his well-groomed beard and long hair pulled back into a stubby ponytail. His eyes sparkled under bushy brows, and his smile was wide and easy.

"I hope so too," I said. "Do you mind if we talk in the kitchen? I have to baste the turkey."

"Of course." He sniffed. "Oh, now I smell it."

"It's only been in the oven for an hour and a half." I led the way past the ornate, curved staircase into the depths of the house, through the archway into our kitchen. To tell the truth, even though it was our kitchen now, I really thought of it as Leo's kitchen. He designed it and he was the master there, teaching the kids how to make pizza and applesauce while tutoring them in math and physics. Even in his grief over Patrick's betrayal, he never stopped helping the kids.

Leo went to stand next to the stove, and I gestured to a stool at the island, although I questioned whether a stool like that could hold Miroslav Blazevic. "Please have a seat."

"It's early for Thanksgiving turkey, is it not?" he asked.

"Well, Mr. Blazevic, my friend Jess is a planner. This oven is new to us, so we had to do a practice turkey to see how it works."

"Please call me Mika," he said. "I think Jess is a wise woman."

"She is," I said. "But that's a lot of turkey to have within two weeks."

I opened one of the oven doors and basted the twenty-three-pound turkey Jess insisted we buy because bigger is better in her book.

"It smells good already," said Mika.

I closed the door and smiled. "It will be great. It's my mom's recipe, perfected over the course of forty Thanksgivings."

"Will you share the recipe?"

"Of course," I said. "Can I get you something to drink?

I'm afraid all I have is coffee, tea, and water. My boys keep our tank continually empty around here."

"Water without ice would be nice," he said.

I gave him a glass and made myself a cup of green tea before sitting down on a stool next to him. "I have to ask. How do you know Betsy?"

"I'm in her knitting group at the library." He grinned at me and I grinned back after I glanced at his meaty fingers.

"Is knitting a challenge?" I asked.

"Yes, but I have mastered it. Knitting is good for the stress, and it keeps the fingers nimble. I have arthritis from a young age and it helps."

"I didn't know that. I'll have to tell my mom."

"Does she live with you?" Mika asked.

"Not yet, but we're hoping to talk her into it." I stirred my tea and asked, "So you've got a ghost problem?"

"Yes," he said, and two spots of color appeared on his high cheekbones.

Leo walked around the island and put his hand on his chest. "He's nervous about people thinking he's crazy."

I nodded and sipped my tea. "Mika, whatever you say is between us. I won't run around town and tell people about your private business."

He heaved a sigh and took a drink of water. "This is good. I am a physical therapist, and no one wants a medical practitioner that is crazy."

"I don't think you're crazy," I said. "I assume Betsy told you about us and this house."

"And Leo Pereyra," he said. "Do you really see him?"

I told him I did, but I didn't mention that Leo happened to be standing right behind him.

"Betsy said you see a lot of ghosts," said Mika.

"I'm not sure what a lot is, but we've seen a few."

He glanced around and searched for his next words. It was

hard. I understood. Jess and I lived in a world where the extraordinary was ordinary. Most people weren't quite ready for that reality, so I waited until he was ready.

"What are they like?" Mika asked.

"The ghosts? They vary, but I'd say overall they're normal people."

He blinked at me. "Normal people?"

"I mean, they're dead people, but they're normal, or they were when they were alive. We're not talking about supervillains or nasty characters, for the most part."

Mika smiled and took another drink. "That's good to hear."

I frowned. "You seem relieved. Don't you know who you're dealing with?"

"That's just the thing, Libby," he said. "We don't."

The Blazevic family had a problem we'd yet to encounter. Mika was married and had two young children. They'd moved into their house on Third Street a little over two years ago with no problems. He was very clear on that. No issues whatsoever until four months ago, when his kids started mentioning a person in the house. It started with his older child, his son Marko, who was eight years old. Marko started telling them about a lady who sat with him at night by his bed. The child didn't seem concerned. The lady was calm and comforting. Mika's wife, Sandra, had had imaginary friends when she was young, so that's what they thought it was. But then their four-year-old daughter, Jelena, said she saw the lady, too, and claimed she'd seen her first by her bed. The children argued about that to their parents' astonishment.

After some questioning, the kids convinced Mika and Sandra that they weren't talking about an imaginary friend. They were seeing an elderly woman wearing a sweater, skirt, and a kerchief on her head. Sometimes she was wearing different clothes, but the kids were certain it was one person.

"And you haven't seen her?" I asked.

He shook his massive head. "No, and Sandra hasn't either."

"What does the woman do?"

"What do you mean?"

"Well, the dead can do things like move furniture and turn off lights," I said. "Those are common complaints. The dead don't like wasting electricity."

Mika stared at me. His mouth opened and shut, but he said nothing.

"I'm serious. They have opinions. We had a case where a ghost kept moving the living room furniture. She wasn't trying to scare anyone. She just didn't like the arrangement."

"She didn't like the arrangement," he whispered.

"Yep. And between you and me, her arrangement made more sense for the flow through the room," I said.

"So what happened? What did you do?"

"We discussed the family's concerns, and we came up with a compromise. The family would move some of the furniture to where she wanted it and she agreed to leave the rest alone and go visit her sister more often."

"That worked?" Mika asked.

"It did. She hasn't moved anything since, but she turns off the lights when they leave the room. We couldn't stop her from doing that, but the dad was all for the energy savings, so we're all happy. The family's getting used to it."

"That is remarkable."

"All in a day's work. So what does she do?"

"Nothing."

"Nothing?"

"Nothing."

I sipped my tea and tried to think of a diplomatic way to ask why he was there. "I'm not sure what the problem is, then."

"The children can see her," he said. "A lot. All over the house and outside sometimes."

"But she's not doing anything to them?" I asked.

"No."

"Does she scare them?"

"Not at first, but she is upsetting them now." Mika gripped his glass so tightly, I feared it would shatter.

"What does she do? Startle them? Please tell me she doesn't show herself as dead," I said with a grimace.

"No, but she's always there. At first, she wasn't, and now the children say she's always talking to them. She won't stop, and she's crying a lot."

That's not good.

"What is she saying?"

"They don't understand her. She doesn't speak English or Croatian. Those are the languages they know."

"That's a new one," I said. "What else?"

Mika glanced around and said, "She's in the bathroom a lot."

"Dead?"

"What?" he asked in horror.

"Sorry. I meant, does it look like she died in the bathroom?"

"No, no. She's in there doing bathroom things."

I raised a brow, and Mika reluctantly told me that their ghost liked to take baths. The kids kept going in the bathroom to find a naked elderly woman in there. Sometimes she was sitting on the toilet and it smelled.

"That is a problem," I said.

"Did you know ghosts can make smells?"

"I did." I glanced at Leo, who looked embarrassed. "It's not uncommon."

Mika shook his head. "I don't know what to do. Sandra

was okay at first. Now she's freaking out, and she wants to move. We can't afford to move."

"I understand completely," I said. "Have you talked to your realtor?"

He nodded. "It's Shelly Kaplan, and I called her. She said no one died there, but that lady must've died there. Why else would she be there?"

I explained that ghosts didn't have to haunt the places where they died. Sometimes they did, but it wasn't required by any means. I thought it would comfort him, but it didn't. If anything, he was more upset.

"You mean ghosts can go anywhere and haunt anyone?"

Cat out of bag.

"Well, yes, but they don't, as a general rule. They usually haunt people and places they love. If she's in your house, she probably loves your house."

"Why is she talking to my kids? They say she's upset."

"Do they think she's trying to get them out of the house? Like she doesn't like them?"

"Oh, no. They don't think that at all. Marko says she's trying to tell him something important, but he can't understand her. The more she tries, the more upset she gets."

"So she wants to be heard. She has a story to tell." I looked at Leo and he nodded. "When do you want us to start?"

"Today. Immediately," said Mika. "We can't go on like this."

"Let me get you our contract so you can check out our terms," I said.

Mika placed his big hand over mine. "Whatever the terms are, I accept them."

Chapter Two

The Blazevic home sat back off Third Street under a pair of massive oak trees that were probably planted at the time they built the house in the 1930s. I wouldn't exactly call it a Craftsman house, but that is what Mika called it. I think of Craftsman as having more wood. The Blazevic house was brick with very little wood, but it did have a wide front porch with thick columns and a pretty front door painted sage green.

I walked up the stairs past a pair of pumpkins that were clearly carved by the kids and not the parents. They were adorably lopsided, and it wasn't clear what they were supposed to be, possibly a cat and Frankenstein.

"When is Jess getting here?"

I jumped and turned around. "Don't do that."

Leo stood on the right side of the porch next to some Thanksgiving decor that was ready to be put up and the porch swing that swayed gently on its silver chains. "You knew I was coming."

"Why do you always appear behind me?" I asked.

"I don't plan it," he said. "It's just the way it happens."

"If you say so."

"I do. Where's Jess?"

I checked my phone. "On her way."

Two lines formed between Leo's eyes.

"Don't worry. I'm early," I said.

A brief smile flashed on his lips. "And you thought I couldn't help with insurance stuff."

"Alright, fine. But don't tell Eric. He's paying me to do the work, not you."

Leo crossed his heart. "You did all the work. I'm just faster with the math."

"You definitely are."

Leo turned around as a car drove into the driveway next to the house and parked under a carport. "Is that Mika's wife?"

"I assume so," I said.

"She's upset."

"Yeah, I got that." I only got a glimpse of Sandra Blazevic's face when she turned in, but a glimpse was all it took. Her face was pinched and her eyes swollen. I checked my phone again. Mika was coming after his last patient, but he warned me it might run long. The patient was chatty, and it was hard to get away. The look on his wife's face made me hope today was a non-chatty day.

Sandra Blazevic walked around her house and came up the stairs with her hands shoved deep in her pockets. Her eyes were even more swollen than I thought now that I'd seen her in the light. Her nose was red, and her blond hair hung in silky curtains around her face.

"Hi," I said. "I'm Libby Forest. Mika told you I was coming, right?"

She nodded.

"Are you not on board? Because if you're not, I can leave. Nobody will be upset. It's fine."

"Mika will be upset," she said in a musical voice that sounded younger than her years. "He thinks he can fix it."

"Maybe he can," I said.

"We have to get out of here," she said. "I hate it, but we have to go."

"What do you think is happening?"

She pulled out a key and said, "I don't know, but if we don't get away quick, it's going to get worse."

She opened the door for me and I went in, followed by Leo. It was a pretty little living room with gleaming hardwood floors and reproduction furniture from the Craftsman era.

"Have a seat," she said. "Can I get you anything?"

"I'm good. Thanks."

"Can I take your coat?"

I unwound my scarf and took off my coat and hat. The house was six blocks from Number Eight, and I didn't have a car that day. The boys took it to school, and Jess had hers.

"Mrs. Blazevic, are you sure you're okay with this?" I asked as she flipped on the gas fireplace and rubbed her hands.

"Please call me Sandra."

"Okay, Sandra. Are you okay?"

"No. We're being haunted by some old witch from the old country and I'm supposed to be calm about it. I'm not."

"What old country are you talking about?" I asked.

"Croatia. Where else?"

"I thought your children speak Croatian."

"They do, but there are different dialects. Even Mika has a hard time understanding the other ones."

"You don't speak Croatian, then."

"No. I met Mika in high school when he was an exchange student." Sandra looked up and smiled for the first time. "We've been together ever since."

"A real love story."

She nodded. "We never fight. Never. But now we are. He

thinks we can stay here, but I listened to his grandmother's stories. I know what can happen."

"What can happen?"

"Spirits can imprint on children and haunt them. That's what she told me about a childhood friend that was haunted by a night hag and went crazy. He killed himself when he was a teenager. We have to get the children away from here."

I glanced past her to Leo, who was horrified, and shrugged. No help there.

"What's a night hag?" I asked.

"It's kind of like a witch. Sometimes called a Mora."

"And they haunt children?"

"That's what she said." Sandra looked around. "Do you see her? Mika says you can see ghosts."

But not witches or hags.

"I don't see anything," I said.

"I knew you wouldn't. We have to move."

"So you think it's the house?"

Sandra nodded.

"I don't mean to be difficult, but why would a Croatian hag suddenly start haunting you?" I asked.

"Well, maybe she's not Croatian. I don't know. She doesn't speak English. Who else would haunt us? The last people that lived here are alive, and their last name is Smith. Nobody gets haunted by a Smith."

"She's panicked," said Leo. "Not thinking straight."

"She could be here right now and we'd never know," said Sandra, and a tear slipped down her cheek.

I looked at Leo, and he shrugged.

"Just because we can't see her right now doesn't mean we won't be able to figure it out," I said.

"That realtor lied to us. I know she did," said Sandra. "Mika says no, but I could tell by the way she kept changing the subject when we were asking her questions about the house."

Sounds familiar.

"Shelly is a little cagey," I said.

"Can you talk to her?" Sandra ground a fist into her palm. "Make her tell you the truth."

"I will do my best."

Sandra came over and sat next to me. She was shaking. "This isn't okay. Did Mika tell you that she's naked sometimes? What kind of ghost shows themselves naked to a child?"

I had no answer to that, and Sandra started crying. I put my arm around her and pulled a clean tissue out of my pocket.

"We're going to find out what's going on," I said.

"Marko says she's upset and yells sometimes."

"She's yelling at the children?"

"Just yelling. He says he's not scared of her, but I know he is. He has to be."

"I have to agree."

The door opened and Mika walked in. "Oh, Sandy. What is it?"

"She doesn't see her." Sandra got up and flung herself into Mika's arms. He was so big, he cradled her two feet off the floor.

"You can't see her?" he asked.

"I haven't looked around yet, but I've seen nothing so far."

Mika tilted his head sideways. "Could someone else see her, perhaps?"

He meant Leo. We'd discussed whether our ghost should come over and take a look. Leo agreed to do all he could, but Mika insisted that Sandra not be told about Leo. He didn't think Sandra could handle it and after meeting her; I agreed.

"Who are you talking about?" Sandra asked.

"Jess," I said. "She'll give it a go when she gets here."

"She just pulled up," said Mika.

The doorbell rang, and he opened the door. Smiling, Jess walked in, looking totally different than she had a mere month and a half ago when we bought Number Eight. She'd gained weight, and her blond hair was smooth and shiny again. That's not to say she wasn't still grieving, but she was better, and that was enough for me.

"Hi," she said. "I'm Jess. How are we doing?"

Sandra cried harder and Mika put her down. "How about you go lie down?" he asked his shaking wife.

"No, she might be in there."

Mika looked at me and I stood up. "I'll go look."

"Good idea," said Jess in the voice she used to soothe her students back when she was still teaching art in school. "How about you fill me in and they can go look around?"

Sandra nodded. "I'm sorry I'm such a mess, but last night was rough. Jelena slept with us because that hag was crying in her room again. She was so loud, she woke up Marko too. We were all in bed together, and I'm so tired."

Jess put an arm around Sandra and helped her to the sofa. "I can only imagine how hard that was. Can I get you some tea or something?"

"I'll get it," said Mika. "Libby, will you come with me to the kitchen?"

"Sure." I followed Mika through their dining room into a small but well-designed kitchen with a farmhouse sink and brand-new cabinets and granite countertops. "We just finished the remodel when this happened," he said. "We took out a loan. We can't move, but my wife..."

"I get it. I really do. It was scary when we moved into Number Eight, but we had to stay. We didn't have the money to go anywhere else."

"But it's good?" Mika asked as he put the kettle on and selected a tea for his wife.

I looked past his shoulder at Leo. "It's very good."

"I wish it could be like that. Did he scare the children at first?"

"Leo? No way. He was great from the get-go, but this is different. He understood us. It sounds like this woman doesn't understand the kids."

Mika shook his head. "I don't think she does. You can ask the children, but they won't be home until later. We usually work until five. Would you like some tea?"

"No, thanks. Do you mind if I just take a look around?"

"By yourself?"

"I won't be by myself," I said.

The big man smiled at me. "I keep forgetting. Is he here?"

"He is."

"Why can I not see him?" Mika asked. "I believe."

"It sounds like you were raised to."

He sighed. "Sandra told you about my grandmother."

"She did. Something wrong with that?"

"No. I loved my grandmother. She was a wonderful lady, but her English was not so good. She told Sandra things, and they got confused with the language barrier."

"There's no night hag?"

He chuckled. "We would not have a Mora here in America, and they don't like children. It is men they want."

"What about the friend that killed himself?"

"Now that did happen, but I think it was schizophrenia."

"So you don't really believe in ghosts?"

"I do. Many people in my family have had experiences with our own that have passed on, and I believe them."

"Good to know. So do you think it could be a relative that speaks a different dialect?"

"I tried saying the basic words, but the children said no."

"Back to the drawing board," I said. "Do you mind if I walk around?"

"You're not afraid?"

I thought about my experience at the shoe factory. Getting chased by a factory worker wielding a wrench and running through a ghost with a severed arm had been a terrifying experience, but I was fine.

"This is my job. I'm all good."

"Be my guest." Mika made Sandra her tea, and I wandered around with Leo through the first-floor bedrooms. There were two and a small bathroom. Then I went upstairs to the children's rooms. Mika and Sandra had decorated them beautifully. Marko's room was painted dark blue with a baseball theme. He also had a framed map of Croatia and lots of family photos. There were several old ladies that would've fit the bill for their ghost, but I assumed Mika had already pointed that out to his son.

Then I went into Jelena's room, and she was a fairy princess with a canopy bed and pink netting. She had a playhouse and a trunk filled with toys and dolls. Her walls also had a Croatian map and family photos. Different ones, but I recognized the people.

"What do you think?" I asked Leo.

"I don't see anyone," he said. "Do you smell anything?"

I laughed. "No. Just you."

"Even now? I feel pretty good."

"Pretty good, but still sad," I said.

"Yes. I suppose so."

"Why can't Mika see you?"

Leo looked at me and said, "I guess I don't want him to." Then he walked out the door. I followed him into a guest bedroom that was empty of anything but the furniture.

"This will not be easy," I said.

"It certainly won't," said Leo.

I wanted to ask why he didn't want Mika to see him, but I didn't. He'd tell me when he was ready.

"I guess we get to visit Shelly."

Leo smiled. "She'll be thrilled."

"Hey, Libby," called out Jess.

I went into the hall and looked down the stairs. "Yeah?"

"You see anything?"

"Nope. You?"

Jess pursed her lips.

"I'm coming." I ran down the stairs and found four people in the kitchen. Mika, Sandra, Jess, and a man who was wearing an old-fashioned double-breasted blue jacket with wide lapels. His pants were light blue and his shoes were brown oxfords. He had a fedora tilted low over one eye and was smoking a cigarette. He looked at me, touched the brim of his fedora, and turned around to walk out through the wall.

Not another one.

"So...what's up?" I asked.

"Do you smell...cigarettes?" Sandra asked.

Jess gave me a slight shake of the head.

"It's Jess," I said.

"What?" Jess exclaimed.

"Your students smoke, don't they?"

"Oh, right. That is true."

Mika looked back and forth between us, his eyes sharp. "Did you see anything up there?"

"No, sorry," I said.

"She's there," said Sandra. "Our children aren't crazy."

Jess put an arm around her shoulders. "We believe you. There's no question that your children are telling the truth. We just have to figure out a way to see her ourselves and talk to her."

"Can you? I don't see how," said Sandra.

I smiled at her and said, "Living in St. Sebastian has taught me that a lot of things are possible that shouldn't be. We will figure it out."

"We'll need to talk to the children," said Jess. "If that's okay."

Mika nodded. "Of course. Tomorrow Marko has his soccer practice in the morning, but we will be done at eleven. Can you come then?"

"Sure," said Jess. "I don't think there's anything going on."

"You know what? We should bring Mariah," I said. "Would you mind?"

"Who?" Sandra asked.

"My daughter," said Jess.

"Why?"

"She sees as well, and she's great with the little ones. Mariah might be able to see the woman. Maybe it's a kid thing."

Mika took Sandra's hand. "I did not think of this. Maybe only children can see her."

"Good idea," said Jess. "Mariah is great with kids, but the boys are great fun. Your son would love them."

"Let's stick with Mariah. We need calm," I said.

"She...won't be afraid?" Sandra asked.

"Not at all. She's used to it," Jess said.

Sandra glanced up at Mika and then asked, "What has it done to her?"

"What has seeing ghosts done?"

She nodded.

"It's helped her." Jess gave her a squeeze. "And it's helped us all. Seeing Leo Pereyra is the best thing that could've happened. Honestly."

Sandra got tearful again, and we said we had to go see Shelly, the realtor. Mika sat his wife down in the living room and put a blanket over her knees before following us out of the house.

"What happened?" he asked as we stopped next to Jess's

Volvo. "What did she do?"

"It wasn't a she," said Jess.

"What?"

Jess explained that while they were standing in the kitchen talking turkey (literally), a man walked through the wall. He said nothing, observed them closely, and lit a cigarette.

For the first time, Mika looked rattled. "Are you serious? There is another one?"

"Yes," I said. "I saw him too, but he wasn't threatening."

I glanced at Leo, who shook his head.

"He just acknowledged me seeing him and left."

"I don't understand what is happening," said Mika. "How can more of them just show up?"

"They can move around at will," said Jess. "They're not tethered to a particular spot."

"So we could get dozens." Mika looked at the heavens and said something in Croatian. I interpreted it as a plea for help.

"I doubt that will happen," I said.

"But you don't know for sure?"

Jess and I looked at each other. We didn't, of course. We were new to the whole ghost thing, and their motivations were as individual as any live human's were.

"First thing is to hit up Shelly for what she knows," I said.

"She won't tell you anything," he said.

"Sandra thinks she lied to you about the house," I said.

He nodded. "That we agree on. She did not tell the truth, but we had no problems until four months ago."

"Nothing happened before that? Nothing?" Jess asked.

The big man thought it over. "No, I can think of nothing."

I patted his meaty forearm. "We will figure it out."

"I hope so." He glanced at his house. "Sandra is getting close to the edge."

So are you.

Chapter Three

Jess drove us out of the old section of town to a strip mall filled with various buffet restaurants and Shelly Kaplan's office.

I turned in my seat and asked Leo, who sat quietly in the back, "So you didn't see that guy?"

"No," he said.

"Did you want to see him?"

"Certainly."

Jess put on her blinker and said, "I wonder why he wanted us to see him and not you?"

"Haven't you noticed that we prefer women?" Leo said.

"You mean ghosts like women better than men?" I asked. "Why?"

"I don't know. But throughout history, women tend to see more ghosts than men."

"Because we believe more readily?" Jess asked.

"Possibly, but I think it's because we want you to see us," said Leo.

"Is that why you didn't let Mika see you?" I asked.

Leo looked out the window. "I thought I wanted him to

see me, but I guess maybe I don't want to be seen by anyone right now."

I turned back around as Jess parked, and we shared a glance. We were obviously not in the anyone category. It was kind of nice to hear, but sad as well. Leo was isolating himself without meaning to. Something that he didn't do in life, as far as I knew.

"I hope Shelly's in," said Jess.

I grinned. "She's going to wish she wasn't pretty soon."

"What's your plan?"

"Not sure yet, but she is going to tell us."

We got out and went in the small real estate office. Shelly and her partner Don were both at their desks and looked up as the bell over the door jangled. Don smiled a welcoming smile. Shelly did not.

"Ladies, welcome to St. Sebastian Realty. How can I help you today?" Don asked.

"Actually, we're Jess and Libby. Owners of Number Eight," I said.

"I know," he said. "I can't tell you how happy we were when you bought that house. Do you love it? All reports say you do."

"We do love it," said Jess. "We're actually here to talk to Shelly about something else."

I looked over and saw Shelly sliding out of her chair and trying to sneak into the back.

"Give it up, Shelly," I said.

"Oh, hi, Libby," she said. "How are you today?"

Don gave her an odd look as she kept edging toward the back. "Where are you going?"

"I'm going to that showing on Huckleberry," said Shelly.

Don stood up. "That's my showing. You need to talk to our best customers."

Shelly looked like she'd rather stick a fork in her eye, but she sat down, wrapping her arms around her waist. Don gathered up some papers and put them in his briefcase.

"Well, I'll be off. Call me if you need anything, Shelly," said Don.

Shelly nodded, and he left with a worried look. Once he'd cleared the parking lot, Jess turned the Open sign to Closed and turned the key in the door.

"Hey," said Shelly. "What are you doing?"

"We don't want to be interrupted," said Jess.

"I do. My business is all about people stopping in."

"Give me a break," I said, sitting down opposite her. "It's all internet now."

"We get walk-ins," she said.

"I doubt that, but if someone comes and pounds on the door, desperate to talk to a realtor live and in person, rest assured, we will let them in."

Shelly took a breath. "Okay. Fine. What happened? Has someone new started haunting you? Because I cannot be held responsible for everyone's afterlife issues."

"No," I said. "That's our department."

"Huh?"

I explained that we investigated people's ghost problems, and we had a new client.

"I had heard that, but what's it got to do with me?" Shelly looked to the side of me. She knew darn well why we were there.

"We work for the Blazevic family," said Jess.

Shelly grimaced and said, "Do not send that man over here! Last time, he broke a chair. A perfectly good chair."

"Are you talking about Mika?"

"Who else?"

I glanced at Jess and then said, "There is another option."

Shelly frowned. "Do you know another man that's larger than Jason Momoa and twice as scary?"

"You think Mika's scary?" Jess asked, astonished.

"Did I mention he broke a chair?"

"By...throwing it?" I asked.

"By sitting on it," said Shelly. "Imagine if he got mad. Do not tell him I'm a problem. I am not a problem."

"Fine, we won't send *him*," I said.

She wrinkled her nose. "What does that mean?"

"It means," said Jess, "who's haunting 312 Third Street?"

"Nobody. There is no old woman haunting that house." Shelly unwrapped her arms and relaxed.

She believes it.

"How do you know?" I asked.

"Because this is St. Seb," said Shelly. "You think I wouldn't have heard about some scary old peasant stalking kids in that house at some point?"

"Have there been kids living there before?" Jess asked.

"Good one," I said.

"Thanks."

Shelly sneered. "Yes, of course. It's a small family house. A perfect starter home." She got on her computer and began typing. "We've sold that house four times. Each time to a family."

The printer behind her started spitting out pages.

"Four times is a lot," I said.

Shelly shook her head. "No, it isn't. I've been in business for twenty-three years." She leaned back and snatched the pages. "Here are the stats for 312."

She handed me the pages and Jess pulled up a chair. We looked over them carefully.

"You'll notice there are no quick exits," said Shelly. "The average stay in 312 is five years."

I checked, and she was right.

"Why did they move?" I asked.

Shelly glanced at her screen. "First one was an out-of-state move for work. Second, needed more space for mother-in-law to move in. Third, time for an upgrade. Fourth, they had twins. Not enough space. Happy?"

"Everybody had kids?" Jess asked.

"Every family, and I never heard a single complaint. I'm telling you, there's no hag in that house."

I put down the pages and eyed Shelly. "What are you lying about, then?"

Shelly's upper lip twitched, and she looked away. "It's a wonderful starter home. It had new windows five years ago, and they upgraded to a tankless water heater. Low energy costs. Can't beat that."

"You're not selling us the house, Shelly," said Jess.

"That's right, and I need to be selling a house. Bread and butter, you know. Have a good day now." Shelly started typing, but we just sat there and stared at her.

"Oh, come on, you two," she said. "You're happy at Number Eight. Why do you have to pester me?"

"Because you didn't tell us about Leo," I said. "You knew, and you didn't tell us."

"But it worked out, didn't it?"

I glanced at Leo, who stood behind her with arms crossed.

"Sure, but it's not working out for the Blazevics," I said. "What are you holding back? They know you didn't tell them something."

"There's nothing wrong with that house." Shelly crossed her heart.

I looked at Jess and she said, "She's lying."

"I know," I said.

"I'm not lying. No one was murdered in that house. No one died in that house," said Shelly. "There's no crazy old woman. There just isn't."

"What about a man?" I asked.

Her mouth fell open. "What?"

"A man. Snazzy dresser, looks to date to the 1930s," said Jess.

Shelly stammered, "There's another one. There can't be."

I looked at the date the house was built. 1941. So I was off a few years, but 1930s wasn't a bad guess. "That house was around then. It fits."

"But there have been no sightings," said Shelly. "None."

"There are now," said Jess.

Shelly rolled her eyes. "Those kids are messing with their parents. Kids do that."

"We saw him," I said. "About half an hour ago."

Shelly clammed up and shook her head.

"You're going to tell us what you know," I said.

"Not my problem. I don't know anything about some man in that house." She didn't meet my eyes. Shelly wasn't the best liar, but she stuck to her story.

"Jess, you have your art supplies with you, right?" I asked.

She jolted to her feet. "Of course. I'll be right back."

"Where's she going?" Shelly asked, shifting in her chair while still not looking at me.

"She's an artist. She's going to draw that ghost for you," I said.

"Why? I won't recognize him."

"You might."

"No."

"Yes."

Shelly wrapped her arms around herself once again, and Jess dashed back to her chair with a huge sketch pad and a large metal case of her favorite pencils. She got to work, and I said, "You know something. You should just tell us."

"I didn't lie to that family," said Shelly, getting a bit squeaky.

"She's hiding something," said Leo.

"I think you didn't tell them everything, just like how you didn't tell us everything."

To Shelly's great relief, her phone rang, and she pounced on it and began telling the caller about the advantages of a condo instead of a house. Five minutes later, Jess finished her sketch and held it out to me. Once again, I was astonished by her gift. A man she'd seen for only a few minutes was fully realized on the page with no detail lost. There was a hint of silver in his sideburns and deep crow's feet around his eyes. She'd drawn his tie pin, a set of four cards, all aces in silver.

"That's amazing," I said.

"Did I miss anything?" Jess asked.

"I don't think so. He's so real. I feel like he could almost talk to us."

Leo walked over and looked. "I've never seen him before."

Shelly eyed us nervously and tried to talk the person on the phone into having a viewing immediately. They refused, and she hung up reluctantly.

"I do have to get back to work," she said.

Jess held up the sketch pad and Shelly winced, but then looked puzzled.

"Who's that?" she asked.

"You tell us," I said.

"I have no idea. I've never seen that man before in my life."

Darn. She believes it.

"Are you sure?" Jess asked, disappointed.

"I swear to you I have no idea who that is," said the realtor.

I sat back and eyed Shelly. "So tell us what you're holding back."

"I really don't know him."

"I believe you, but there's something else."

She shook her head.

"You know that we have connections," I said.

"You moved to town five minutes ago," she scoffed.

"With dead people."

Shelly flushed and looked around nervously. "If you're talking about Leo Pereyra, I happen to know he wouldn't hurt a fly. He was a lovely person."

Leo got misty and turned away.

"Not Leo. Although he did chase people with phantom bees, and I hear that's not fun," I said.

"He's not going to do that to me," said Shelly, but she didn't sound as sure as she had.

I glanced at Leo's back and said, "No, he's not, but he isn't the only game in town."

"The confederates never leave the hospital," she said.

"Not them." I turned to Jess. "Were the guys out at the Horny Hotel this morning?"

"Oh," Jess said with a smile. "As a matter of fact, they were."

"Do you think you can summon them?"

Shelly leaned forward. "Who are you talking about?"

"They don't always pay attention. There are a lot of ladies that love the hot tub right now," said Jess. "But…"

Leo turned around, winked at me, and pop, he was gone.

"Give it a minute," I said.

"What are you going to do?" Shelly asked.

"Wait for it," said Jess.

The realtor's voice got loud. "Wait for what?"

"Tell us what you know," I said.

"I don't know anything."

There was a pop, and the four fur trappers appeared by the door.

"Hey," said Boy. "What's you doin' there?"

Boy didn't wait for an answer. He wandered off. Keeping his attention was the impossible dream. A guy who'd forgotten both his name and how he died couldn't be counted on. "I never been here before."

Wheeler, Johnny, and Jedidiah were more reliable. I started breathing through my nose and said, "Show them your drawing."

Jess held up the portrait, and the ghosts walked over to the desk, passing through Shelly.

Shelly gasped, shivered, and said, "What is that? What is that?"

"You're okay. They're not upset," I said.

"Who? What's happening?" she asked. "I'm so cold."

The trappers gathered around Jess and she dry heaved a little. "Do you recognize this guy?" she asked.

"No, ma'am," said Wheeler.

"That looks like one of them snotty ghosts that says we smell."

Oh lord, you smell so bad.

"Do you know him?" I asked.

"Nope," said Jedidiah. "Is he a watchman or something?"

I looked at Jess, and she pinched her nose.

"What's a watchman?" I asked.

Leo appeared and said, "He's asking if the man is a cop."

"Oh," said Jess, looking closer at her portrait. "Why do you ask that, Jedidiah?"

Jedidiah pointed at the man's left arm. "He's got a gun."

"Does he?" I asked Jess.

"I don't know. I didn't mean to draw that."

The trappers conferred and agreed that they thought the man had a weapon under his arm. Leo bowed to their knowledge on the subject, since they'd lived during the frontier era when weapons and death were an everyday occurrence.

"But you don't know him?" I asked. "You've never seen him at the hotel or in town?"

The trappers talked it over and agreed that they hadn't.

"What is going on?" Shelly asked. "Who in the world are you talking to?"

I leaned forward. "I think you believe in ghosts."

"What?"

"You believe."

"I never said that," the realtor said nervously.

I drummed my fingers on her desk. "You never said that ghosts didn't exist. You just said there wasn't some old hag in the Blazevic house."

"There isn't," she said.

"So you believe in ghosts?" Jess asked with a smile.

"I don't know."

"Yes, you do." I turned to the trappers. "Can you please let her see you?"

The four of them harrumphed and complained. Shelly wasn't deemed worthy of seeing them. She had a look about her that said she'd turn up her nose at them. Shelly did look snotty with her pink suit and enormous bow tied under her chin. They didn't seem to mind that Jess was still pinching her nose and gagging a little. I was on the edge of dry heaving, and they didn't notice that either.

"Okay," I said. "I understand."

"Understand what?" Shelly asked.

"That you might be mean to them."

Our realtor couldn't comprehend what I was saying. Mean to ghosts? Was that a thing? Why would they care what she thought?

"If that's it, I think you should go," she said primly.

"See," said Wheeler. "Snotty."

"Then, how about this?" I asked. "You let her smell you."

"Is you saying we stink?" Boy came over and leaned in close, changing his smell to rotting. I can't describe how bad it was, but I did throw up in my mouth a little.

"No, no," I squeaked out. "Let her smell your opossum."

"Opossum smells good."

A TRUNK, A CANOE, AND ALL THE BARBECUE

Jess's eyes were watering, but she said, "It's a matter of taste."

Wheeler shrugged. "How about you show us a little titty?"

Leo stomped over, and the papers on Shelly's desk began to flutter. "What's happening?" she asked.

"Do not say that to them!" Leo bellowed. "Do you want me to do to you what I did at the factory?"

The trappers backed away, apologizing profusely.

"You want the opossum?" Wheeler asked. "You got it."

Nothing changed for Jess and I, but Shelly drew back with wide eyes. "What...what is that?"

"That," I said, "is the smell of 1812."

"1813," said Wheeler.

"What year is ya'll talkin' 'bout?" Boy asked.

"You never knew the year," said Jedidiah.

"Did so."

They started arguing over what year the opossum was from. They'd all eaten opossum at different times, but they'd never actually known each other in life.

"So how do you like that?" Jess asked, waving a hand at Jedidiah, who held his favorite opossum by the tail. It was rotting and looked like roadkill. I'm guessing that's where the chronic diarrhea that killed him came from.

Jedidiah came over and held out his opossum next to Shelly's head.

"Oh my. Oh my." She grabbed her trashcan and started breathing hard.

"That's enough, boys," I said.

"Aw," said Boy. "It was just gettin' good."

"Let's make her chuck it," said Johnny.

"Now, boys, be nice," said Jess. "I think we've made our point."

Wheeler sauntered over to Jess and got her eyes watering anew. "You gonna be doin' more pictures?"

"I can."

"I want one of me when I was young," he said. "We didn't have no mirrors."

"Consider it done," said Jess.

"Huh?"

"I will do it."

Wheeler snapped his fingers, and Shelly slumped back in her chair. "Oh, jeez. That was..."

I pulled out a tissue. "Oh, we know."

"You want to tell us about that house now?" Jess asked.

Shelly got her own tissue and wiped her mouth. "Fine, but it's not going to help you, and I'd appreciate it if you don't spread it around that I didn't tell the Blazevics everything. It didn't have to be disclosed."

"They already know you didn't tell them everything, but we won't make it worse," I said.

Shelly took a breath and told us that there had been a death on the Blazevic property, but it was before there was a house built, and the body wasn't in the house's footprint, more like the end of the backyard.

Jess held up her portrait. "This guy?"

She shook her head. "I don't think so. He doesn't look like the type."

"What type?" I asked.

"The dead man was a builder, and he was old."

"How old?"

"Oh, gosh. I don't know," said Shelly. "At least in his sixties or seventies."

Leo came over, having regained his composure. "Ask her if he was murdered."

"Was he murdered?" I asked.

"I don't think so. I only know about it because my grandmother knew the family. She just said he died on Third when they were first building there before Pearl Harbor and the war. The Abbotts built on the spot. They were the first owners."

"So 1941?" Jess asked.

"I think so, but she didn't give a date," said Shelly.

I looked back at the portrait. He looked earlier than 1941.

"So you see, this has nothing to do with some old woman, and I swear I don't know anything about that man or anything else at the property. I didn't tell the Blazevics or anyone else because nothing's ever happened there. Nothing."

"Are you sure?" I asked.

She held up her hands. "I would tell you. Just don't bring back that smell."

"She thinks we stink," said Jedidiah, holding out his opossum.

"No, no," said Jess. "Don't do that. She told us what she knows."

The trappers grumbled, and Jess promised them all portraits of them in their youth. That got them to go back to the Horny Hotel. Well, that and they remembered there was a water relaxation class happening in fifteen minutes and there promised to be plenty of bikinis for them to gawk at.

They popped off, and we stood up.

"Thanks, Shelly," I said. "That wasn't so hard, was it?"

"I think I'm going to throw up."

Jess nodded. "It does help."

Shelly stared at us as we turned around her sign to Open. "Please do not come again," she said.

We grinned at her.

No promises.

Chapter Four

We arrived back in downtown St. Seb as a few snow flurries started landing on the windshield. Lots of the old houses had their Thanksgiving decor up, but we hadn't gotten around to it. To tell the truth, I didn't really have Thanksgiving stuff. I love Thanksgiving, but Christmas was my family's real decorating holiday.

"Hey, Leo," I said. "Did you used to decorate Number Eight for Thanksgiving?"

No reply.

I turned in my seat and found the back empty.

"He didn't get in," said Jess.

"Oh, I guess I just assumed he did," I said.

"He's really not okay."

"What do we do? If he were alive, I would make him food and hug him."

Jess smiled. "Like you do for me. Thanks for humoring me with the turkey."

"No problem. It turned out great," I said.

"Has Mariah said anything about it?" Jess asked.

"About the turkey?"

"Thanksgiving."

"Not really. She's been busy," I said.

Her lower lip trembled. "Hal loved Thanksgiving."

I nodded. It was going to be hard. We'd gotten through Halloween, Hal's absolute favorite thing, pretty easily. The kids were crazy busy with all their ideas. We did a haunted mortuary and a battle of the bands. There wasn't much time to think about Hal not being there, but Thanksgiving would be quieter.

"We'll get through it," I said.

"It's your second year without your dad," said Jess. "How do you feel?"

I looked over at her. My friend. My sweet, wonderful friend thinking of me when she didn't have to. Most people wouldn't.

"I'm okay. We'll make all his favorites, and Mom's coming. So that's good."

"Did she book her ticket yet?" Jess asked, looking more cheerful.

"She did, and she's staying through Christmas, unless you object."

"Are you kidding? That's the best news I've heard since I don't know when." She put on her blinker and turned off Elizabeth and onto Mina.

"Where are we going?" I asked.

"The *Sentinel* to see Tank," said Jess.

"Don't you want to go home?"

"I did, but now I don't. Let's help the Blazevics."

I needed to get back to work, but I agreed. When Jess looked happy, I'd learned you had to go with it or the opportunity might not come again.

"We can't stay long," I said. "The kids will be home soon, and they won't get on their homework unless we're there."

"Leo will probably be there," said Jess.

"Probably. Do you think we're asking too much of him? Patrick was a tremendous blow."

"I think the kids are keeping him going," she said. "They're a second chance."

"If only we could think of something we could do for him," I said.

Jess turned on the street where the former Great Missouri Shoe Factory loomed large. A lot had changed in the last month. I'd had a run-in with the resident ghosts, some angry, mistreated factory workers, and Leo had caught wind of it. Literally. He smelled them on me and went to the factory and kicked butt. At least, we assume that's what happened. There was a huge ruckus, and the factory appeared to be on fire for a period of time. Tank said that there were some explosions too, but when the dust cleared, nothing had happened, except that the factory ghosts had been MIA ever since.

"Do we dare?" Jess asked as she pulled up to the parking lot.

"Tank says it's safe now," I said.

Jess grimaced and pulled into the newly paved lot. Before my run-in, Tank had blocked it off with heavy chains, and debris from a car the ghosts destroyed had littered the cracked pavement. Now it was clear of all the broken glass and rubble, with sharp lines for parking spaces and a friendly sign that told visitors where the St. Seb *Sentinel* offices were.

"I'm still nervous," said Jess.

"You're not alone in that," I said.

"Oh my gosh. I forgot. Are you too freaked to go in?"

I got out and said, "I don't think they'd dare bother me again."

Jess bit her lip and we went in the *Sentinel*'s door to find the office that was in the old accounting section to be quiet as usual, except for a skinny man snoring on the sofa.

"Slow news day," said Jess.

"When isn't it?"

"McCann's market is opening that burrito bar."

"I'm not sure that counts as news."

Tank stirred on the sofa. "It counts. We can't have a battle of the bands every day."

"Thank goodness," I said. "The cleanup was a nightmare."

Tank sat up and stretched. "Oh, man. That was a great nap."

"Sleeping on the job," said Jess. "What kind of example are you?"

"The kind that knows when nobody's coming to see me," said Tank.

"We're here," I said.

"You don't count." Tank stood up and went to his coffee bar. "What can I get you?"

"Information," said Jess.

"I assumed that. Coffee? Tea?"

I asked for peppermint tea and Jess got a latte. Tank was a surprisingly good latte maker. Caffeine was important for a newspaper in sleepy St. Seb.

"So did you see the parking lot?" he asked.

"We did more than that," said Jess. "We parked in it."

"Pretty exciting."

"We hope not."

"Don't worry." Tank glanced at the door to the factory floor. "They haven't been back. Did you see how fast construction is going?"

We had, and I, for one, had serious reservations about condos for the upwardly mobile going into the factory. Those ghosts were no joke, but Tank had put a lot into the plan, and every unit was sold.

"Seems to be moving right along. When will they be finished?" I asked.

"Six months, maybe less." He brought us our cups and

then sat down behind his desk. "So what's up in the world of our local ghost negotiators?"

I blew on my steaming cup and said, "Mika Blazevic hired us. Do you know him?"

Tank chuckled. "Who doesn't? Mika doesn't exactly blend in."

"Did you know he's got an afterlife issue?"

"I didn't, but Mallory knows his wife, Sandra. Mallory says Sandra's been acting funny at their book club meetings. She thought maybe it was marriage troubles. Mal's seen it before."

"It's not the marriage," I said. "This has to remain between us."

"You know I hate that. I am a newspaperman. I love a good story."

"We don't know if it's a good story," said Jess.

"If you two are here, it's a good story." He steepled his fingers. "If Mika and Sandra give the go-ahead, can I do it?"

I shrugged. "Sure. We don't care."

"Right on. What's ya got?"

"Have you ever heard of anything weird about their house?" Jess asked.

"Um...where do they live?" Tank asked, with his fingers poised over his keyboard.

"312 Third Street."

Tank got to typing, scanned his database, and then shook his head. "Nothing's popping up, except a garage sale three years ago."

"It doesn't sound familiar to you?" I asked. "Anything on Third Street?"

Tank sat back and said, "Nothing's coming to mind. What's happened?"

Jess and I told him about the old lady, and the newsman paled.

"No wonder Sandra looks ill and tearful," he said. "That's a nightmare."

"It really is, and that's not all," I said.

"Does this get weirder?"

"I'd say it's low on the weird scale."

"Alright."

I told him about the man in the Blazevic kitchen and Jess opened up her sketchpad.

"Do you recognize this guy?" Jess asked.

Tank took a look. "No, but I wish I did. He is cool."

"He was, now that you mention it," I said. "He looked like he was from the 1930s, and Shelly told us there was a dead body on the property in 1941. What do you know about that?"

"How in the world did you get Shelly to tell you that?" Tank asked.

"The fur trappers are very persuasive," said Jess.

"She can see them?"

"She can smell them."

He drew back. "You said that's bad."

"And useful," I said.

"How devious of you, but I applaud the results. Shelly is notoriously close-mouthed about properties," said Tank.

"Did you know there was a death on Third Street?" Jess asked.

"I didn't. Just a bit before my time. Was it a murder?"

"Shelly didn't know. It was an older man, sixties or seventies. She thought he was a builder," I said.

"What's he got to do with that old lady and this dapper gent?" Tank asked.

"We have no idea, but we have to start somewhere."

Tank stood up. "You probably won't like this, Libby, but it's back to the microfiche."

I made a face, but Jess got up. "I can do it."

"We'll all do it," I said. "I'm just having flashbacks of severed arms and whatnot."

"He's not out there," said Tank.

"You didn't know he was out there before," I pointed.

"A fair point, but I'm pretty sure he's not there now." He went to the door and opened it. "By the way, his name was Willy Tuggle. He died in 1915 when his arm got caught in the machinery and was severed. He bled to death."

"Poor Willy," said Jess, walking bravely through the door.

"It gets worse. The factory owners blamed Willy for the accident and refused to pay any money to his widow," said Tank.

I took a breath and walked out. The factory floor was quiet, but I grabbed Jess's arm and held on tight. "Was it his fault?"

"I think not," said Tank, leading the way in the same direction where I'd seen the wrench-wielding maniac, but he didn't appear.

"Why not?" Jess asked.

"The equipment was run-down, and what little safety guidelines there were at the time were ignored. The other workers supported Willy, but the owners had pull and they paid nothing."

"That's a good reason to haunt the place," I said. "Not that I want him back, that is."

Tank led us to a room marked Storage Two and stopped with his hand on the knob. "I keep thinking if he shows up again, you two can help him."

"Help him do what?" Jess asked, her voice growing tight.

"Do whatever he needs to do," said Tank.

"If I never see that guy again, it'll be too soon," I said.

Tank smiled. "Understood. Now, this room isn't exactly clear, but it won't hurt you."

"Er...what do you mean?" I asked.

"Remember how Taylor, my intern, said there was green fog?" he asked.

"Yeah."

Tank opened the door, and there was a green fog. Honestly, I'm not sure *fog* did it justice. It was more solid-looking than fog. It looked like you could slice it and put it on a plate.

"What in the world is that?" Jess asked, backing up.

"Nobody knows."

"You must have some idea."

"Not really," said Tank. "It's just here."

"That's freaky," I said.

"You get used to it." He walked in, and we looked at each other.

Jess squeezed my arm. "Do you think this is a good idea?"

"Do you want to look at the microfiche?" I asked.

"Not so much."

Tank popped his head out. "Ladies, are you coming?"

I glanced back at the empty factory floor. How bad could it be? There wasn't any blood. That's where my standards now were. No blood. We're okay.

"Let's do it," I said.

"You first," said Jess.

"Coward."

"Guilty as charged."

I walked in through the fog and, though it looked solid, it wasn't at all. I couldn't feel it other than an odd, tingly sensation that made me want to pee.

"Okay, Jess?" I asked.

"Okay," she squeaked out.

We found Tank behind the bank of fog at a microfiche station with piles of boxes all around. "We're not quite organized. Help me find the 1940s. They're in here somewhere.

The previous editors were dedicated to preserving all our copy, so we've got it."

We rooted around and finally found a pile of the 1940s over in a corner under the 1960s. Jess found 1940 and 1941 in the same box, and Tank got the reels loaded.

"Here we go," he said. "She didn't say when in 1941, did she?"

"Before the war," I said.

"Before the war for us or everyone else?"

"Pearl Harbor."

"Starting with November and we'll go backward," said Tank.

It took about twenty minutes, but we found the death of John K. Tunny III on March 3, 1941. Shelly was right that he died on the property. Partially. Tunny actually died on two lots. The Blazevic property and the one behind them before much construction had begun. The article said that workmen came in on the morning of March fourth, ready to dig out basements and found Tunny dead. He wasn't just a builder. He was the guy financing the project, and he owned the entire company. No one knew why he was at the property, but he did check up on his worksites frequently. The coroner labeled his death as natural causes but didn't put it down to a specific cause. Tunny was obese and an alcoholic. He had significant heart and liver disease and was drunk at the time of his death.

I sat back in my seat. "So not a murder."

"Hold on," said Tank, and he went through a couple of weeks of issues. "I saw something. Here it is."

Jess and I squinted at the faded newsprint on the screen.

"Tunny family claims foul play," read Jess. "They thought it was murder."

The article laid out the Tunny family's feelings on their patriarch's death, and it added up to not knowing why he was there, having left home after a mysterious phone call at nine in the evening. His wife and children claimed he was sober at the time, and he drove off in his brand-new Packard. The car wasn't at the Third Street location and was never found. Where was the car? The family demanded an investigation and got nowhere. Natural causes put an end to any police interest. The family said they were hiring a detective named Vic Delaney to investigate. He came from St. Louis and was highly recommended.

"Any more articles?" I asked.

Tank scanned through and found one small article saying that Vic Delaney had been unable to locate Tunny's car or discover the reason that he'd left the house on the night of his death. Case closed.

"I can't see how this connects to the old lady," said Tank.

"Neither can I," said Jess.

"It probably connects to that guy in the kitchen," I said.

"Do we care?"

I shook my head. "Not so much. The Blazevics can't see him, and he's not doing anything to them. Let's look for old ladies and mysterious deaths."

We spent an hour going through the 1930s until we all had headaches.

"I don't think it's here," said Tank. "St. Seb has never had much of an immigrant population. There was a large German segment, but they came in the 1880s."

"It's weird that this just started up four months ago," I said.

"Something must've happened," said Jess. "Did something happen in town?"

Tank shut down the microfiche and stood up. "Nothing that I can think of, but let's take a look."

He led the way through the fog and closed the door behind us. The factory floor remained quiet. I found it eerie somehow, not that I preferred rampaging ghosts, but I had a sense that they were there, watching in silence.

"Okay?" Jess asked.

"I'm good."

We went back in the *Sentinel* office and found Taylor, Tank's intrepid intern, at a desk, typing away with a donut in his mouth. He saw us and the donut fell out and hit the keyboard with a powdered sugar plunk.

"Oh, I didn't know you were here," said Taylor. "I'm just working. Working at working."

Tank rolled his eyes. "They're not here about you."

"I didn't think they were. Why would they be?"

Tank looked at us. "You make him nervous."

"I'm not nervous. Why would I be nervous?" Taylor asked.

We all knew why Taylor was nervous. He and Mariah had been circling each other for a couple of weeks. They'd met for group dates, if you wanted to call them that, at the bowling alley and the movies, but that night was their first proper date. Just the two of them. Taylor had actually asked Tank to ask Jess if it was okay to ask Mariah out for real. It was oddly old-fashioned, but Tank said that's how you know that a guy really likes a girl. He gets very careful not to put a foot wrong. If he didn't care, he'd ask her out and let the chips fall where they may.

"Everything's fine," said Jess, although she wasn't completely on board with Mariah dating so soon after Hal's death. She thought it was a sign of neediness. I thought it was a sign of getting on with her life, but Jess wasn't ready for that either.

"It really is," I said. "We've got a new case."

Taylor brushed off his keyboard and said, "No kidding. A murder? Tell me it's a juicy murder."

"It is not a juicy murder," said Jess.

"Not that we know of," I said.

"So there's a chance?" Taylor asked.

"There's a chance."

The kid bristled with excitement. His help was key to solving Leo's murder, and it got him a fat scholarship to a prestigious journalism program. His articles on the investigation were excellent, I had to admit. "What can I do?" he asked.

We told him what we were up to, and the boy beamed after he looked at Jess's sketch.

"It's the detective," he said.

"What is?" Jess asked.

"The guy in the house," I said.

Tank nodded. "That had occurred to me too."

"Why would the detective hang out there?"

Taylor pointed at us. "Unfinished business. He didn't solve the case."

"Could be, but we have more pressing matters than a maybe murder in 1941." Tank sat down and started typing. "Four months ago. What happened four months ago?"

"Can I do it?" Taylor asked. "Can I?"

"Can you do what?" Jess asked.

"Look into that detective?"

Tank shrugged. "Be my guest."

"Name?" Taylor asked.

"Vic Delaney," I said. "He worked in St. Louis. That's all we have."

"That's all I need," said the eager intern, and he got to work with powdered sugar still on his handsome face.

I drank some of my cold tea and asked, "So anything happen on Third Street four months ago?"

Tank stopped typing. "Nope. Nothing interesting on there or anywhere else. Normal stuff. Mayor's husband got caught drunk driving. Frank Owens streaked at the Town and

Country Fair. Mabel Mathews poured weedkiller on her neighbors' begonias over an American flag tiff."

"They were fighting over the flag?" I asked. "Did her neighbor burn it or something?"

"Not a chance. Hazel had too many flags displayed on her house and yard, in Mabel's estimation," said Tank.

"How many did she have?" I was thinking three or four.

"Three hundred."

It took a second to compute that.

"How?" Jess asked.

"Hazel is both patriotic and determined. Basically, you couldn't see her yard or house from the street. That includes her mailbox, so the mailman started delivering her mail to Mabel next door, and then you have two ninety-three-year-olds ready to fight to the death."

"How did Mabel find Hazel's begonias?" I asked.

"Second-floor window box. Mabel is great at distance spraying," said Tank.

"And you think that's normal?" Jess asked.

"For St. Seb, yeah."

"But nothing that would affect the Blazevic house or kids?" I asked.

"Sorry, no. They're a nice family. Mika's a fantastic physical therapist. I haven't heard a peep about them. Taylor?"

Taylor stopped typing and said, "He's cool. Works with all our athletes. I never heard anything else about them."

"It would help if you knew where the old lady was from," said Tank.

"The kids don't know the language," Jess said.

"Play them," said Taylor.

We all looked at him and waited, but the kid was back to typing and not paying attention.

"Taylor, focus," said Tank.

"Huh?"

"Play what?"

Taylor stopped and thought for a second. "Oh, yeah. Play the languages for the kids."

The three of us frowned, and he sighed with exasperation. Adults. We're so slow.

"Get on YouTube or something and play people speaking different languages. See which one sounds right."

Tank snapped his fingers. "Kid, you are smarter than you look."

Taylor grinned. "Thank goodness. My grandma calls me a pretty boy, and it's not a good thing."

"It is where Mariah's concerned," I said, eliciting a blush, and Taylor retreated to his typing.

"When are you going to interview the kids?" Tank asked.

"Tomorrow," said Jess.

"I suggest you ask Leo about getting that woman to let you see her."

"He can't see her either," I said.

"Oh, I guess that makes sense. He'd have just asked her what was going on," said Tank. "Maybe he can figure something out."

"We don't want to press him."

Tank sat back and asked, "Still not doing so great?"

"No. The Patrick thing hit him hard," said Jess. "I wish he would talk to you or Kip at The Poet's Garden."

"Kip would love that, but he told me he hasn't seen Leo."

"I guess he doesn't want anyone to see him," I said. "Mika believes, and Leo couldn't reveal himself to him."

"Why not?"

We shrugged.

"Sounds like he needs to read his own grief column," said Tank. "Has he looked at *Departures at 8*?"

"Not that we know of," I said, standing up. "Thanks for your help."

Tank walked us to the door and shook our hands. "Let me know what happens with the kids. This could be an interesting feature."

"No ghosts," I said. "The last thing I need during my divorce is Derek saying I'm a crackpot."

"The boys didn't tell him?"

"Not so far."

Tank's thin features grew worried, but he didn't say anything, and that worried me.

Chapter Five

We were about to walk inside Number Eight when Jess stopped with her hand on the knob. "Do you hear something?"

I froze and listened. "Music?"

"Leo must be back." Jess smiled and opened the door.

If Leo was at home, the first sign was usually music. This time, three young voices were belting out Blondie's "Call Me" from somewhere in the depths of the house. We grinned and took off our coats and hung them on our new wrought-iron coat rack.

"That sounds like Samantha singing with Mariah and Keely," said Jess. "Should we record it for Sylvia?"

I shook my head. "Sam would be horrified."

Samantha Otto was Leo Pereyra's granddaughter. She was a step, but no one in the family thought of Leo as anything but blood. Sam had been incredibly shy, but she seemed to be coming out of her shell after meeting Mariah and Keely. Keely was a Fischer. The Ottos and the Fischers had been like the Hatfields and the McCoys until we solved Leo's murder and proved the downtrodden Fischers had nothing to do with it.

The family had fresh energy to them, and Keely had bonded with Mariah and Samantha immediately. The three were now inseparable.

We headed for the kitchen slowly, not wanting to interrupt the sound of joy coming from our kitchen. The girls started singing together after our Halloween battle of the bands and had joined the high school show choir. Hearing them sing was one of the few things that seemed to lift Leo's mood.

I walked in clapping as the girls finished the song. Samantha looked like she wanted to crawl under a rock, but Mariah and Keely took bows and did jazz hands.

"Pretty good, huh?" Mariah asked.

"You know it was." I patted Sam on the back. "Good job."

"Excellent," said Jess, looking at Poptart in his bed, purring away. "So you haven't seen Leo, I take it."

"Nope," said Samantha. "He's still so sad, but my dad says he won't talk about it."

"How is your dad?" I asked.

"Okay. He says he's processing it."

I couldn't imagine what Eric Otto was going through. Finding out his own brother killed their beloved stepfather out of greed and desperation was a blow to end all blows.

"He did kinda get some of it out, though," said Keely.

"How'd he do that?" Jess asked.

Samantha ducked her head and said that her dad had gone to the cemetery where Patrick was buried and, in her words, completely lost it. He'd screamed and kicked over the stone and was getting ready to pee on the grave when the caretaker came out and stopped him.

"Did it make him feel better?" I asked.

Sam nodded. "I think so. He was a lot more normal after that."

Mariah went to the kitchen table and grabbed a large black

book, Leo's *Departures at 8*. "We looked it up. Leo said that a burst of anger can release the grieving person from pent-up rage and help them start the real grieving process."

"He would know," I said. "Now, if we could just help Leo with his process."

The girls looked at each other.

"We have an idea," said Keely as she twisted a long lock of hair around her finger.

"Great," I said. "Let's have it."

Sam took the book from Mariah and flipped through it until she got to a specific page. "Here it is. Leo told a man that was grieving the loss of his mother *not* to avoid the sense memories that were bothering him and making him feel."

"Okay," said Jess. "How does that help us?"

"He said to delve into those memories and feelings. The man didn't want to have any of the food that his mother made because it reminded him of her. He didn't want to hear her favorite music or even smell a cleaning product she used."

I pulled the turkey out of the warmer and set it on the island. The intense Thanksgiving smell instantly made me think of my dad. It was our second holiday season without him. I wanted to throw the turkey out the window.

"How is that helpful?" I asked.

"Leo said he had to pick a memory that he'd been avoiding and purposely face it. An easy one at first, like her lemon cleaner, and work up to the harder stuff like her food or her perfume."

"Are you saying we have to desensitize Leo like people do when they're afraid of spiders?" Jess asked. "First a picture of a spider, etc."

Keely nodded eagerly. "Exactly. Mariah says Leo doesn't come in the kitchen much anymore."

"He doesn't," I said. "I hadn't thought about that."

"It was the place where he spent a lot of time with the boys," said Mariah.

"Right," said Jess. "But we can't make him do anything."

"But we can make the food he loved."

Jess shook her head. "We don't know what that is."

"I do," said Sam. "He talked about it at our house. Just a little. My dad said one of his favorite memories of growing up was when Leo's mom came to visit. She always made her special soup. Dad said they would all sit here at the island and stay up late talking. Leo said that was his favorite soup and a favorite memory, too, but then he got upset and left."

"What's the soup?" I asked.

"Albondigas soup," the girls said in chorus.

Jess and I looked at each other. I'd never heard of that soup before.

"It was a family recipe," said Mariah. "It has meatballs."

"That sounds good," said Jess. "Did you get the recipe?"

Sam wrinkled her nose. "We don't have it. Dad said it was Leo's mom's secret recipe. It's the Pereyra family comfort food."

I walked over to Leo's recipe cabinet and opened it. "Leo must have his mother's recipe. Let's look."

We divided Leo's recipe collection between us and started looking through the loose recipes and the binders. Leo was a kind of recipe packrat. He had everything, and he loved all kinds of food.

While we were looking, the back door burst open and the boys came in, laughing and punching each other.

"Idiot. You should've talked to her," said Henri.

"I'm not talking to her," said Max. "You talk to her."

"I don't like her."

"Everybody likes her." Then Henri turned around and spotted Sam at the island. They both froze and blushed.

Max looked around at our silent faces. "What?"

A TRUNK, A CANOE, AND ALL THE BARBECUE

"Nothing," I said. "Have you seen a recipe for albondigas soup?"

"Nope. What's that? Guess what? You'll never guess, so I'll tell you." Max spread his arms wide. "We're in charge of the Christmas pageant."

Henri forgot his nerves, and the boys went into a rousing chorus of "We are the Champions." My boys are nothing if not confident.

When they finished, I said, "No, you're not."

"Huh?" Henri asked.

"You are not in charge."

"We are so," said Max. "Mrs. Johns gave it to us today."

The assistant principal hates me.

"What did I ever do to her?" I asked.

The girls started laughing, and my boys frowned. The expression didn't fit well on their faces. Their father didn't call them The Eggs for nothing. They were always sunny-side up, and in turn their frowns turned upside down.

"Oh, you're joking," said Max. "Good one."

"It's going to be amazing," said Henri. "The best one ever."

"How would you know?" Mariah asked. "You've never seen a Christmas pageant."

"That's why it will be the best," said Max. "No rules. No boundaries."

"No sense," I said. "Mrs. Johns may have put you in charge, but you shouldn't be in charge."

"All we have to do is organize the little guys and get a program ready," said Max.

"Did you say little guys?" Jess asked.

"The elementary kids. They do the pageant," said Henri. "Usually the high school drama teacher heads it, but she had a nervous breakdown. What is a nervous breakdown, anyway?"

"What I'm about to have," I said.

Sam shook her head. "Oh, guys. Don't do it. Last year was a disaster. Three kids peed on stage."

Max pointed at her. "We'll get Depends."

"Everybody pees before going on stage," said Henri. "Oh, and treats for the ones that don't pee. Kids love treats."

Max came over to Mariah. "You make the treats. We got lactose intolerant, peanut allergies, gluten allergies, and one that has epileptic fits if he sees a strobe light, but I guess that's not a food thing."

"What kind of treat has no lactose, peanuts, or gluten?" Keely asked.

"I don't know, but you can handle it," said Max.

"Nobody said we were doing it," said Mariah.

"You don't want to let the little guys down, do you?" Henri asked with hound dog eyes.

Sam glanced at him and said, "My mom has special recipes for allergies."

Henri ran around the island and hugged her. "You're a genius."

Sam looked like she might faint, but couldn't stop smiling.

Max held up his hands, forming a window. "I'm thinking the musical version of *A Christmas Story*."

"Is that a thing?" I asked.

"Heck, yeah. It was on Broadway."

"I'm saying no to Broadway."

Max and Henri high-fived each other. "We can do it."

"Please don't do it," said Mariah. "They're little kids."

"Yeah, guys," said Sam. "My cousins were in it. They couldn't remember what they were supposed to do, and they didn't have any lines."

"How old are the kids in this thing?" I asked.

"Kindergarten through fifth," said Henri. "The best years."

No wonder there was peeing.

"When does this have to be decided?" I asked.

"It's decided. We're doing it," said Max. "We have a month to pull it together."

"A month?" Jess asked. "What's the drama teacher gotten done so far?"

"Nothing," said Henri. "We have free rein."

"You better start planning right now," I said.

The boys shook their heads.

"Can't. Meeting the guys for pizza," said Max.

I held up my hands. "We have turkey. Eat turkey."

"Later, Mom," said Henri. "Hey, can you look at costume design? Thanks."

"Where's Leo?" Max asked. "We have to tell him."

"We don't know," said Mariah.

"Guess what, Mom?" Henri asked.

I don't want to.

I said nothing, and nothing was required with my boys.

"Dad's coming," said Henri with absolute glee.

I grabbed the counter and took a calming breath. "Coming where?"

"To the pageant, of course," said Max. "He's gonna love it. You know all those shows he put on in high school and college. It's gonna be just like that."

"You already invited your dad to the pageant?" Mariah asked in astonishment. "It, like, *just* happened."

"We're gonna invite him on Thanksgiving," said Henri. "You know he'll come. He never misses our stuff."

"Derek is coming to Thanksgiving?" Jess asked, as astonished as her daughter.

"Yeah," said Max. "We can't have Thanksgiving without Dad."

My beautiful boys looked at me with sparkling eyes and I said the only thing I could say. "Right."

"Great," said Max. "Are you guys coming to pizza?"

"Us?" Samantha asked.

"Yeah," said Henri, suddenly shy. "You should come. It'll be fun."

Keely nudged Sam and said, "Sure, we'll come, but Mariah's going out with Taylor."

The boys nodded sagely.

"The big date," said Max. "Shouldn't you be doin' stuff?"

"Like what?" Mariah asked.

"Waxing your lip. Trimming your leg hair."

"Gross. Shut up. I don't have a hairy lip." Mariah chased them out of the kitchen, snapping a towel at them. Within an hour, the house was empty, and we had a twenty-three-pound turkey to eat between the two of us. I wanted pizza.

"Do you remember when we used to go out on Friday nights?" Jess asked.

"Vaguely."

"Want to eat the turkey in front of the TV?"

"Absolutely," I said.

"Should we carve it first?" Jess asked.

"Nope."

Chapter Six

"How long do turkey comas last?" Jess walked into the kitchen the next morning with hair that looked like she'd taken a teasing comb to it and wearing a pair of stained pajamas.

I looked at the clock. "Going on twelve hours for me."

"Coffee," she groaned.

"Hey, Jess, would you like some coffee this morning?" I asked.

Jess went to the kitchen table and collapsed into a chair. "Yes, please."

I poured her a cup and brought it with a bottle of soy milk to the table. "Feeling rough?"

"What happened to us? We used to do stuff. We were wild."

I yawned. "You were wild. I was your sidekick."

"You did stuff. We used to go to see bands at two o'clock in the morning and drive to Philadelphia just because we could."

"That was a terrible trip. Some turd stole my purse, and you got lice at the motel," I said, refilling my mug.

"My point is that we were fun." Jess pointed at a greasy spot on her chest. "Do you see this? Do you?"

"I see it."

"It's turkey grease because I fell asleep at eight o'clock in the evening with a turkey wing hanging out of my mouth," said Jess. "Me. I did that. The girl who climbed out of her hotel window in London to go to drop acid at the Hippodrome."

"Do not tell the kids that," I said.

"I saw the Chili Peppers play wearing only tube socks."

"Where was that?"

"The Netherlands."

"Where were your parents?"

"Who knows? I was fun, and now I'm covered with grease. I didn't know you could go to sleep at eight o'clock. It's like we're eighty. No. Older. Your mom doesn't go to sleep that early," said Jess in full rant mode.

"Yes, she does," I said.

"Neither does mine. I got a text from Felicity last night. She was just getting in from dinner with her publisher. It was midnight in LA. My mother is more interesting than I am."

"She's always been more interesting than me."

"Are you listening?" Jess asked. "My husband is dead and I'm covered in grease."

"The two are probably connected," I said.

"What?"

"We used to have partners. Well, you did, and I had Derek when he was around. This is a new life, and it's exhausting. I've worked for two hours already this morning and it's Saturday."

Jess reached across the table and patted my hand. "That's terrible. Let's send the trappers to visit Derek."

"He doesn't believe," I said. "It's pointless."

Jess put her head down on the table. "I want to be happy again."

"We were happy last night. That was an excellent documentary."

"Do you even hear yourself?"

"Jess, I love you, but I'm not dropping acid at the Hippodrome."

"It's closed, I think."

"For good reason," I said. "So how was Mariah's date?"

"Boring," said Jess.

"What?"

Jess looked up. "Well, not boring, just nice."

"We want it to be nice," I said.

"They went indoor mini golfing."

"Oh, that's sweet."

"She should be having a wild, fun youth like I did," said Jess.

I shook my head. "I'm totally against that."

"What? Don't you want her to experience things?"

"No."

"I don't understand you."

I scooted my chair and put my arm around my best friend. "Mariah has experienced plenty. She lives with a ghost, for crying out loud. She needs safety and stability. Why do you think you liked my parents so much? They were super boring."

Jess blew her nose on a napkin. "They weren't that bad."

"Square dancing, Jess. Remember the square dancing?"

She chuckled. "Do I smell?"

"Like Thanksgiving. It's a good thing. Hal loved Thanksgiving."

Behind us, Poptart started hissing and then streaked up the stairs.

"Leo?" I asked.

Our ghost appeared next to the island and surveyed the mess. His recipes were strewn everywhere. "What happened here?"

"We were looking for something for…Eric," I said.

Leo perked up. "A recipe? What does he want? I remember all his favorites."

This is going to help.

"Sam doesn't think you have it."

"I'm sure I do," he said. "Which one does he want?"

"Your mother's soup. Albondigas soup, I think."

Leo froze, and I thought I'd miscalculated.

"Is that the wrong name?" Jess asked.

"No."

"Do you have it?" I asked. "We didn't see it."

Leo started to look odd, like he had when we were investigating his death and mentioned his kids.

"Don't disappear. We didn't mean to upset you," I said.

"I won't. It's just that I don't have that one," he said, looking sadder than ever. "I can't help Eric."

Talk about a wrong turn.

"Your mom didn't give it to you?" I asked.

"No. She never wrote it down. She said she would teach it to me, but she didn't get the chance," said Leo. "I died first."

Jess looked like she would burst into tears, and I wanted to kick myself.

"What about your family?" I asked. "They must have it."

"No one else was a cook. Just me." Carol's chair appeared, and he collapsed into it.

I slapped my hand on the table and stood up. "That's it. We are not boring and it's not too late."

"What are you talking about?" Leo said.

"Jess thinks she's boring and you think it's too late," I said. "We're investigating a ghost who's haunting children and a possible 1930s detective. That is not boring. And you." I pointed at Leo.

"Me?" Leo asked with his big dark eyes all sad and endearing.

"You're a master cook. You know what's in that soup. Let's make it."

"She never taught me."

"Nobody taught Jess how to be a mother, and she's a great one."

"Nice," said Jess. "Thanks."

Then a miracle happened. Leo stood up and the chair disappeared. "The meatballs were pork and beef."

"That's a start. Jess, go take a shower. I'm going to google that soup. We have an appointment at eleven."

Jess scurried off to take a shower, and Leo looked livelier than he had in weeks. "Do you think we can do it?"

"It's going to take a few tries, but we'll get it," I said.

"I can't even taste it," he said.

"You smell it and Eric can taste it."

Leo smiled. "Have you been reading my book?"

"The girls have."

He turned away. I think he may have wiped away a tear.

Armed with a shopping list, I dragged Mariah out of bed and forced her into jeans and a hoodie.

"Where are we going?"

"To the Blazevics' house to see that ghost."

"It's too early."

"It's ten to eleven," I said.

Mariah tried to get back in bed.

"And we have to go shopping for Leo's soup."

"*The* soup?"

"We have a plan to help *Eric*, and Leo is totally on board," I said, glancing toward the door, but I didn't see him.

"Can't we do all that later?"

"We have an appointment. The kids need us. The old lady is freaking them out."

"Take the boys," said Mariah.

"Are you kidding?"

"They always get out of stuff because they're crazy."

"True story, but you're who we want on this occasion," I said.

Mariah eyed me from under the curtain of hair that hung over her face. "Really? Why?"

"You're patient. The kids will respond to you."

"Kids love The Eggs. That's why Mrs. Johns gave them the pageant."

"We don't want a performance," I said. "We want two little kids to give us information that they don't know that they know."

"Max and Hen *are* crazy," she said.

"Yes. Please get up."

Mariah went over to her little dressing table and ran a comb through her hair and put on lip gloss. "Alright. Fine. I hope Leo's going."

Leo popped into the door and said, "I wouldn't miss it."

Mariah grinned at him and then me. He was better. That much was obvious. We went downstairs and joined Jess in the car. Driving the six blocks was a must. It was freezing, and I was still having turkey effects. The coffee hadn't helped much.

Jess parked in front of the house and carried her sketch pad with her. She told Mariah that we were going to ask the kids if they'd seen the man without revealing that he'd been in the house. Sandra could not handle it.

"Fine with me," said Mariah. "Can we go to The Grind afterward? I need quiche."

"How do you know they have quiche today?" Jess asked.

"Sam's working this morning."

I knocked on the door, and Mika answered immediately.

"Whoa," said Mariah.

"I should've warned you," I whispered.

Mika waved us in with a big, joyful smile, but his eyes had deep grooves under them. "Thank you very much for coming, and you must be Mariah."

His hand engulfed Mariah's, and she stared a little. "Hi," she said.

"Are you good with the children?" he asked.

"Pretty good. I babysit, or I did before we moved here," said Mariah.

"And...you aren't afraid?"

"Of kids?"

Mika laughed. "Of ghosts?"

Mariah joined in his laughter and winked at Leo, who stood by the fireplace. "No. I'm pretty much used to them now."

"That is good to hear." Mika gestured to the sofa. "Please sit down."

"Can Mariah look around a little?" I asked. "To see if she sees something."

"Certainly."

A tiny little blonde girl ran in and skidded to a halt beside Mika and stuck two fingers in her mouth. Mika scooped her up and nuzzled her with his beard, making her screech and us smile.

"This is my darling, Jelena," he said. "Jelena, this is Jess, Libby, and Mariah."

The little girl didn't speak, but she did wave at us.

"Are the kids' rooms on this floor?" Mariah asked.

"They are upstairs." Mika squeezed his daughter. "Do you see the lady this morning?"

Jelena shook her head, and he said, "Go ahead. You never know."

Mariah took off and crossed paths with a little boy that clearly took after Mika. He was a very large eight-year-old.

"Hi," he said. "Are you the ghost hunters?"

"We're more like ghost detectives," I said.

"Dad says you have a ghost," said Marko.

"We do," said Jess. "But he isn't scary. He's part of the family."

Marko looked around. "Where is he?"

"He's feeling shy right now," I said. "He might let you see him after we know you better."

The boy made a face, and Mika told him to sit down as Sandra came in. She looked worse than her husband, with eyes more swollen than the day before.

"I didn't realize you were here already," said Sandra. "Can I get you some coffee? I just made a pot."

"I'd love some coffee," I said, and Jess agreed.

Sandra went to the kitchen and Mariah came back. "Sorry. I don't see anyone."

Mika sat down in an oversized armchair with Jelena still in his arms. "That is a shame. I hoped a young person would see her."

"That was our hope too," I said. "But we're not done."

Jess opened her sketchpad. "Can you describe her to me?"

Marko shrugged. "Old, and she doesn't speak in English."

I pulled out my phone and opened the YouTube app, as Taylor suggested. "Maybe you can help us identify her language? Can you do that?"

The kids nodded, and I tried Spanish first. They said no. That wasn't it. Then I tried German. No. Italian. No. French. No.

"Do something a little more rare," said Mariah. "Russian."

I tried Russian, Turkish, Mandarin, Korean, and several

other languages, and they were all no. The kids started asking to go watch TV or play their games, even though Sandra tried to keep them engaged with snack and juice.

"This is so boring," said Mariah. "I need something to do. How about we do something while the adults talk?"

"What?" Marko asked with mild interest.

"I see you've got sketchpads like my mom's. Let's draw."

The boy made a face. "I don't like drawing."

"Why not?"

"My teacher says we have to draw nice things. Nice things are boring."

Mariah looked at Mika and Sandra and they nodded, so she got the crayons and pad. "Nice things are totally boring. You are so right. Let's draw something interesting for a change."

Mariah started working, and it wasn't but three minutes before Jelena left her father's protective embrace to join Mariah on the floor at the sofa table where a dragon was emerging. Then Marko came over.

"How big for the wings?" Mariah asked.

"Big," said Marko.

"That's not a size. Show me."

The kids started giving instructions, and Mariah drew an amazing dragon to their specifications. Then she got them drawing, showing them how to make eyes and claws.

"So," said Mariah. "Was the lady with you last night?"

The kids nodded.

"What was she doing?"

"Crying," said Marko.

"Where was she crying? In the hall?"

"No," said Jelena. "In my room."

"In your bed?"

"No. She was walking around."

I leaned forward. "Can you show us how she was walking?"

Jelena jumped and started pacing while wringing her hands. Then she hurried back to her pink dragon that was surprisingly fierce.

"She does that all the time," said Marko.

"She paces?"

"Uh-huh."

Mariah pointed at her dragon's bared teeth. "Is she ever like that?"

The kids agreed that the old lady didn't make mean faces. She never had. They saw her as sad or distraught.

Mariah tickled Jelena's nose with a lock of her long blond hair. "Does she have hair like mine?"

"No. She's old," said Marko.

She held out the crayons. "Show me the color of her hair."

He picked grey, and Mariah tickled Jelena's nose again. "Is it straight like mine or curly like your brothers?"

"Curly," said Jelena, focusing on her dragon.

"Is her skin your color or darker?"

Jelena looked up and focused on me. "Her color."

I grinned. Jelena's skin was extremely pale, and I looked tan in comparison. I leaned over to her and widened my eyes. "Does she have my eyes?"

Jelena shook her head. "They're not as pretty."

"Thank you, Jelena," I said. "Are they blue?"

She wrinkled her nose. "They're weird. I don't like them."

We all looked at each other, and Sandra's hands shook.

"Why don't you like them?" Mariah asked.

Jelena worked on drawing claws and didn't answer.

"Marko, are the lady's eyes weird?"

He nodded. "They don't look like your eyes."

"How are they different?" Jess asked, quickly sketching an eye. "Show me."

Marko reluctantly left his dragon and stood next to Jess. "Can I touch it?"

"Sure," she said, and Marko rubbed the pupil until it was almost indistinguishable from the colored part. Then he went back to his drawing.

Jess held up the drawing and Mika said, "She has cataracts."

"Oh," I said. "Of course."

Sandra sank back in her chair and gave us a weak smile. I pulled up several photos of people with cataracts, and the kids chose an eye that looked right to them.

"So it sounds like she had blue eyes, but they're all blurry now," said Mariah. "How about her nose? Is it a big, manly nose like your dad's, or a little delicate one like your mom's?

Her nose was neither, and it took a while to discover that the lady's nose was rather bulbous. Mariah showed incredible patience and worked through all the lady's features and then her outfit. She wore a flowered kerchief over her curly grey hair and a heavy cream-colored sweater with buttons and a pattern around the neck. Jelena described a plaid skirt that was below the knee. Then Marko said her shoes looked like men's shoes, but Jelena was offended and described them as brown lace-ups with no heel.

Jess sketched as the kids worked on their dragons with Mariah. Mika and I talked about life in St. Seb while Sandra held onto her coffee mug like it was a life raft.

Finally, Jess turned her portrait around and asked, "Is this the lady?"

Sandra gasped, and Jelena clapped. "It's her. It's her."

"How did you do that?" Marko asked.

"You told me what to do," said Jess.

The boy got up and looked closer. "It's really cool. Can you draw dragons like Mariah?"

"She taught me," said Mariah.

"That's her?" Sandra asked. "She doesn't look…evil."

Marko returned to his drawing. "She's not mean, Mom. Jeez."

"She's looks like an old lady from my country. Very traditional," said Mika.

Jelena grabbed Mariah's hand. "Can you draw Beatrice?"

"Who's Beatrice?" Mariah asked.

"Her favorite doll," said Sandra.

Jelena got up and tugged on Mariah's hand. "Come see Beatrice."

"Okay. Okay. I'm coming." Mariah held Jelena's hand, and they went in search of Beatrice.

"Your daughter is wonderful," said Sandra.

"Thank you," said Jess. "We like her."

"She's available for babysitting?" Mika asked.

Jess nodded. "She used to babysit all the time. She's taken the Red Cross training and everything."

"Is she busy tonight?"

Sandra stiffened. "We can't go out. What if something happens?"

"My love, we haven't been out in over four months," said Mika. "We need a break."

Sandra pointed at the portrait. "What about her?"

"You heard the kids. They're not afraid, and Mariah has more ghost experience than we do."

"I don't know."

"I do."

"Mom!" Mariah's voice echoed from somewhere in the house.

Sandra jumped to her feet, spilling coffee down her front. "What happened?"

Mariah ran into the living room. "She's here."

"The lady?" Jess asked.

"Yeah."

"Can you see her?"

"No, but Jelena says she's in her room," said Mariah. "We might get some more details."

We all dashed up to Jelena's room, except for Sandra and Marko. Mika persuaded the shaky Sandra that she didn't need the stress. We could handle it. I was surprised that she didn't come, but I was relieved. The room wasn't all that big, and Mika would take up half of it.

Mariah led the way into Jelena's room, where the little girl was curled up on her bed with a beautiful porcelain doll with real hair and an ornate Victorian outfit. Leo went and stood by the window, looking around. There was frustration on his handsome face, and he shook his head at me.

"This is Beatrice," said Jelena proudly. "Baba gave her to me."

"My mother," said Mika. "Beatrice is a family heirloom."

"You should draw her, Mariah," said Jess. "Draw them together."

"I'm not that good," said Mariah.

"I beg to differ," I said. "You obviously are. So... Jelena, the lady is here right now?"

Jelena nodded and fussed over Beatrice's bonnet.

"What's she doing?" Mariah asked.

"Crying."

"Can you show me?"

Jelena gave Mariah her doll and mimicked a distraught woman wringing her hands.

"That's really good," I said. "Where is she right now, Jelena?"

Jelena pointed at the window.

"Inside?"

She nodded.

"Can you show us, sweetheart?" Mika asked, and Jelena got off her bed and went to the window. She kneeled down in front of her toy box and began wailing and wringing her hands.

It was bizarre seeing a child doing that, and I quickly said, "That's really good. Does Beatrice have other clothes?"

Jelena jumped up. "Do you want to see?"

"I do," said Mariah, and Jelena went to find a small wooden box that was filled with Beatrice's other clothes, all original and beautiful. I went over to the toy box. It wasn't your typical bought-it-at-IKEA toy box. It was the size of a coffee table, wood, and obviously antique. There were two faint lion heads painted on the front and brass studs decorating the bands of iron strapping that made it look sturdy for travel.

"Where did you get this?" I asked.

"The trunk?" Mika asked, pulling his gaze from his daughter happily changing Beatrice's outfit with Mariah.

"Yes. Is it a family piece like Jelena's doll?"

He chuckled. "No. We bought at an antique mall."

"When?"

The smile dropped off Mika's face.

"Are you okay?" Jess asked.

"A few months ago. I'm not sure."

"Four months?" I asked.

He relaxed. "No. Longer. Memorial Day weekend."

Leo waved at me. "Ask Jelena when she started seeing the old lady. It was probably a while before she told her parents. Kids keep secrets that might distress their parents."

I went over to the bed where Mariah was helping Jelena but watching us carefully. "Jelena, when was the first time you saw the old lady?"

"I don't know," she said.

"Was she like she is now the first time?" Leo asked.

I repeated the question, and Jelena shook her head.

"What did she do at first?" Mariah asked as she selected a delicate little shoe for Beatrice.

"She sat on my bed," said Jelena.

"Was she saying anything?" Mika asked.

"Uh-huh."

"Was she upset?"

"Not yet."

I touched Jelena's little hand. "Was she trying to talk to you?"

"Uh-huh."

"Did she get more upset when you couldn't understand her?" Leo asked.

I repeated her question and Jelena nodded.

Mariah smoothed Beatrice's skirt. "Why didn't you tell your mom and dad about her?"

Jelena shrugged.

"Did you think they'd get upset?"

She nodded.

I turned to Mika. "It wasn't four months ago."

Mika looked like a tree that was about to be blown over. "Yes. I see."

We worked it through with the little girl and discovered that the old lady had been there before the Fourth of July and before their vacation in mid-June, but not before her birthday on May seventh.

"It's the trunk," said Jess. "It has to be."

"I bought it," said Mika. "I wanted an antique."

I went over and patted his rock-hard arm. "It's not your fault. Who would think that trunk came with a...passenger."

I looked at Leo and he said, "People are attached to places and things. She's attached to this trunk."

"Let's look it over," I said. "Did you see any names or dates or anything?"

"No. The dealer said it was an antique blanket chest." He pulled it out from the wall and we emptied it out together. There were no identifying marks anywhere, just some fresh scrapes on the bottom that probably didn't affect the value. A lovely cloth covered the inside. It wasn't some cheap wallpaper, but instead a nice, dark satin with pretty bouquets printed on it.

"This is a special trunk," I said. "Maybe a bridal trousseau."

"And she doesn't like toys in it?" Mika asked.

Leo frowned. "That seems like an extreme reaction to toys. We understand that things change. If I had to guess, I'd say she likes children best. That's why they can see her."

I leaned over and looked at the bottom. "Was this staining already here?"

"Yes. Sandra tried some stain remover, but it didn't come out. What do you think it is?"

"I don't know. The fabric is dark. It didn't smell or anything?"

"No. It was musty, but it's old."

"Did the dealer say how old it was?" Jess asked.

"He was guessing, but he said 1900," said Mika.

"What about the provenance?" I asked.

"The what?"

"Where it came from? Where'd he get it?"

"I didn't ask," said Mika.

I stood up and googled vintage trousseaus. Nothing looked like that trunk. "Did he say if it was French or anything?"

"No, but..."

Jess and I looked at him with excitement.

"What?" Jess asked.

"He seemed eager to sell it," said Mika. "I guess I now know why."

"How did you know he was anxious?" I asked.

A TRUNK, A CANOE, AND ALL THE BARBECUE

"He lowered the price without me asking and he said he needed to make room for more inventory."

"The dealer knew," said Leo. "You need to talk to him."

"Do you have the receipt?" I asked.

Mika nodded, and he closed the trunk before picking it up.

"Daddy, what are you doing?" Jelena asked.

"We have to take it back," he said.

Jelena's adorable little face scowled at him, and she crossed her arms over Beatrice. "It's my trunk. You can't take it."

"Sweetie, if we take it back, the lady will go with it."

"No."

"We can't keep it."

"Mine." Jelena gave Beatrice to Mariah and climbed off her bed to go toe to toe with her gigantic father. "You can't be mean. You said we have to be nice."

"Nice to the trunk?" Jess asked.

"Nice to the lady," said Jelena. "She's upset."

Mika put the trunk back. "I can get you a different trunk. A better trunk."

"No. You said we'd find out what's wrong with her." Jelena blinked back tears and Mika looked at us.

"We can go to that dealer and trace the trunk," I said.

"How will that help?"

"We have to start somewhere, and we have Jess's drawing. If we get the provenance, we might find the family."

Jess nodded. "It's a start. And if we find where it came from, we might discover what language she's speaking."

Jelena put her little fists on her hips. "It's mine."

"Your mama will not be happy," said Mika.

The tiny girl responded by leaping into her father's arms. He cuddled her and sighed. "Sandra will want it gone."

"Ask what the lady is doing now," said Leo.

I touched Jelena's thigh. "What's the lady doing now?"

She twisted around and looked at her trunk. "Nothing."

"Is she crying?" Mariah asked.

"No."

"Can you show us what she's doing?" Jess asked.

Jelena clasped her hands together, pressed them to her chest, and craned out her head.

"She looks..." I trailed off.

"Eager," said Leo.

"Exactly," said Jess.

"What?" Mika asked.

"Your ghost thinks we're going to help her," said Mariah, and Jelena nodded.

"She's smiling a little," said Jelena.

"Give us a shot," I said. "It's worth a try."

"You're going to help her?" asked the little girl.

"We're going to try our hardest," I said.

She smiled and asked Mariah, "Can you stay and play?"

"I can't, but maybe I can babysit you sometime," said Mariah.

"Tonight. Tonight."

Mika grinned. "Are you busy?"

"I'm not."

Mika kissed Jelena's cheek. "You will be a good girl."

She threw her arms around his neck. "Yes!"

"Sounds like we have a plan," said Jess.

Several.

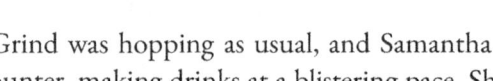

The Grind was hopping as usual, and Samantha was behind the counter, making drinks at a blistering pace. She grinned at us, and Sylvia came out from the back, carrying a tray of custard tarts.

"Haven't seen you in a couple days," said Sylvia, and she looked behind us.

"He went to check on the boys," I said.

She smiled. "Good. I hear we have a plan."

"News travels fast," said Jess.

"With girls, always."

We ordered, and Mariah went behind the counter to help. "We're starting the soup today."

"Can I help?" Sam asked. "I'm off at two."

"Sure," I said. "I have to work, so it's all you three."

"I thought you were going to the antique guy," Mariah said.

"I can't, but we'll go tomorrow."

"What antique guy?" Sylvia asked as she gave us our drinks.

I waved her over, and we went to sit down in an alcove. Jess showed her the portrait and told her what we were up to.

"I know that antique mall," Sylvia said. "They have good stuff. I got a lot of our decorations there."

I showed her the receipt that Mika had given us and a picture of the trunk.

"I remember that trunk," she said. "I was going to buy it and put a glass top on it so we could use it for a table here."

"Why didn't you?" Jess asked.

Sylvia's beautiful face grew puzzled. "It was the strangest thing. The girl at the counter when I went to negotiate the price talked me out of it."

"She didn't want to sell you her trunk?" I asked. "Why?"

"It wasn't her trunk. For a second, I thought it might be a racial thing, but it wasn't. She said the dealer was iffy and I'd do well to steer clear of him. She showed me a bunch of other trunks and I bought two. She was really nice, but she had a thing about the dealer."

"Or the trunk," I said.

"It seemed more like it was him and she was nervous. She didn't want me to tell anyone what she said."

I held out the receipt. "Do you recognize the name?"

She shook her head. "I don't know if she ever said it."

"That is interesting," said Jess. "They know something."

"And you're going to find out what?"

"I hope so," I said.

Sylvia leaned over toward us. "If you could solve Leo's murder, you can do anything. How is Leo?"

"Same," said Jess. "But the soup idea perked him up, but it's supposed to be for Eric."

"Sam told him, and he's on board. Eric hates seeing Leo like that. He was never depressed in life that Eric remembers. He mourned the grandparents, of course, but he could always see goodness around him."

"How is Darren doing?" I asked.

"I think he's still in shock and feeling guilty," said Sylvia.

"Guilty?" Jess asked. "What for?"

"If he hadn't been named in his grandmother's will, Patrick wouldn't have killed Leo."

"That wasn't his choice," I said.

"He still feels terrible. Darren would've given the place to Patrick if he'd known what would happen."

"I can't imagine how he feels," said Jess. "His own brother."

"Patrick was the favorite. I'm sure you've figured that out by now. The shining star. The most fun. Won the most awards. Most likely to succeed. How did this happen?" Sylvia asked, not really to us, but in general. The unanswerable question. Why?

"All we can do now is help them cope with it," I said.

"Speaking of soup. Eric has some ideas. I'll email them to you."

I showed her our base recipe, and she agreed that was a good start.

"So...how was the big date last night?" Sylvia asked. "Sam won't tell me anything that Mariah said."

Jess rolled her eyes.

"What? It was bad. How could it be bad? Taylor's a good kid."

"It wasn't bad," I said. "Jess is mourning her misspent youth and thinking Mariah's night of mini golf is not up to par."

Sylvia nodded. "I was working at Samantha's age. Alone in New York. Staying out all night. Hitting the clubs. My daughter is happy with Netflix and a pizza."

"You understand," said Jess.

"Yes, but I was lucky to get through it unscathed. Others weren't."

I sipped my coffee. "Please tell her that."

"I want Mariah to have fun," said Jess.

"Your kind of fun?" I asked.

Jess grimaced. "Maybe not that extreme."

Sylvia smiled and said, "Extreme. I like the sound of that. Do tell."

Jess told. It's amazing how you can know someone for decades and still not know everything. For Jess, *Home Alone* wasn't a movie. It was a lifestyle.

Chapter Seven

When I walked into the kitchen shortly before eleven the next day, I found Max and Leo standing motionless at the stove. Henri was at the kitchen table with every school book he had and twice as many notebooks and folders. Apparently, when you have a lot of tests, papers, and assignments due on Monday and Tuesday, you wait until Sunday to start any of it.

Any other kid might've had the sense to look chagrinned. My boy just grinned. I pointed at Leo and Max, and Henri shrugged before picking up a turkey sandwich. Thank goodness. We still have so much turkey.

Our less-than-alive neighbors, Peg and Vern, came over to spend Saturday evening with us, as usual, and were full of leftover recipes. Some included Jello. As much as I wanted to humor those two, I was not suspending two pounds of shredded turkey in what Peg called her Perfect Salad with unflavored gelatin, carrots, cabbage, and peppers. Using apple juice instead of water gives a special zing, or so I've heard.

I'd already agreed to watch back-to-back episodes of *Marcus Welby M.D.*, and that was bad enough. I could kick

Jess for buying the DVDs on eBay, but Peg and Vern were so happy. They just loved that Dr. Welby. Jess almost bought *Hee Haw* for them, but I got to her in time. That's where I drew the line. One minute, Jess was bemoaning our boring middle-aged life and the next she was all excited to sit on the sofa with ghosts, watching their favorite show. I didn't know what was happening, but we weren't doing *Hee Haw* or, God forbid, *Lawrence Welk*. I'd avoided antidepressants so far, but that would nudge me over the line. The Jello recipe would punt me over.

Jess came in behind me and said, "I give up. What are they doing?"

"It's not right," said Leo.

He and Max turned around. Max had the funniest look on his face.

"Are you okay?" I asked.

"Can you get high off sniffing soup?" Max asked.

"I don't think so."

"I feel funny."

I went and got my son, steering him away from the ghost who was back at sniffing the soup. Samantha and Mariah had made it the day before. I thought the soup was fabulous. Lovely little meatballs in a tomato broth with peppers and onion. Leo thought the soup smelled nice, but it was not his mother's soup.

"There's something missing," said Leo. "I can't put my finger on it."

"What did Eric say?" I asked.

"The same, but he doesn't know what it is."

I poured some coffee in a travel mug so we wouldn't have to go by The Grind. Sylvia was making cinnamon rolls. I couldn't resist those, and I was just being able to button my jeans again.

"Where are you going?" Leo asked without turning

around.

Jess got her own travel mug. "The antique mall."

Leo turned around and asked, "Do you want me to come?"

I didn't. The cats needed herding, but that wasn't the right answer.

"Always, but look at those two," I said. "They're already distracted."

"We're not distracted," said Henri. "We were never tracted."

I looked at the ceiling.

"Hey, Mom," said Max. "We figured out the theme of the Christmas pageant."

"Is it do your homework, get As, and scholarships?" I asked.

They snorted.

"We are so scholarshipping," said Henri.

"So many scholarships," said Max.

Jess crossed her arms. "Oh, yeah. How do you know that?"

"Mom and Dad got scholarships," said Henri.

"They don't get passed down," I said.

The Eggs laughed, and I kind of wanted to set them straight, but who knows? They seem to pull everything off with little effort, so maybe college would be the same. I hoped so. Derek wouldn't even discuss who was going to pay for college, and the boys' funds weren't going to cover it.

"Well, on that optimistic note, we're off," I said.

"Wait," said Max. "We didn't tell you our theme. It's about you."

A middle-aged mom that can't remember to wear deodorant?

"Me?" I asked.

"Yeah," said Henri. "We're basing the whole thing on your favorite movie."

Jess laughed. "You're basing a Christmas pageant on *Murder on the Orient Express*?"

Max pointed at her. "That would be super cool."

"That's not Mom's favorite movie," said Henri.

"It's not?" I asked.

It was. 1974. Lauren Bacall, Ingrid Bergman, Sean Connery, and Albert Finney as Hercule Poirot. Perfection.

"No," said Henri. "Your favorite movie is *Love Actually*. Dad told us."

Jess looked at me, and I shrugged. "Favorite Christmas movie."

"See," said Max. "We know."

Henri pulled up a photo on his laptop of the movie's Christmas pageant with the kids dressed as sea creatures. There were lobsters. I did love that movie.

"So you're doing what?" I asked.

"An ode to *Love Actually*," said Max. "It'll be great."

"Do I have to make lobster costumes?"

"Somebody has to," said Henri.

I looked at Leo and he said, "We'll talk about it."

"What's to talk about?" Max asked. "I'm emailing Mrs. Johns. She is going to love it, and Ethan's little brother plays the drums. This is going to be epic."

My kid started typing, and we left. There was nothing to say other than, "I don't know how to make a papier-mâché lobster."

"I wonder how they're planning on handling the Billy Mack video with the sexy girls," said Jess as we got in her car.

"I forgot about that," I said. "Are you worried about the body doubles' sex scenes?"

"I am now."

Jess may have laughed most of the way to the Fond Memories Antique Mall, but I was sweating. The Eggs didn't really see the world the way other people did, and I couldn't imagine what they'd decide to include because they thought it was funny. It would be funny. Flipping hilarious, but also might have parents banging on our door, yelling.

"It's fine," said Jess, wiping tears off her cheeks. "I love those two. I needed that."

"I didn't. What are we going to do?"

Jess made a swimmy motion with her hand. "Go with the flow."

"That's not a whole lot of help," I said.

"Speaking of help, let's track down that trunk and get paid so you can afford college if all those scholarships don't pan out."

"Very funny."

"I think so," said Jess, looking around the parking lot. "Are we sure it's open?"

I checked the website on my phone. "Opened at eleven."

We got out and went to the door, passing an ancient Dodge Caravan with a plethora of cat stickers on it. I love Poptart, but not that much, apparently. We opened the door that set off a buzzer that sounded like a whiny violin and went to a large square kiosk that had signs for checkout and customer service. There were six registers and nobody manning them.

"What do we do?" Jess asked.

"Shop," I said. "We need another coat rack."

"Yes, we do. I didn't realize Mariah and I had so many coats."

I pulled out the trunk receipt and said, "Let's start at booth fifty-one."

We looked left, right, and forward. Three ways to go and no hint of an organization.

"I guess we just wing it," said Jess. "It'll be like a treasure hunt."

"This place is huge," I said.

"A long treasure hunt." She took my arm. "Remember when we went to the vintage clothing mall in London."

"That place was awesome," I said.

"I still wish I'd bought that flapper dress."

"You would've rocked that fringe."

"Do you think it's too late?" Jess asked.

I laughed. "I'm sure they sold it twenty years ago."

"For fringe."

"No. You get to decide on fringe, but I say you're still in there."

She smiled and chose right. We wandered through the huge warehouse-sized antique mall stuffed with booths that specialized in everything from vintage records to jewelry to furniture. If there was an organizational plan, I couldn't detect it, but the deeper we went, squeezing between pie safes with their punched-out tin panels and Victorian brass beds, the more unsettled I felt.

Jess took my arm and whispered, "Do you feel funny?"

"Yes, very much so."

"We should've brought Leo."

"He had to handle the boys and figure out the soup," I said.

She squeezed my arm tight. "Did you see that?"

"Um...maybe," I said. "What did you see?"

That's when the sound of giggling erupted in front of us.

"You nasty little guttersnipes!" yelled a young woman.

A group of giggling children in ragged clothing ran down the cross aisle in front of us, chased by a bride in an Edwardian gown with a veil, flowers, and long train.

We ran to look and watched as the bride chased the children, trying to smack them with her bouquet. One of them, a boy with a split lip and a stack of newspapers under one arm, jumped up and snatched her bouquet. He dashed away, holding it high like the Olympic torch.

"How dare you!" the bride yelled, and chased the children around the corner.

"So that happened," said Jess.

"And so is that." I pointed at a booth filled with antique books where the man we'd seen at the Blazevic house leaned on a cane. He wore a different outfit, a three-piece suit with a pocket watch chain dangling from the pocket of his vest, but he managed to appear casual despite his formal attire.

"Do you think we should introduce ourselves?" Jess asked.

"Something tells me he knows exactly who we are," I said, nodding to him, and he responded with a smile and a touch to the brim of his hat.

"Okay. Let's keep looking."

We wandered through the mall and finally found the correct booth out of sheer luck. We smelled a fire and heard raucous laughter, following it to a booth filled with military antiques, uniforms, footlockers, and weaponry. Sitting in the center of the booth was a group of WWI soldiers gathered by a small cast-iron stove, playing cards. They reminded me of the trappers, although the smell was totally different. They were cooking something in a black pot on the stove, but it wasn't opossum, thankfully. It smelled like beef stew, but it was hard to tell with the amount of smoke the stove was emitting.

The soldiers didn't notice us and kept playing cards, giving me time to really see them. I suspected they were close to their deaths in the timeline, considering their conditions. Two had bare feet that were hideously swollen, red and blotchy. One had blood running down the side of his face, and another was missing a leg.

I jumped when Jess spoke.

"Excuse me," she said, and the soldiers looked up in surprise.

"Ma'am?" asked the one missing a leg.

"Sorry to interrupt your game, but do you know where

Booth Fifty-One is?" Jess asked.

They scratched their bristly chins, and I was struck by how young they were. There weren't very many bristles.

"Yes, ma'am," said the bloody one in a West Virginia accent. "Right there."

He pointed, and we turned around to see a booth that was more ramshackle than the others with no discernible theme like the other booths. It had everything from a blue Pan Am travel bag to a 1920s dresser to a tuxedo that might've stepped out of *The Great Gatsby*. It was totally disorganized and looked like a garage sale exploded.

I turned back to the soldiers. "That messy one?"

The men laughed.

"The old man don't do much on it anymore," said the man with the bad feet.

"Do you know the old man's name?" Jess asked.

"He don't see us."

I paused and then asked as I caught sight of the man in the suit approaching, "Do many people see you?"

One man laid down a card, causing the others to curse and throw down their own cards.

Laughing, the winner said, "Not so much. You are the first in a while." His accent was upper class, and I noticed his uniform was better quality than the others.

Jess stepped closer. "Do you see a man over there by that refrigerator?" She pointed at the man who watched us, still and expressionless.

"A what?" asked West Virginia.

"That big white box."

The soldiers turned and looked. Then they shook their heads.

"Sorry, ladies," said the one without the leg. "You know we cain't always see each, right?"

I smiled. "We know, but it doesn't hurt to check."

"Thank you for your service," said Jess as she turned away.

"Huh?" the soldiers said as one.

Jess turned back and said it again, causing confused frowns.

"Thank you for your service to our country," she said. "We thank our soldiers now for their sacrifices. It's normal."

The men got both misty and excited. Now they were interested. They got up and gathered around Jess, showing her their medals and pictures of their families. While she was busy, I went into Booth 51 and started going through the piles of, well, crap. There were boxes of cheap paperbacks from the seventies, a collection of rusty iron skillets, and old golf bags with random clubs in them. Some things had tags on them and others didn't. Nothing showed where the items may have come from, and there wasn't a dealer name either.

Jess joined me and held out her phone. "They are so sweet. I'm going to see if I can find their families."

"What for?" I asked.

She turned back to the men, who'd resumed their game but waved happily at us. "Their stuff is in that booth. The families might like to get it back."

"Did they know each other when they were alive?" I asked.

"No, but they're good friends now."

"Did they die in the war?"

Jess shook her head. "Not all of them."

"Seriously?"

"Tucker got gangrene after the amputation, and that killed him. McSally got shot in the head while on patrol, but the rest survived," said Jess.

"I'm shocked," I said.

"Me, too." She turned back to the booth. "This is a mess."

"Tell me about it, and nothing looks like it might be related to Jelena's trunk. We need to find someone who works here."

Jess looked past me. "Maybe she does."

I turned to see a woman wearing a seventies blue jumpsuit. "You think she's alive?"

"Check out the hair."

The woman had chunky highlights in her blond hair and curtain bangs.

"You might be right, but they didn't invent those bangs yesterday."

"May as well try it," said Jess. "She kinda matches Sylvia's description of the clerk who wouldn't sell her the trunk."

"Didn't she have brown hair?" I asked.

"People change their colors all the time," said Jess.

"Yes, they do."

We worked our way through several booths to catch up with the woman who was going through the mall with a clipboard in hand.

"Excuse me," I said. "Hello."

"Oh," she said, turning to look at us with eyes that were rimmed with blue liner. Not a good sign. "I didn't know we had any customers yet."

We came up to her and Jess asked, "Do...you work here?"

"Yes, I do," she said. "I'm Dawn. How can I help you?"

Dawn?

"Dawn, that's an unusual name for someone your age."

"I'm twenty-five," said Dawn with an adorable frown.

"And you work here?" Jess asked.

The frown deepened. "Yes."

"With the customers like us that come in?"

"Um...who else would I be working with?" Dawn asked as she edged away from us.

"Sorry," I said. "I guess since it's an antique mall, we expected someone older."

Dawn smiled and said, "I get that a lot. I just love vintage. This is a great job for me while I finish my master's."

Good sign.

"What's your degree in?" Jess asked.

"Public policy."

Excellent sign. Was that even a thing in the seventies?

"That sounds difficult," I said.

"It's fascinating. I love data and microeconomics."

It sounded like she was alive, but that outfit? She even had the platform heels. We could be there all day trying to figure out if she was alive, so I reached out and poked her shoulder. Solid.

Dawn stared at me. "What are you doing?"

"Nothing. That is an extraordinary outfit. Where did you get it?"

She told us about a vintage booth on the other side of the mall that specialized in the seventies.

"I love to dress in vintage. The customers like it," said Dawn. "Are you looking for seventies clothing?"

"Actually," said Jess, "we're looking for a couple of things. A coat rack and information."

"Coat racks we have," she said with a smile. "I don't know about information."

"I'm hoping you know something about that booth over there," I said, pointing at the mess.

Dawn wrinkled her nose. "We have way better stuff than that."

"We can tell, but we have a particular interest in that booth."

"How so?"

I pulled out Mika's receipt and showed it to her. "Do you know anything about this trunk?"

Dawn handled back the receipt. "Sorry. I didn't sell that. I wasn't working."

"How do you know?" Jess asked.

"That's not my handwriting."

We chuckled.

"Of course." I pulled out my phone and found a picture of Sylvia. "Do you recognize her?"

"Oh, yes. She's hard to forget. I sold her some things for...a coffee shop, I think."

"You are dead on," I said, pulling up a photo of Jelena's trunk. "She tried to buy this trunk, but you talked her out of it."

Dawn looked away. "Why do you ask?"

"The family that did buy it asked us to find out its provenance," said Jess. "Don't worry. They don't want to bring it back. They just want to know the history."

She relaxed a tad bit. "Well, I can't tell you that. I have no idea where it came from."

I pointed. "But that booth sold it?"

Dawn nodded and made a face.

"What's wrong?" Jess asked.

"Nothing."

I held up Sylvia's picture. "Why did you warn her off buying the trunk?"

"I really shouldn't say anything." Dawn shivered, and the hairs on the back of my neck went up. Then, suddenly, there was a man standing behind her. Jess and I sucked in breaths and Dawn's eyes widened.

"What's wrong?" she asked.

The man came around the side of her, so close he was almost touching her. He wore a shiny pinstriped suit and held a Tommy gun in one hand like a gangster out of a black-and-white movie.

"Nothing," I said.

The man sniffed Dawn like a predator and then winked at us.

"We... ah..." Jess trailed off as the man looked her up and down.

Dawn swayed, and I asked, "Are you okay?"

"I just feel…"

The other man, the one with the cane and pocket watch from the Blazevics, walked over and jerked a thumb at the gangster. "Beat it."

The gangster sneered at him. "She's seen me."

"She ain't seeing you now."

"I can make her." He sniffed Dawn again, and she paled as she looked around. "Do you smell something?"

I nodded. The gangster's smell was dive bar at three in the morning, stale cigarettes, alcohol, and pee.

"What is that?" Dawn asked.

I took her arm and met the eyes of the other man. He was older now, in his fifties with lots of laugh lines and too much sun exposure.

"I said beat it." He jerked his thumb, and the gangster looked ready to defy him, but the man said, "You don't want to test me."

Then the gangster shrugged and sauntered away.

"You need to sit down," said Jess, and she grabbed a bentwood rocker from a nearby booth. We sat Dawn down and I got her a mint. In the short time we'd been dealing with ghosts, I'd discovered that mints helped. I can't say why.

Dawn sucked on her mint and apologized. "I don't know what came over me."

And you don't want to.

I glanced at the man with the cane who'd retreated to stand by another booth. "It's fine."

"Sorry we're bothering you about the trunk," said Jess. "We're helping out the family."

Dawn nodded. "I can't tell you where it came from."

"Why didn't you want to sell it?" I asked.

"I would've if she insisted."

I squatted next to her. "Why would she have to insist? You

sell antiques. A sale's a sale, isn't it?"

"Well... the dealer is..."

"Less than honest," suggested Jess.

"Oh, no. Not the dealer himself. Hugo Olsen is a nice man, but he's getting up there, and his son is more involved."

"And that's not good?" I asked.

"The stock has gotten weird." Dawn explained that she'd started working at the antique mall when she was still in undergrad, and back then, Hugo Olsen's booth mainly offered midcentury furniture, books, and artwork. His sales were steady and everyone liked him, but as he got older, the furniture was harder for him to deal with, and his son started helping. Hugo came in less and less. Dawn hadn't seen him in a year, but she talked to him on the phone sometimes. He wanted to know why sales were down, and she would refer him to his son.

"We've had issues," said Dawn.

"Like what?" Jess asked.

"The other dealers complain about the state of the booth and the quality of the stock. They don't like being near a booth that's unprofessional, and some people think the stuff is...not clean."

"Not clean as in stolen?" I asked.

"There's been a few questions on that, but I mean clean as in clean."

Jess and I looked over, and I have to admit *clean* wasn't the first thing I thought of, but the whole antique mall did have a dusty feel about it.

"We had some customers freak out," said Dawn. "I didn't want your friend to have any issues when we have so many nice things that haven't had problems."

Oh!

"What are they freaking out about?" I asked.

"They didn't say, they just ran out, and I mean all the way

out," she said.

"Of the building?" Jess asked.

She nodded. "One lady was screaming. Well, more than one. Several."

Jess and I looked at each other and then at the booth. I hadn't seen a thing, and I was fairly confident that I would if something were there.

"How do you know it was that booth's fault?" I asked.

"I saw it happen one time. A woman was in the booth and she just started screaming," said Dawn. "Another time, a man came and yelled at me about playing jokes in the booth and that it wasn't funny. I didn't know what he was talking about. The other dealers think there might be mice or dead mice. One of the dealers swears she smelled something rotting."

This is getting worse.

"When's the last time that happened?" I asked.

Dawn thought for a second. "Oh, I guess it's been a while. A few months, maybe."

"Could it be six months?" Jess asked.

"I don't know." Dawn took a breath and stood up. "I go home for the summer, so I don't know what happens then."

The man with the cane moved into my eye line and smiled. He unnerved me for a second, but I got it together and asked, "Has it happened this fall since you've been back?"

"Let me think," she said. "You know what, I don't think it has."

The man nodded and walked away.

"Can you give us Hugo Olsen's address?" Jess asked. "We really need to talk to him."

Dawn put the rocker back and said, "I'd have to look it up. I think Hugo lives out in the country. Dutzow or someplace like that."

A voice came from behind me and said, "Are you talking out of turn, Dawn?"

A TRUNK, A CANOE, AND ALL THE BARBECUE

"Mr. Burgess," said Dawn, going stiff. "I didn't see you there."

We turned around and a man in his late sixties, wearing a flannel shirt and a fleece vest, eyed us with suspicion. "I noticed."

"These ladies have some questions for Mr. Olsen."

"I'll be happy to answer any questions," he said. "You should go man the front. We've got people flooding in."

He was obviously full of it, but Dawn scurried off, leaving us with the guy that sold Mika Jelena's trunk. No two men could have the same out-of-control eyebrows, ear, and nose hair. At least, I hoped not. That was a lot of nose hair. Mika wasn't exaggerating.

"I hope you can help us," I said as the bride, now regal with her bouquet back, walked by. Mr. Burgess glanced at her and then us. He saw her, but he barely registered the knowledge on his face. I knew on instinct he would never admit it to us.

I held out the receipt. "You sold this trunk?"

Mr. Burgess barely glanced at the receipt. "Possibly. There are no returns for Booth Fifty-One."

Why am I not surprised?

"They don't want to return it. They want to know where it came from," I said.

"I have no knowledge of individual dealers' stock."

"Why were you so eager to sell the trunk?" Jess asked.

Mr. Burgess's eyes narrowed. "I don't know that I sold it."

I pulled up the photo of the trunk that Dawn instantly recognized. "This trunk. You sold it to Mika Blazevic."

"I don't recall the trunk or anyone by that name," he said.

I showed him a picture of Mika from his company's website. "This is Mika Blazevic."

"I'm sure I would remember him."

I'm sure you do remember him.

"Look," said Jess. "We're not trying to cause a problem. The family wants to know the provenance of the trunk. That's not an unusual request, is it?"

Mr. Burgess struggled with that one and finally said, "No, but I can't tell you anything."

"Okay. Fine," I said. "Why were people screaming in Booth Fifty-One?"

He was ready for that one. "They weren't."

"No screaming and running out?"

"No."

"How about a rotting smell?" Jess asked.

"I don't know what you're talking about," said Mr. Burgess. "Now I have to get back to work. Let me walk you out."

Jess and I crossed our arms.

"We're not allowed to shop?" I asked.

His cheek twitched as he struggled for an appropriate response.

"Looks like you could use the business," said Jess.

"We do very well," he said, affronted.

"None of the people here can buy anything," I said.

His cheek twitch got worse, and I smiled as the guttersnipes dashed around us, jumping at him and yelling about how he was a fat bastard.

"I don't know what you mean," said Mr. Burgess.

One boy pulled down his pants and mooned him, then ran away, yelling, "Made you look."

The other followed suit, and we started laughing. The ghosts took such joy in harassing Mr. Burgess, it was impossible not to enjoy it.

"Stop that," he demanded.

"Having a good time?" Jess asked. "Never."

"We take it as it comes," I said.

A boy flicked a ghostly booger at me and I pretended to

catch it, delighting him to no end.

"It's time for you to go," said Mr. Burgess. "I'll show you—"

I turned to the boys who were taking turns throwing dead rats and mooning Mr. Burgess, who clearly wasn't popular. "He's trying to make us leave. Do you think we have to go?"

A raucous jeering started behind us, and the boys surrounded him.

"Stop that. Get out of here, you filthy ragamuffins!" he yelled.

"He called us filthy," said Jess. "How dare he!"

"Not you," Mr. Burgess said.

"Then who?" I asked. "We're the only ones here."

The man with the cane appeared behind Mr. Burgess and tipped his hat to us, enjoying every minute of the dealer's discomfort. I gave him a salute and said, "He won't say who he's talking about. Is that fair?"

"Yeah," said Jess. "We all deserve to be acknowledged, don't we?"

"What are you doing?" Mr. Burgess asked.

"Shopping," I said. "Ta-ta. Have a good one all by yourself."

Mr. Burgess let out a string of colorful curse words, and it was just his luck that a family that seemed very much alive happened to be within range. They made faces and hurried away while Mr. Burgess swatted at the children, delighting them even more.

"You just have to talk to them," said Jess.

"You don't know what you're saying," he said.

"Well, they're not whirlpooling us, so I think we do," I said. "Come on, Jess. Let's find a coat rack."

She hooked her arm through mine and put her nose in the air. "I'm sure we'll find plenty of help."

And we did.

Ghosts are helpful, and Jess was right. Everyone wants to be acknowledged, even if they're dead. Before long, we had a paddleboat captain, a young man from the Shawnee tribe circa 1820, and a fifties housewife giving us a tour. Doris was the most helpful. They'd torn down her house to make way for the antique mall and she'd been there ever since, finding the activity and changing stock amusing.

She and Hokolesqua knew where all the coat racks and hall trees were. Hokolesqua only spoke a little English, but he was happy to point out the advantages and disadvantages to each piece. Doris knew the style. He knew the defects. The paddleboat captain had a whiskey flask and proved you could be a drunk ghost should you choose to be. He wasn't very helpful with the antiques, but he proved to be an excellent source of information on Mr. Burgess, who he also disliked intensely. All the ghosts did. We would've liked to have gotten more out of Bill, but he was too drunk to stay on one topic for long. He did know that Mr. Burgess was friends with Hugo Olsen's son, Steve, and he was getting some cash under the table for putting up with the mess in Booth 51. Bill called Steve a rubbish man, and I gathered he sold a lot of stuff online. Bill was very interested in computers, and unlike Doris and Hokolesqua, he had a basic understanding of what they were and did. He'd seen Mr. Burgess looking at Steve's stock online. Unfortunately, he couldn't tell us more than that because he had a second flask and drained that, passing out in an aisle where the bride had to step over him to continue her promenade.

With the help of Doris and Hokolesqua, we picked out an Edwardian hall tree, found a cart, and wheeled it to the front, where Dawn was helping some living customers who were buying antique books to class up their living room.

When she was done, she checked us out and passed me a slip of paper.

"Don't tell Mr. Burgess," she whispered.

I glanced at the paper and grinned. Hugo Olsen's address. "Thanks. You're a sweetheart."

She smiled and said, "If there's anything else I can do, just call. I'm usually the one that answers the phone. Mr. Burgess can't be bothered."

That was the moment Mr. Burgess came sprinting by, chased by the children, the gangster, and a woman in a long dress and bonnet, who was throwing rocks at his head. We watched him run down a long aisle, yelling, "Stop it, you dirty scum bastards!"

Dawn's mouth hung open, and when he turned a corner, disappearing with a string of foul language hanging in his wake, she asked, "Did that happen?"

"What exactly?" Jess asked.

"Mr. Burgess running and yelling about bastards."

She really can't see.

"I'm afraid so," I said. "He might have an issue."

Dawn leaned forward. "He's the bastard."

"You'll get no argument from us," said Jess.

I signed my credit card receipt and Dawn asked, "Do you want help out?"

People were coming in to shop, so we said we could handle it and we wheeled our purchase out into the cold and flurries. I hadn't given the size of the hall tree any thought, but it fit in the Volvo, just barely.

After I returned the cart and got in, I showed Jess the address. "To Hugo's?"

"Where's Dutzow?" she asked.

"Beats me. Ask Google." I asked, and we went, not knowing what was in store. Every day is an adventure when you can see the unseen.

Chapter Eight

We drove onto the bridge at St. Sebastian half an hour later. The sun had come out, and the flurries vanished, so we had a clear view across the bridge. You'd think that would be a good thing, but it wasn't.

"So across the bridge and five or six miles," I said. "I hope he's home."

"Sunday afternoon. We have a good—" Jess slammed on the brakes. A car behind us screeched to a halt, nearly hitting us, and I screamed so loud, I hurt my own ears.

A man was standing on the railing, holding onto a cable and looking down into the churning river.

"What do we do?" Jess asked.

"Help," I said as I jumped out of the car.

The car behind us honked, and I held up a hand, approaching the man slowly. "Hello there," I said, shivering in the wind coming off the icy river.

"Libby!" Jess called out to me. "I'm calling."

I gave a thumbs-up but didn't look back. A man behind me yelled, "What are you doing? Get moving!"

"Hello," I said. "I'm Libby. Can I ask what you're doing?"

The man on the railing turned to look at me. He wore a suit with his tie askew and his shiny dress shoes were slipping on the slick railing. His eyes were so empty, I felt a chill of hopelessness in my soul.

"Please tell me—"

He jumped, or rather, he vanished after he jumped. Just gone. I bent over as the honking of a multitude of cars assaulted me. Jess ran over and dragged me back into the car. Then she jumped in and hit the gas. We did our own fishtailing and sped off the bridge with hearts still pounding.

"That was..." I couldn't even put it into words.

"Terrible," Jess said. "So real. I thought he was real."

I put my hand on my chest. "We're going to have to figure something out. We could have an accident."

"We had to stop," said Jess. "He could've been real."

"He was real," I said, feeling my heart pound under my sweater. "It happened. He did it."

"Maybe," said Jess. "He disappeared when he stepped off. Maybe he didn't really do it in life."

"Why reenact that or remember it or whatever?"

"We'd have to ask him."

"I don't want to," I said.

The last thing I wanted was to see those eyes again. I was seeing a death, and suddenly I wanted to call Derek. He saw Hal die. He knew. Had I been understanding enough about that? I couldn't even remember what I said. The pain had been so raw and overwhelming.

"You were amazing," said Jess.

"Huh?"

"You just went. You didn't even think about it."

I smiled. "That seems more like a you thing."

"Back in the day, it would've been," she said. "I rubbed off on you."

"Well, you were right behind me."

"We always made a good team," said Jess, turning at the sign for Dutzow.

I nodded. The ghost thing just got a whole lot more complicated. I was grateful Jess was there. A team was definitely in order.

We drove through the tiny town of Dutzow and it appeared to boast a small grocery store, a feed store, a barbecue joint, and a winery. Hugo Olsen's house sat on a dirt road just past the short main drag.

"I totally want barbecue," said Jess.

"I'm right there with you. Afterward."

Mr. Olsen had a long driveway that could've used some shoring up. There were a lot of ruts, and Jess bottomed out twice. She grumbled until the house came into view.

"Oh, it's lovely," said Jess.

"I didn't expect that," I said.

She grinned. "I expected a trailer like the Fischers used to have."

"Me too."

Mr. Olsen's house was far beyond a trailer. It was a log home with a wide front porch and pillars. Everything about the house was neat and tidy, but there was a collection of large metal sheds off to the right that weren't in the best of shape. One was open, and we could see it was stuffed to the rafters with junk that ranged from coolers to furniture, with a canoe crammed in the corner. There were wagon wheels, planters, and birdbaths scattered around the sheds in various states of disrepair.

"That looks more yard sale than antique dealer," said Jess.

"I wonder where he's getting that stuff," I said.

Jess parked next to a panel van, and we went to the door. My heart was back to beating normally, but I'd be lying if I didn't admit that I was nervous about knocking. Anything could happen. The bridge taught me that.

A TRUNK, A CANOE, AND ALL THE BARBECUE

Luckily, Jess had no such trepidation and knocked straight away.

"You seem more like yourself," I said.

"I don't know who I am without Hal," she said.

While I tried to think of an answer to that, an elderly man with a walker answered the door. "Can I help you?"

"Hello," said Jess. "We'd like to ask you some questions about a trunk you sold six months ago."

Mr. Olsen squinted at us behind thick bifocals and said, "I don't do the selling anymore. I'm retired."

"Your son, then," I said.

"He's not here."

"Where can we find him, then?"

Mr. Olsen shook his head. "He's a busy man, and we don't take returns anymore. That's his policy."

"We know," said Jess, smiling her most winning smile. "We're just helping a friend. He wants to know the provenance of an item he bought."

"No returns," he said.

I nodded. "He doesn't want to return it. His little girl loves it. He just wants to know where it came from. If it's American or perhaps European."

"People like to know provenance, don't they?" Jess asked.

Mr. Olsen nodded. "It is important for sales. I always tried to know everything I could about my items."

"Then you understand," I said.

He smiled, showing off a set of false teeth that could've used some brushing. "Of course, but Steve isn't here right now."

"Does he live with you?" Jess asked.

"He looks after me. I'm lucky. He's a good boy."

"I'm sure he is. Do you know when he'll be back?"

"He's at his girlfriend's house. I don't know."

"Do you have his number so we can call for an appointment?" Jess asked.

"What are you asking about? No one asks Steve questions like they did me," said Mr. Olsen, growing a tad suspicious.

That's interesting.

I got out my phone and held it out with the picture of the trunk displayed. "This is the item we're asking about. Do you recognize it?"

The old man squinted at the screen. "What is that?"

"A trunk."

He frowned. "A trunk?"

"Yes. Pretty ordinary," I said, fudging a bit.

Mr. Olsen leaned in closer. "Where did you get it?"

"We didn't buy it," said Jess. "A friend did."

His frown deepened. "What's inside?"

"Nothing," I said. "But it has some pretty fabric."

He jerked upright. "Where did you get it?"

"They bought it at the Fond Memories Antique Mall," said Jess, and the old man instantly started backward, dragging his walker.

"Go on now," he said.

"Mr. Olsen," I said, "you recognize that trunk. Please tell us where you got it from."

"I've never seen that before in my life," he said.

"You obviously have," said Jess. "Just tell us and we won't bother you again."

"I'm an old man and I'm retired." He slammed the door in our faces.

I knocked and shouted, "Mr. Olsen. We only want to know where it came from. Whatever's going on isn't your fault."

He reached up and pulled down the shade to cover the window, and we heard the locks being locked.

"I guess that's the end of that," said Jess.

"She must've haunted them," I said. "And they sold it without worrying about who was inheriting the problem."

We walked back to the car, and Jess shook her head. "I think it's more than that."

I got in and put my hands over the heat vents while Jess turned us around. "What makes you say that?"

"That's a pretty extreme reaction to a simple question," she said. "They probably bought it without knowing. What's the harm in saying where they got it?"

"You're right. All he has to do is tell us they bought it at another antique mall or something, and we go away," I said. "What's the problem?"

"There must be a big problem," said Jess. "Barbecue?"

"Yes, please."

She drove us back into the one-horse town that had a very busy barbecue place. Dutzow BBQ was full, and we agreed to eat at the bar to avoid waiting. The place smelled fantastic, and I wanted to order everything but settled on a burnt ends sandwich and sweet potato fries. Jess surprised me by ordering a real lunch, ribs and slaw.

"What? I'm starving," she said.

"I'm just happy you're eating," I said.

The bartender, a middle-aged guy covered in tattoos and leather, offered us drinks. Jess got coffee, and I indulged in a spiced hard cider. Very alcoholic and very good.

I sipped the cider and asked, "So, should we hang around and wait for Steve to get back?"

"It could be all day," said Jess. "I doubt he's going to be any more forthcoming than Hugo."

"I guess we could get Leo to pay them a visit."

"We don't know if they can see," she said.

"They know something. It's a fair bet."

"I'd rather go with a sure thing."

I propped my elbows up on the bar. "I don't think there are any sure things anymore."

"Larry Fischer is still scary," she said. "And he owes us."

"You want to sic a furious Fisher on old Mr. Olsen?" I asked.

"Do you have a better idea?"

I took a drink and let it warm me through before I said, "I'd like to have a try with Steve first before we call in reinforcements. This is our job. We should try to do it ourselves. Besides, you never know. Maybe Steve will see sense and just tell us. It's the easiest thing to do."

The bartender sidled over and said, "Are you talking about Steve Olsen?"

We perked up, and I said, "We are. Do you know him?"

"I do. Not a bad guy. What do you want with him?"

"Information," said Jess. "It's easy."

The bartender chuckled. "Good. Steve doesn't do hard."

"What do you mean?" I asked.

He put his hands on the bar. "It's like this. If there's a right thing and an easy thing, Steve goes with easy every time without a thought. Don't get me wrong. I like Steve. Great guy to have a beer with, but I wouldn't want to trust any big decisions to him. Another cider?"

"Don't mind if I do," I said. "I hope I don't get wasted."

"It's cooked down, so the alcohol isn't much." He poured me a second cider and refilled Jess's coffee cup. "So what are you trying to get out of Steve?"

I told him about the trunk, the ghost-free version, and that got him puzzled.

"Old Hugo wouldn't tell you where it came from? That's weird. I've known him forever. He was always honest and upfront."

"Not about this," said Jess.

"Mind if I look at it?"

A TRUNK, A CANOE, AND ALL THE BARBECUE

I showed him the trunk, and he shook his head. "I don't recognize it, and I've been in the Olsen house a lot."

"Where do they buy from?" I asked.

"Auctions were Hugo's thing, but he doesn't get out much anymore," said the bartender.

"What about Steve?" Jess asked.

"I can't see Steve hanging out at an auction all day. That's effort."

A woman called out, "Order up number eighty-three."

"Hold on." The bartender went and got our food. It was drool-worthy without a doubt, and it took effort to stay focused.

"I just asked Lynn," he said. "She knows Steve too. She says he's into the storage thing."

Jess and I looked at each other between mouthfuls. I swallowed and asked, "Storage thing?"

"You know, like *Storage Wars*. He buys storage units full of junk and then sells it."

I wrinkled my nose. "That explains all the random stuff in the sheds out at the house."

"And at the antique mall," said Jess.

"What's he selling there?" asked the bartender.

We told him about the mess and how other dealers were complaining.

"Sounds like Steve," he said. "Lazy as the day is long."

"The house looks well cared for," I said.

He chuckled. "That's Steve's sister. She pays for a housekeeper, but Steve takes credit."

"So you think he won't help us find out about the trunk?" Jess asked.

"You'd have better luck going to the storage places."

I wiped sauce off my chin and said, "We'd have to know where to go."

"Google it," he said.

"There must be places all over," said Jess. "How would we know which one is the one he's bought from?"

He refilled Jess's coffee again and said, "Like I said, Steve is lazy. He's not driving far. Look for the closest place that does auctions."

I googled storage auction and found several places. A blonde woman with nearly as many tattoos as the bartender came out smiling and introduced herself as Lynn, the pit master. We told her she was a genius, and she glowed with pride.

"Ned said you were asking about Steve's business," she said.

I told her why we were asking and she looked at the list on Google.

"Steve's in here a lot. I've never heard him mention St. Peters, but he has talked about driving down to Rolla."

I looked at the map. They were about the same distance. "He told you he buys storage units?"

"Bragged about it is more like," said Lynn. "That man is always on the lookout for the easy score. He buys the units online. He doesn't even go in person to check them out."

"So he could buy from anywhere," said Jess.

"He could," said Ned, "but he wouldn't. Steve's not going to spend hours driving anywhere if he can avoid it."

Lynn nodded. "He'd go with the easiest option. I'd go down to Rolla and see what they say."

"Who are you doing this for, anyway?" Ned asked.

"The Blazevic family in St. Seb," I said.

Lynn and Ned threw up their hands.

"That's Mika's trunk?" Lynn asked.

"Yes."

"Love that guy. He got me through my knee replacement."

Ned poured me another cider on the house. "He did my

rehab after my motorcycle accident. Love that man. Made me tough it out. I'd be walking with a limp if it weren't for him."

The love for Mika and his family was strong. Our entire lunch was on the house. They took my number and promised to call the next time Steve came in so we could corner him.

We left Dutzow Barbecue with full bellies, new friends, and a plan. You can't beat that.

Chapter Nine

Rolla Storage Solutions' website said it was open, and they had three abandoned units on an auction site. I saw nothing in the pictures worth buying, but the bids were up to a hundred bucks on all three.

We drove into a seedy area filled with pawn shops, bail bondsmen, and, my favorite, a sewer cleaning shop next to Intimate Desires Adult store. The storage place was a block away. You wouldn't be finding me storing anything there, but apparently, no one else had an issue. The facility was huge, with hundreds of units in various sizes.

"It's not as crappy as I thought," said Jess.

I pointed at the cameras as she parked. "Lots of security and fresh paint."

"If the cameras work."

"Huh?"

"Places put those up for show. They've been doing it forever," said Jess.

We got out, and I asked, "How do you know that?"

She smiled at me. "Felicity put it in a book."

"Was it based on you not getting on security cameras back in the day?"

She smoothed her ponytail and said, "Could be."

"Did Hal know all this stuff?" I asked.

"If you didn't, he didn't." Jess headed for the office, and I followed the way I used to when she was cooking up a plot to have fun. And we had fun, a lot of fun. I was only arrested once, but the judge vacated the arrest, having pity on me for being young and stupid. Same for Jess, although there were a couple of underage arrests for drinking and public lewdness. Skinny dipping was taken seriously back then.

Jess went into the office, all smiles. She could always charm people with Derek's kind of confidence. I stood behind her and waited while she rang a little bell on the counter.

She looked over her shoulder and said, "Get up here, Lib. I need you to bat those blue eyes."

"You don't need me to do anything," I said. "You're in the zone."

"I don't have a zone anymore."

I didn't answer, but I did go to the counter. We waited, listening to some indistinct chatter in the back. It sounded like a soap opera was on and a group was watching.

No one came out, so Jess rang the bell again and a yawning man about fifty came out. His name tag said Perry. He had significant scarring on the side of his face and a limp.

"I'm sorry. I may have dozed off," Perry said with a smile. "What can I do you for?"

Jess smiled and said, "We hear you sell abandoned storage units."

He nodded and handed her a card. "We do. You can buy them online."

"Actually," I said, "we're interested in a unit that you've already sold."

Perry straightened his polo and said, "A sold unit? Which one?"

"We're not sure. It would've been sold over six months ago to Steve Olsen."

"Oh, Steve. I know him," said Perry. "Did he send you?"

"Not exactly," said Jess. "We're trying to track down a piece he sold. The provenance is important."

Perry shook his head. "Can't help you. I have nothing to do with what's in the units. I just open the unit when the buyers come to haul the junk away."

"So you would've opened the unit for Steve, then," I said.

He shrugged. "Maybe."

"Do you have records on which units were sold to who?"

"That's private and confidential."

I shook my head. "There's no such thing as buyer storage unit confidentiality." It sounded good, but I had no idea.

"I don't know anything about what Steve does or why he does it," said Perry.

Jess's eyes narrowed. "You think Steve's up to something."

"No, I don't."

"You do too," I said. "You're getting all sweaty."

He wasn't, but that made him nervous, and he started to fidget.

"Libby, show him the thing," said Jess.

"The thing?" I asked.

"The thingy we're looking for."

"Oh, that thingy." I showed Perry the picture of the trunk, and I'm pretty sure he recognized it, but he had the air of someone who just didn't want to deal with it.

"Sorry," he said.

New tactic.

"It's for a little girl," I said. "Her dad bought her the trunk and they want to know the history. Is that so bad?"

"No," he said.

"Show him the picture, Jess," I said.

"Which one?"

"Of Jelena that Mariah sent you while she was babysitting."

Jess held out her phone and showed Perry a photo of Jelena and Marko holding up their dragon drawings.

"Cute kids, but I still can't help you," said Perry.

I wished we had Larry with us. Even if he didn't spit in people's hair anymore, he looked like he spit in people's hair, and that would probably be enough for Perry. A stiff wind could've blown that guy over.

"We're trying to do a good thing for a little girl," I said. "Who would it hurt to tell us which unit that trunk came out of?"

"Steve wouldn't like it," said Perry.

"He doesn't need to know, and it really isn't a problem for him."

Perry crossed his arms and said, "There's nothing I can do."

Jess was about to make another argument when a group of guys in track uniforms came out of the back. They were in their late teens and smelled of sweat and beer.

"Come on, Perry," said one. "Help the ladies."

"It's for a little girl," said another.

Perry grimaced and made a little waving motion at them that he tried to conceal from us.

"You got the list on the computer," said a third. "It would take you a second."

"Do it, man," said another.

The space behind the counter was getting tight, and Perry was truly sweating.

"If that's all, ladies," said Perry. "I need to get back to work."

"Do you call watching soap operas work?" Jess asked, and the boys broke out laughing.

"She's got you, bud."

"Taking a nap during our stories."

"Super hard working, Perry."

Perry kept a straight face and said, "I have the TV for company."

"What are we?" asked one boy. "Chopped liver."

I smiled and batted my eyes. "It's for Jelena. She's only four."

"Come on, Perry. Come on," the boys chanted, but he shook his head.

Jess and I looked at each other, and there was only one thing to do.

"Come on, Perry. Come on," we chanted, getting the boys to pump their fists and making Perry look nauseous.

"Why did you say that?" he whispered.

I grinned. "All the cool kids are doin' it."

The boys broke out in gales of laughter, slapping each other on the back and, if I'm honest, getting smellier. Boys. What are you going to do?

"Can you…"

"See them?" Jess asked. "Yes, we can."

"Who do you see?" Perry whispered.

The boys turned their backs to show their names.

"Harris. Jones. Clark. Hill. Green," I said. "Mueller. Barnes."

Perry held up his hands. "Enough."

Jess and I waved at the boys.

"Hi. We're Jess and Libby," I said. "New to seeing the dead. How are you?"

Some of the boys jumped over the counter, and others walked through it. They all wanted to talk. Perry was one of the few that could see them, and he wasn't very interesting.

Plus, they'd known him forever, and he was never the most exciting guy.

"Hey," said Perry. "Enough of that. We were always tight."

The boys joshed him for a bit and then we got to hear their story. They went to the track sectionals. Won. Got drunk in the parking lot with the bus driver and crashed on the way home. Perry was one of the few survivors. He first saw them at the crash site and thought he'd gone insane, since he knew they were under sheets.

"That must've been startling," said Jess. "Libby passed out the first time she saw our ghost."

The boys loved that, and we gave them our history. It was probably a mistake. They didn't know there were so many people in St. Seb that could see ghosts and they decided on a field trip. I told them about the trappers and how they loved company. So that might be a win-win.

"So," I said, leaning on the counter, "what do you say, Perry? Can you give us that unit or what?"

Perry sighed.

His former teammates began chanting again.

"Oh, fine. Since I'll never hear the end of it, let me look." Perry flipped up the end of the counter and let us into the office, where he went to the computer and quickly looked up the auctions that ended over six months ago.

"We don't have a lot," he said.

"Does Steve buy from any other storage places?" Jess asked.

"Not that I know of. He doesn't like to drive."

That fits.

"He's not exactly a go-getter," I said.

"No, he isn't," said Perry, and his teammates agreed. They weren't crazy about Steve. Harris caught him peeing on one of the units, and they were all deeply offended. I was surprised, since I figured boys would pee anywhere, but they took it like Steve was peeing on Perry. Not okay.

"He bought six units before May," said Perry. "They were dirt cheap, and he said he got some good stuff."

"Do you know what was in them?" Jess asked.

"We don't inventory. Unit auctions are a crapshoot. Sometimes you get lucky and sometimes you don't."

"What about pictures?" I asked. "I saw pictures on the auction site."

"Oh, yeah. I take those." Perry went in and pulled up pictures of the units one by one. On the third, we got lucky.

"What's that?" Jess asked, pointing at a corner of the open unit that was stuffed with stuff, including rugs and the canoe we'd seen at Mr. Olsen's house.

"What?" Perry asked.

Green put his hand through Perry's head, causing him to yelp and shiver. "Don't do that! Now I've got brain freeze."

"Sorry," said Green. "But that looks like a corner of a trunk."

Still shivering, Perry blew up the photo.

"That's it," I said. "That's the trunk."

"Oh, yeah. I remember that unit. There was a real bidding war on it. Steve paid a pretty penny."

"Why was it so popular?" I asked, looking closely at all the stuff.

"The rugs and the canoe. All those boxes. They were pretty neat and labeled."

"Whose unit was it?" Jess asked.

"I have no idea. It was an old one from back in the day," said Perry.

"You don't have the credit card and info on file?"

Perry leaned back in his chair. "This may come as a shock to you, but not everyone wants to put their real names on their storage unit."

A TRUNK, A CANOE, AND ALL THE BARBECUE

"Don't they have to?" I asked. "You ask for ID, don't you?"

"Sure," said Perry. "And we require a credit card now, but we used to take cash, and there's nothing to stop someone from using a fake ID. What am I gonna do? Run a credit check on every dude that wants to hide his stuff from his wife? I don't think so."

"But the credit card would have to match the ID."

"People fake both. We've had stolen cards used. Sometimes people don't check their statements. We had a granny who was paying for a unit here for twelve years before her son took over her finances and discovered the charges."

The boys were horrified, but a new episode of *Coronation Street* started playing and they got distracted. Perry rolled his eyes. "They love that show. Puts me to sleep."

"Nice of you to play it for them," said Jess with her eyes going moist.

"Least I can do," Perry said softly. "It makes them happy."

"Can you find out what you do have on that unit?" I asked.

Perry typed away on the computer and said, "Yeah, I thought so. This unit was in the original section. No records on the computer. Let me look through the files."

Jess and I watched *Coronation Street* with the boys while Perry dug into his records. It didn't take too long, since the unit had been abandoned and the file was in that drawer.

"Here we go," he said, opening a slim manila folder with tattered edges. "Jeez. This is old."

"When did they start renting it?" Jess asked.

"March 29, 1990."

"Wow," I said. "That's forever ago."

"When did you declare it abandoned?" Jess asked.

"March, but it should've been a lot sooner," said Perry. "My fault. It wasn't on the computer. Normally, when the unit's payment doesn't come in, it gets flagged, and we start trying to contact the owner. We give them ninety days to pay or get their stuff."

"How long since that unit paid?" I asked.

"Three years." Perry's cheeks colored. "It didn't pop up, and it wasn't until I was doing an inventory of the old units that I noticed that there hadn't been a payment."

I bent over and peered at the accounting sheet in the file. "Cash payments?"

"Yes. He came in every five years and paid for another five," said Perry.

"So it's been eight years since he's been in?"

Perry looked at the sheet. "That's right, and before you ask, I have no idea who it was. We do take cash payments from the old-timers, but I couldn't tell you about this time. Eight years is a long time, and Glen took the last payment. He's long gone."

"If we found him, do you think he might remember?" Jess asked.

"You two are determined," said Perry. "No, I doubt it. Glen was a pothead. He was lucky to remember the day of the week. We fired him for sleeping in the units."

"Well, what's the name on the contract?" I asked. "I can barely see it."

Perry held up the sheet. "Unit 15 belonged to T. Jones. If that isn't generic, I don't know what is."

"How about a phone number? You had to contact him somehow," said Jess.

"We tried. No luck. It was a landline that was disconnected."

"What's the address?" I asked. "Is it here in town?"

"Yep." Perry gave me the address, and I plugged it into Google. "That can't be."

"What?" Jess and Perry asked.

"It's a Dairy Queen."

Jess sighed. "Awesome."

"You know, it probably wasn't always a Dairy Queen," said Perry. "They tear down old houses all the time."

"Do you know when they built the Dairy Queen?"

He looked at the photo I pulled up. "Looks fairly new, but I'm not a Dairy Queen guy."

I groaned. "Do you remember anything else about that unit? Anything we can trace?"

Perry sighed. "We sell abandoned units all the time. There's been some pretty amazing stuff in them from time to time."

"Like what?" Jess asked.

"We had a mint-condition 1969 Mustang once."

"Are you joking?" I asked.

"Nope. That's the kind of thing I remember. And one unit was filled with mannequins. Nothing else. Just mannequins. Almost gave me a heart attack when I opened it. Another unit had six kayaks and crates of bedpans. That was memorable."

"Did Steve say anything about it?" I asked.

"Let me think. That was a busy time. It ebbs and flows. We had a ton of unit turnover around then. I was run ragged." Perry looked down at the paperwork.

Jess elbowed me. "What about them?"

I looked over at the ghosts. Why not?

"Hey, guys?" I walked over with the trunk photo on my phone. "Do you have a second?"

"No," said Harris. "Tracy's about to con Charlie into paying for an abortion."

"She's not even pregnant," said Green.

The boys were on the edge of their seats, but I said, "It'll only take a second."

"Shush."

I grabbed the remote and paused the show, causing a huge ruckus.

"It's fine," I said, holding out my phone. "Do any of you remember this trunk or the stuff that was in the unit where it was?"

Most of the boys could barely be bothered to look with Tracy on the screen, frozen in mid-scheme, but Hill and Clark did a double take.

"Yeah, I remember that," said Hill. "Perry complained about that."

"Huh?" Perry swiveled in his seat.

"You were so mad that Steve bothered you about that unit," said Clark.

"He bothered me?"

Harris looked over, tapped his temple, and said, "He forgets stuff, so we help him remember."

A muscle twitched in Perry's jaw, but he didn't deny his memory issues.

"The head injury?" Jess asked.

He nodded. "I've never been the same. The guys...help me keep track of things. I remember the big stuff like mustangs."

"I'm glad they can do that for you," I said.

"I couldn't have held a job without them, but please don't tell anyone. The owners don't know that I have problems from the accident, and I'd like to keep it that way."

"Your secret is safe with us," said Jess. "So Steve bothered you?"

"I don't really remember that," said Perry. "Guys? Why was Steve bothering me?"

"He needed help moving the stuff, and you were busy," said Clark.

"Oh, right," said Harris. "You argued about it."

Perry slapped his forehead. "I forgot about that. I was so busy with customers. I'd have had to close the office to do it."

"Then you didn't move anything with him?" I asked.

"No." He looked at the boys and they shook their heads, but Green said, "Mr. Thompson did."

A zing of hope went through me. "Who's Mr. Thompson?"

"Long-term customer," said Perry. "I don't remember him being here, but that's not unusual. Boys?"

The boys all agreed that Mr. Thompson had been there that day, paying his bill in person and getting his wife's Easter stuff out of his unit.

"Which unit is it?" I asked.

Perry reached for an old-fashioned ledger, but Green said, "Unit 16."

"There you go. Right next to T. Jones."

"Do you have a number for Mr. Thompson?" Jess asked.

"That I have." Perry found Mr. Thompson's file and called. Mr. Thompson answered on the first ring and was confused about what Perry was asking until he mentioned moving a canoe. Mr. Thompson was seventy. He was surprised that Steve asked him, but he was in good shape and was able to do it easily.

"Did you move anything else?" Perry asked.

Mr. Thompson said he'd moved a lot of things. Steve was very insistent and he couldn't get away. It was easier just to do it. Perry asked about the trunk, and the old man wasn't sure. Then I texted him the photo, and he remembered it well because that trunk was one of the sticking points with the moving. It was incredibly heavy, and Mr. Thompson wanted to empty it out, but Steve insisted they move it full. That was the last thing Mr. Thompson moved, because lifting it into Steve's van hurt his back.

"Ask him if he saw what was in it," I said.

Perry asked, but Mr. Thompson said that Steve stopped him from opening it. He thought there must be something valuable inside and was very curious. He thought he might take a peek when they got it in Steve's van, but Steve didn't turn away for a second.

"Did he see anything that might identify the owner?" Jess asked.

Mr. Thompson said it was a lot of closed boxes labeled with names and dates. He didn't look inside. He just moved them with Steve. Perry thanked him and hung up.

"I can't think of anything else to do," said Perry.

"Do people have to come into the office to get their keys or anything?" I asked.

"No. They have their own keys."

I went and picked up the remote. "Guys, do you ever remember anyone getting into Unit 15?"

The boys didn't remember anyone ever going in there, and Perry said the unit was pretty hard to open, since there was considerable rust on the door tracks.

"I don't think it'd been opened in a long time," he said.

I turned on the soap and the boys went back to being engrossed. I couldn't imagine Max and Henri being interested, but I guess being dead changes everything.

"Thanks a lot for your help, Perry," I said. "We really appreciate it."

"I don't think it was much use, but I'm happy to help," he said.

"Wait a minute," said Jess. "We didn't ask Mr. Thompson."

"Ask him what?" I asked.

"If he's seen anyone in Unit 15. He's had his unit forever, hasn't he?"

Perry looked at Mr. Thompson's information. "1987."

"Maybe he has," I said. "Do you think I can text him, or would that be weird?"

Perry shrugged. "He didn't mind the photo. I don't see why you can't text."

I went ahead and sent a message. Mr. Thompson answered immediately, saying he'd seen no one at the unit. The storage place was usually very empty. I thanked him, but then a few seconds later, he texted again. His wife had seen a man one time in the unit about ten years ago. She pulled up in her car. He saw her and quickly closed the unit and drove away.

"What did he look like?" I texted.

"About fifty. Just normal," texted Mr. Thompson.

"What about the car?"

"She doesn't remember."

"Anything else she remembers?" I asked.

"She only remembered because we never see anyone there and he was weird about closing it and getting in his car. She didn't even get out before he was driving away."

I thanked him again and told Jess and Perry.

"Why does that make me nervous?" Perry asked.

"Because you're human," said Jess. "And we humans know something's off when we hear it."

"What do you think he had in that trunk?"

The old lady.

"I have no idea, but we're going to find out," I said. "Jess, we need the sketchbook."

Jess ran out and came back with her drawings. She showed them to Perry and the boys. None of them had seen the old lady or the man who'd appeared in the Blazevic's kitchen and had been following us around.

"Sorry," said Perry. "Who are they?"

"We don't know yet," said Jess.

"Then how did you draw the pictures?"

We smiled, and then Perry laughed. "Of course. Silly me. You saw them."

I explained about the trunk and the Blazevics.

He shook our hands and said, "I sincerely hope you figure it out. That's awful what's happening to those kids."

We thanked him and the boys and turned to the doorway. The man stood there, leaning on his umbrella with his hat pulled low. He smiled and nodded at us. Then he was gone. Not the way Leo left with a pop. It was more a whisper and somehow more disturbing.

"What?" Perry asked from behind the desk.

He didn't see him. I wonder why.

"Nothing," I said. "We got a lot to think about."

"Good luck."

We were going to need it.

Chapter Ten

Dairy Queen was a bust. In terms of information, that is. In terms of the Oreo Hot Cocoa Blizzards, totally solid. Jess had a tiny kid's cone like an insane person and asked the entire staff about the building, the area, and anything she could think of, but the staff had no clue. Even the manager didn't know anything. She'd moved there a year ago. The building had been there for years, but that's as good as it got.

We drove home with information, but I wasn't sure what to do with it. Steve was the one to talk to, but with the way Mr. Thompson talked, he would not be forthcoming about the trunk.

Jess turned into the driveway and said, "We can't tell Mika and Sandra."

"Tell them what?" I asked. "We don't really know anything."

"I know you're thinking what I'm thinking."

I got out and said, "What am I thinking?"

Jess joined me and lowered her voice. "That she was in the trunk."

I grimaced.

"See. I knew you thought that."

"I was, but why would Steve hide it? He just bought the unit. He didn't kill her. All he had to do was call the police. It's not his fault."

We walked up to the front door and Jess said, "Didn't want the publicity?"

"Any publicity is good publicity."

"With bodies?"

"He'd have been on the news and talking about the business," I said. "He might've gotten new customers."

"Maybe it's not that, then," said Jess. "Something obviously stolen. Loads of money, like from a bank robbery."

"I wish we had a better description of that guy who owned the unit."

Jess opened the door. "I wish we had a full name. T. Jones. What the heck is that? It even sounds fake."

I walked in and stopped in the foyer. "Do you smell that?"

Jess smiled. "They're at it again."

"If at first you don't succeed," I said.

We walked back to the kitchen where we found the kids, all the kids, about fifteen in all. Ethan and Sam were at the stove with my biggest stock pot. Max and Henri were at the kitchen table with Keely, Mariah, and a bunch of kids I didn't really know, but had seen a few times. I would've been irritated that they didn't ask if they could have people over if Leo hadn't looked so happy, standing in a corner watching the hive of activity.

"Are we having a party that we weren't told about?" I asked.

"Mom," said Henri. "You're back."

"We are back. What are you doing?"

"Planning the pageant," said Max. "It's a whole thing. We had to have a crew."

Henri pointed at the kids around the table. "Mom. Jess. The crew."

"Hi, crew," I said, and the kids waved.

"Did you get your homework done?"

"Yeah, yeah. It was easy," said Max. "We study grouped it. Strength in numbers. Try the soup."

Sam and Ethan waved, and we went over.

"Another version?" I asked.

"My abuela's recipe," said Ethan. "Want to try it?"

We both tried the Estes family recipe, and it was great, but when I looked at Leo, he shook his head.

"Love it, but what did you do with the other pot of soup?" I asked.

"Tell me you didn't throw it out," said Jess.

"No way," said Sam. "We wouldn't do that."

"So..."

Mariah came over. "We took it to the senior center. Ethan's grandma says they take donations, and they were super happy to get it."

Ethan nodded. "They were going to package it up and send it home with people, but everyone wanted it, and it was gone before they could do it."

I hugged them all. "What a wonderful idea. Would they take turkey soup? We've got to do something with that turkey."

"Sure," said Ethan. "They love getting homemade stuff. My abuela brings in her tortillas and people draw straws to get them. Mr. Szmanda's daughter makes pierogies."

I got the turkey out of the fridge and popped it in the Crock-Pot with water. I turned it on low and went back to work. The house cleared out about seven and we sat down to eat the Estes family soup.

"What's wrong with it?" Mariah asked.

Leo stood there with his arms crossed. "I don't know, but it isn't right. Something's missing."

"A secret ingredient," said Henri.

"The plot thickens," said Jess.

"Not thick enough?" Max asked.

Leo laughed. "It's not a stew."

They all went back and forth, but I found myself not thinking about the soup or even the trunk. I was back on the bridge and feeling chilled again by those eyes. What was he doing? Of all the ghosts we'd had contact with, none had been like that.

"Libby?" Leo asked. "Everything okay?"

I couldn't tell the kids about that horror, so I said, "Yeah, just tired."

"Sorry you didn't figure out where the trunk came from," said Henri. "But you'll get it."

"Yeah, you will," said Max.

Mariah nodded. "It's pretty cool that you found where it came from."

"Just the storage unit," said Jess. "We still have to find the owner of that unit."

"I told Jelena that you would fix it."

"Were the kids okay last night?" I asked. "We didn't see you this morning."

"They were great. I made grilled cheese with sourdough, cheddar, provolone like you taught me. They loved it, and we drew dragons and watched Christmas movies. They are so ready for Christmas."

"Was the lady there?" Max asked.

"She was, but I can't see her," said Mariah. "I thought maybe she'd let me see her if I was there for a while, but she didn't."

"What was she doing?" Jess asked.

"The kids said she was quiet, like she was waiting for something. I think she's waiting for you to solve it."

She might wait a long time.

"I hope we can," I said.

"There is one thing that happened," said Mariah.

I braced myself. "Another ghost?"

"No. Jelena doesn't want her to leave."

"Who?" Leo asked.

"The old lady."

Leo smiled. "She's attached."

"To a woman who keeps her up all night crying?" Jess asked.

"She's not scary. Jelena likes her when she's not crying, and she hasn't cried since you two were there."

"You made an impression," said Leo.

"Then why won't she let us see her?" I asked.

He shook his head. "Her reasons might not make any sense, even to her. I didn't want anyone to see me until you came. I couldn't have told you why. Now I know, of course."

We all got quiet. Leo had hidden himself for nearly twenty years because somewhere deep inside, he knew Patrick had murdered him and he couldn't face it. The old lady must be going through something similar. I hoped her body wasn't in that trunk at some point. How could Mika keep the trunk? Sandra would lose her mind, not that I blamed her. Being in a former funeral home was one thing. Having a trunk coffin in my kid's room was another.

"I didn't mean to put a damper on the mood," said Leo.

"It's cool," said Max. "We just feel bad."

"I don't want you to feel bad."

Max and Henri grinned. "You can make it up to us."

Leo smiled and crossed his arms. "Oh, really? How can I do that?"

"Help us with the Christmas pageant," said Henri.

"Sports were my thing."

"Sports. Musicals. Same thing," said Max.

"They are not."

"We have faith."

Leo agreed to help, and Mariah was on kitchen duty, so I took my laptop up to my room to answer some more emails. I'd forgotten how relentless the insurance game was. People were in distress and needed help immediately. Eric wasn't a nine-to-five kind of guy, either. He worked all the time, according to Sylvia. When people needed something, he was on it no matter what. I knew where he got that from. Leo would never have told a grieving family that it was Sunday or late at night or that he was busy. He'd have dropped what he was doing and been there for them. He was a good example to my boys. The world had a shortage of kindness, and I took that thought right into bed, where I answered emails about a leaking fridge ruining hardwood and a daughter who'd been driving for three days and hit a car in the McCann's parking lot at seven that night.

"Libby?" Leo's voice came through my door.

"Come in," I said.

Leo walked through my bedroom door and came to the foot of my bed with a concerned frown on his face. He was still wearing his mortician outfit, and I found myself longing for Zorro or his cover band getup. Anything that reflected his old happy self, but I feared that black suit was there to stay.

"What happened?" he asked.

"We told you all what happened?"

"Jess is crying again."

I closed my laptop. "What? Did she tell you why?"

"I didn't want to intrude," he said.

"That's my department." I started to slide off my bed, but Leo said, "What happened to you?"

"Me?"

"I can tell, Libby. I know you," he said.

"It's nothing."

The armchair appeared, and he sat down to wait while I figured out what to say.

"You can't mention it to the kids," I said.

"I understand."

"There was an incident on the bridge."

Leo got stiff. "Did someone do something to you?"

I pulled the covers up to my chin. "Not to me. To himself."

Leo listened in that patient, kind way of his, and I found myself tearful for no particular reason.

"It's so crazy. I wanted to call Derek. I never want to call him," I said.

"You're compassionate, and you had a similar experience to Derek. You watched someone die."

"But it wasn't real."

"It was real," said Leo. "It happened."

"But why would he show that to us? Why would he relive it?"

"We don't always know why we're drawn to certain things in life or in death."

"Do you know who that was?" I asked.

"Tell me more about what he looked like," said Leo.

I described the man, and Leo shook his head. "I didn't bury him. We don't get a lot of suicides in St. Sebastian."

"Hold on. John the mover said people jump off the bridge. It's a thing."

"It is a thing, but that doesn't make it common," said Leo. "And it's not usually St. Sebastian natives."

"People come from out of town to jump off the bridge?"

"Sadly, yes."

"Why?"

"I don't know," he said. "It draws them."

"Do you think we could help him?"

"The man on the bridge?"

"Yes."

He smiled at me. "It's kind of you to think that."

"So you don't think we can?"

"I don't know."

I nodded and got out of bed. "Do you want to come with me to see Jess?"

"No," he said. "I'll sit here awhile."

I knew he would say that, but it disappointed me all the same. "I'll be back."

Leo nodded, and I went out to Jess's room down the hall. I knocked, and she answered in a muffled voice, "Don't make a big deal out of it."

I went in to find her crying in bed. That happened often enough that I was starting to hate the sound of Air Supply. "Did something happen?"

"No. It's stupid." She blew her swollen nose and burst into tears again.

I sat on the end of her bed. "Come on. We did pretty good today, considering we've got a ghost we can't see and an antique dealer that's shutting us out."

"It's not that," said Jess.

"What then?"

"You saw me today."

I eyed her and tried to figure out where this was going.

I've got nothing.

"I see you every day," I said.

Jess blew her nose again. "I was happy."

"And that's bad because…"

"Hal is dead," she said.

"I don't mean to be difficult, but you've been happy since it happened. I've seen you," I said.

"Not like that."

"Like what?"

"It lasted for a long time, and I wasn't even thinking about Hal," said Jess with a fresh set of tears.

Leo. Come in here. Come on, Leo.

"You can't think about him all the time," I said.

"I should," she said.

"Says who? If you say the internet, so help me."

"I think I should. Instead, I'm feeling like I used to," said Jess, looking more guilty than I'd seen her in years. Jess was about as big on guilt as I was on shame. We don't do either much at all.

"That's good, right?" I asked. "You're recovering."

"No, like I used to."

"I don't get it."

"Before Hal. When it was you and me running around and having fun. Before careers and kids. Before. I didn't miss it. I didn't think I did."

I moved up beside her and put an arm around her trembling shoulders. "You'll figure it out."

"It's like I didn't really like that life with him, and I did. I loved it."

"But it wasn't you like you used to be. It's a new you," I said.

Jess cried on my shoulder and Mariah came in with big eyes. "Is everything okay?"

"She misses your dad," I said.

"I thought you had a good day."

I smiled through my own tears that came without warning. "That's why she misses him."

Mariah climbed onto the bed. "It's okay, Mom. Dad would want you to be happy. Leo wanted Carol to be happy. He was sad that she never got over it."

"He said that?" Jess asked.

"Yeah. He's kinda upset about it."

Max and Henri came into the doorway.

"What are we doing?" Max asked.

"Are you having movie night without us?" Henri asked.

Mariah rolled her eyes. "Yeah, dirtbags. We're having a crying movie night."

The boys made faces. "That's not so much fun."

"No kidding."

I explained what was happening to the boys, and they considered for a minute and then left. I wasn't sure if they just didn't want to deal with it or if they were up to something. To my relief, they came back ten minutes later with supplies.

"It's movie night," said Henri, putting an enormous bowl of popcorn on the bed.

"TV night," said Max.

"Yeah, TV night."

The boys climbed on the bed, and Max grabbed Jess's remote off her side table.

"What are you doing?" I asked.

"Hal said that *Golden Girls* makes Jess happy," said Henri.

"We're doing what Hal said." Max turned on the TV.

"You're crazy," said Mariah.

"And brilliant," said Henri.

"Most of all, humble," said Jess, wiping her eyes.

The boys turned and looked at her.

"Was Hal wrong?" Max asked.

"Hal was never wrong," she said. "Press play."

He pressed play, and we all curled up for a *Golden Girls* marathon on a Sunday night. It might not have been the best idea on a school night, but no regrets.

Chapter Eleven

Eric Otto looked up from behind a pile of paperwork and smiled as I walked in the main office to drop off some signed paperwork. He was a different man than the one I'd met weeks before Halloween. His color was good, and he no longer seemed as weighed down. Seeing a ghost had done that for him, and he never expected that to happen or that Leo's murder would be solved.

"My favorite person," he said, waving me into his office.

"One of them, anyway." I went in and put a container on his desk.

"You and Jess are in the top ten. What's that?"

"The new albondigas soup," I said.

"Sam said it wasn't right." He picked up the container and popped open the top. "Cold, and it still smells good. What's wrong with it?"

"Leo doesn't know," I said. "I was hoping your taste buds could lend a hand."

"Happy to help." He looked at my empty hands and asked, "All good?"

"Yep. We are all caught up. The Campanoses' fridge has

successfully ruined the entire first floor's hardwood, and the basement needs water abatement. Reba Porter never wants to drive again, but the damage is minimal."

"Fridges and hardwood," said Eric. "A match made in hell, and people never realize what's happening until it's too late."

"Especially when they're in Florida with their dying grandmother," I said.

"That's worse. You've got them in a hotel?"

"The bed and breakfast down the street from Number Eight, and two estimates will be in today."

Eric kicked his feet up on the desk and said, "And now we wait for the Thanksgiving disasters."

"How many garages last year?" I asked.

"Only one by some miracle. Our worst was five years ago. Four garages and two houses."

"Frozen turkeys?"

"Three frozen turkeys, two grease fires, and one family dispute that ended in a drunk uncle driving through the breakfast nook. No injuries. Thank goodness."

"Have you thought of doing a public service announcement? You can't fry frozen turkeys."

Eric smiled. "Sylvia thought of that after the bad year. She puts up signs at The Grind and all over McCann's Market. It's helped."

"She's brilliant."

"That she is," he said. "I don't think I have anything else right now. You can join me in kicking up your heels."

"Actually, I can't," I said.

"Oh, right. You're on the Blazevic case," said Eric. "How's that going?"

I made a face. "We're trying to figure out a way to get Steve Olsen to tell us what he knows about Jelena's trunk."

"You're sure he knows something?"

"Positive."

"I wish I could help, but I don't know that family."

"And I thought you and Sylvia knew everyone," I said.

Eric got up. "Not quite. It's almost lunch. I'm going to have the soup. Want to share?"

"I've had plenty. I have another question, though."

"Shoot."

"It's about the bridge."

Eric stopped at the door and turned around. "Did you see something?"

"I did. We did. Jess and I."

He winced. "Bad?"

"Could've been worse," I said.

"It's never good when someone says that. Come to the break room with me."

I followed Eric to the break room and waited while he heated the soup. Then he sat down and tried it, groaning in pleasure.

"Is it right?" I asked.

"No, but it is darn good," said Eric.

"What's wrong with it?"

"It's missing something."

"That's what Leo said."

"My dad is always right," said Eric. "So what did you want to ask me about the bridge?"

"Have you insured any of the jumpers?"

"You get straight to the point, don't you?"

"Sorry."

"No worries," he said, blowing on a spoonful. "I hate beating around the bush, and the answer is no."

"Never?"

"Never. They're always out-of-towners, and we haven't had one in years."

I got myself a bottled water and asked, "How many years?"

"I don't know. Six or seven."

"Who was it?"

Eric studied me over his bowl and then said, "A woman, mentally disturbed. It wasn't her first try, as I recall."

"Any men?"

"You saw a man?"

I told him about the incident on the bridge, and he shook his head. "Doesn't sound familiar. You should ask Tank about it. He'd know or would have it in the *Sentinel*'s archives."

"Maybe later," I said. "First things first."

"Good luck with the Blazevics' trunk, and thanks for everything with Sam."

"What's everything?" I asked.

"Everything. She's very happy and getting more comfortable in her skin every day. I think seeing Leo has helped."

"Her or you?"

"Both."

I put the cap on my bottle and was going to ask if there was anything else I should work on, but my phone buzzed.

I smiled and said, "Yes. Yes. Yes."

"Who is it?" Eric asked.

"Dutzow Barbecue," I said.

"If you're going, I want in."

I smiled and held up a finger. "Hello."

Ned was on the line and whispered that Steve Olsen just walked in to have lunch.

"Can you keep him there for a while?" I asked.

"How long's a while?" Ned asked.

"I'll leave right now, but I'm in St. Seb."

"No problem. We can be a touch slow."

I thanked him and smiled at Eric. "You want something? I'm going."

Eric didn't smile back. "Are you going by yourself?"

"Jess is working at the Horny Hotel. It's me, myself, and I."

He looked at his phone. "I have an appointment. Can't skip it. Who can go with you?"

"I don't need help," I said. "It's a public place. Ned, the bartender, will look after me."

Eric heaved a sigh. "Ned's good people, but I'd feel better if you had Jess or someone."

"Why exactly?"

"You're onto something. I don't know Steve Olsen, but he might not be pleased."

"Would Leo suffice?"

"He can't do anything," Eric said.

"Wrong. He can tell you if something's happened," I said.

Eric thought about it and said, "Dad? Hey, Dad? You hear me?"

Leo popped in next to me and I jumped. "Oh, you're trying to kill me."

"I didn't realize you were there," said Leo. "What's going on?"

Eric explained, and Leo's eyes became intense. "I will have her back."

"Thanks, Dad."

The ghost and I went to my car. The boys weren't happy, and I had to practically wrestle the key fob from them. I got in and Leo sat beside me in his mortician suit.

"I don't suppose you have something more appropriate to wear?" I asked as we drove toward the bridge.

"What's wrong with this?" he asked.

It makes me sad.

"It's not very detective-like," I said.

"You're wearing a flowered blouse."

I grinned at him. "I need a deerstalker hat."

"Please don't wear one of those. Only Basil Rathbone could pull it off."

"My dad loved him in the Sherlock Holmes films."

We chatted about the various Sherlocks, and Leo was shocked to find out there was a modern version. I promised to watch the series with him when we drove on the bridge and my stomach tightened up.

"Libby?"

"I'm okay."

"Do you see him?"

"Not yet."

And there he was. The jumper. Right where he'd been the last time. Same suit. Some shoes slipping on the railing.

"Oh, God," I whispered.

"He's there?"

I nodded.

"I don't see him."

I wanted to stop. Everything in me said to stop and help, but I couldn't help. He was beyond help, far beyond. I kept driving, and we passed him. When I looked in the rearview, he was gone.

"Do you think he hates me?" I asked.

"Libby, dear, he couldn't possibly," said Leo. "He didn't know you then, and he doesn't know you now."

"He could," I said.

"Have you seen him anywhere else?"

"No. Just on the bridge."

"Then he doesn't know you."

I glanced over. "Sometimes you're in the room and not visible."

"He's not in the house, Libby," said Leo. "I wouldn't allow that."

"Can you stop it?"

"Yes." Leo's tone had a finality to it, and something told me not to inquire, so I didn't, and we drove toward Dutzow as fast as I dared.

A TRUNK, A CANOE, AND ALL THE BARBECUE

Steve Olsen sat in a booth by himself with a huge platter of meat in front of him. No sides, just meat. I think that says something about a person. I'm just not sure what it says.

I leaned on the bar and said to Ned, "My boss is worried about me approaching him. What do you think?"

"I think Steve's a wuss," said Ned.

"I agree," said Leo, and that's saying something. Leo was nothing if not charitable.

"A wuss, huh?" I asked.

Lynn joined us and said, "I think he's too lazy to go after you. Steve's more the 'play dead and hope you go away' type."

"Is he a super loser or what?" I asked.

Ned poured me a Coke and said, "Not a loser exactly. Just a guy who always takes the easy way."

"If it weren't for his dad, I don't know where he'd be," said Lynn.

"He never had any other job?" I asked.

"Not that I know of," said Ned. "There's nothing wrong with working in the family business, except that Steve stopped doing the family business."

"What do you mean?"

"I asked around after you and Jess were in. Steve stopped doing the real antiques as soon as Hugo stopped being involved. Now it's whatever junk he can get ahold of and get a minuscule profit on."

I sipped my Coke and said, "As long as he is profitable, I guess."

"I think he is," said Lynn. "But here's the thing, I don't think Hugo knows they don't actually deal in antiques anymore. My dad's in the VFW with Hugo and he says that Hugo talks about all Steve's great finds."

"There could be stuff in the storage units," I said. "That's where he got the trunk."

"Have you seen *Storage Wars*?" Ned asked. "You're not finding high-class antiques in those things."

"Hugo thinks they've got high-class antiques?"

"My dad said he does."

"Did you tell your dad about the storage units?" I asked.

"Not a chance," said Lynn. "Dad would tell Hugo immediately. It's a brothers-in-arms kinda thing."

Ned nodded. "Vietnam vets. They stick together."

"Yes, they do," said Leo. "I did a lot of work for the vets."

I glanced over at Leo and then at Ned and Lynn. They didn't see him, and it was odd to have a three-way conversation when they couldn't know who else was there.

"Hugo was in Vietnam?" I asked, picturing that little old guy and his walker.

"He was. Two tours," said Lynn. "My dad only did one. One was enough."

"I feel bad," I said as I watched Steve forking huge amounts of meat into his gullet.

"About what?"

"Steve did something and his dad is going to find out," I said.

"Maybe it won't be so bad."

Maybe.

I stood up and said, "Wish me luck."

Lynn grinned at me. "My money's on you."

"Do I look tough?" I asked.

"You have two boys?"

"Yes."

"Then you're tough. Go get that lazy creampuff."

I turned to walk toward Steve's table, and "creampuff" wasn't totally off. He was short and doughy, sitting at the table in an extreme slump, so he didn't have to lift the fork too far. I wasn't sure how old he was. Midforties maybe. He'd lost most of his hair, and what he had left was a strange orange color that didn't look remotely natural, but I couldn't imagine why anyone would dye their remaining hair that color. The closest description I could think of was creamsicle. Good Humor had nothing on Steve Olsen's hair.

"Excuse me," I said.

Steve pointed at his glass without looking up. "More water."

"Okay. Are you Steve Olsen?" I asked, because I couldn't think of a better opening.

"Yeah. Are you going to get the water?"

Leo stood beside me. "Unbelievable."

I smiled at Leo and slid into the booth. "No."

Steve looked up with his fork halfway to his open mouth and froze. His pale blue eyes widened as he stared. Suddenly, I was happy that I'd put some effort into my look for the day: hair, eyeliner, lipstick, not to mention my silk blouse and diamond earrings. I looked like a serious woman sitting across from a not serious man and he knew it.

"Who are you?" Steve asked, leaving the fork suspended midair.

I held out my hand. "Libby Forest."

He frowned and reluctantly shook my hand with the weakest handshake I'd ever had from a man. It was also very moist. Yuck.

"You're not getting me water?" he asked.

"Not all women want to get you water," I said.

"Aren't you a waitress?"

"Do waitresses usually sit at the tables?"

Steve thought about it, but he didn't reply. He started eating faster. Steve wasn't big on chewing or closing his mouth.

"So I'm here on behalf of the Blazevic family," I said.

"Who?"

I grabbed a napkin and wiped up the bits of meat he sprayed on the table and my hands. "Mika Blazevic bought a trunk at your booth in the Fond Memories Antique Mall."

"No returns. All sales final."

"They don't want to return it. They want information."

Steve glanced up and continued to eat, increasing his speed.

"They want to know the provenance on the trunk," I said. "Do you know what trunk I'm talking about?"

Steve's eyes grew squinty. "No."

"I think you do."

"Nope. Go away. Eating."

"If he could see me…" Leo balled up his fists, and I shrugged.

"Mr. Olsen, I need to find out—"

"Go away."

I leaned back to avoid the increase in spraying. "Mr. Blazevic wants an answer, and he's not the sort of man to take no for an answer where his children are concerned."

"I don't know nothing about any kids," said Steve.

I pulled out my phone and held up the picture of the trunk. "What do you know about this trunk?"

He didn't look. "Not my trunk."

Leo swiped a hand through his head, and Steve jolted upright like someone had shocked him. "What was that?"

"What?" I asked.

"I was. It was. Cold. I'm cold."

"It's winter."

Steve started shoveling food into his mouth again and I said, "I know you sold this trunk."

"No, you don't," he said.

"I have the receipt."

"All sales final. No returns."

"I don't think he's very bright," said Leo.

I looked up and said, "No, I don't think he is."

Steve glanced at me and asked, "Who are you talking to?"

"Don't worry about that." I held up the photo. "Worry about this trunk."

"Not my trunk."

"You bought it at auction from the Rolla Storage Solutions in March," I said.

"Says who?" Steve said before trying to shove a piece of meat the size of a saucer in his mouth.

"Records. Facts. Witnesses."

"No witnesses."

"Mr. Thompson helped you move the canoe, and he said you had a very curious attitude about this trunk. Why's that, Steve? What was in the trunk?"

"Nothing," he said.

"I thought it wasn't your trunk."

"It's not."

"It is. There was something heavy in that trunk, and I want to know what it was," I said.

"I don't know what you're talking about," said Steve, waving at Ned. "She's harassing me."

Ned waved and gave me a thumbs-up.

"That guy's a jerk," said Steve.

"So are you," I said. "What was in that trunk?"

"Nothing. Jeez. What is with you?"

Leo leaned over me. "He's not going to tell you."

"I see that," I said.

Steve looked at the air beside me and looked at me like I was crazy, so I grinned at him like I was.

"You are going to tell me what was in that trunk," I said.

"I'm not telling you nothin'," Steve said between bites.

I pulled up the photo I'd taken of Jess's drawing. "Who is this woman?"

He didn't look. "I don't know."

I threw a sugar packet at him.

"Hey," he said.

"Hey. Tell me who she is," I said.

Steve glanced up and shrugged. "I don't know."

For the first time, I believed him. I glanced up at Leo and he said, "I don't think he recognized her."

"Figures," I said, and Steve looked up to see who I was talking to, but I was looking at him.

"You done?"

"No, I am not. Who's this?" I showed him Jess's drawing of the man from the Blazevic house.

"You don't quit," said Steve.

"That's right, so just tell me."

"I've got nothing to say."

I leaned back and crossed my arms. "You don't want me to call in reinforcements."

Steve chuckled as he shoved in the remaining brisket on his plate. "Who've you got? The PTA?"

"Larry Fischer."

He looked up. "Who?"

"Oh, please," I said. "Everyone knows the Furious Fischers around here. Larry Fischer. He's been known to spit on people, among other things."

"How do you know him?" Steve asked with a new wariness.

"I did him a solid and now he owes me," I said.

"Larry isn't the kind of guy who does things for free."

That did surprise me. Larry was absolutely the kind of guy who did things to help people. He just didn't get the publicity for doing it. Larry was a kind of stealth nice guy, especially since we solved Leo's murder.

"You don't really know him then," I said.

"I do. He bought some crap from me."

"I'm sure crap is right."

"Screw you."

I held up my phone with my finger poised over Larry's contact info. "Shall I just give Larry a call, then?"

"Yeah, right," said Steve. "You don't know that guy."

I tapped the call button, speaker, and Larry answered, "Hi, Libby. What's up?"

Steve paled, and his fork stayed in his stuffed mouth.

"Hi Larry," I said. "Could you do me a tiny favor and tell Steve Olsen that you know me?"

"Steve, the junk dealer?" Larry asked.

Steve sputtered and swallow the bite that was so large, it looked like it hurt his throat.

"That's the guy," I said. "He's right here. I have you on speaker."

"Sure," said Larry. "Can I ask why?"

"I'll explain everything later."

Larry cleared his throat and said, "Hey, Steve. I know Libby and she's a friend. Will that do it, Lib?"

I looked at Steve as he started eyeing the exit. "I think we're good. Thanks."

"See ya later."

"See ya, Larry." I cut off the call and said to Steve, "So that was Larry, and he likes me. He thinks you're a junk dealer. How about that?"

Steve guzzled his remaining water and asked, "What do you want?"

"You know what I want."

He yawned. "Wow. I'm tired. I can hardly keep my eyes open."

"Seriously?"

Steve wadded up his jacket and leaned against the wall.

"People were freaking out in your booth at the antique mall. What was going on?"

"Sleeping."

"There was a smell," I said.

Steve started breathing heavily, and all I could do was stare. The man was actually trying to sleep his way out of talking. I looked over at Lynn, who shook her head in amazement.

"What an idiot," called out Ned.

Steve twitched at that, but he didn't open his eyes. I started throwing the sugar packets one by one. "Open your eyes, ya loser. I'm not giving up."

I ran out of sugar and started smacking him with my hat. "Answer me."

Ned walked over and slapped Steve's bill on the table. "Pay up, opossum boy."

Steve didn't move.

"This guy," said Ned. "New low."

I smacked him again. "Call an ambulance. Maybe he's had a heart attack."

"He'll have to pay for that," said Lynn as she joined us.

I looked at Leo and made a gesture with my hand.

"I don't want to torture him," said Leo.

"Someone has to get this loser to respond," I said.

Ned cracked his knuckles. "I could punch him. I might be a little out of practice, but bar fights are like riding a bike. You never forget how."

Steve responded, but not like I thought he would. He started jumping around the booth. "Hey. Hey. Hey."

"Hey yourself, idiot," said Ned. "Answer the lady and pay—"

Steve shook and started jittering his way across the booth. "Hey. Hey. Hey."

"What the!" Lynn cried out, and Steve fell onto the floor. He rolled onto his side and began spinning like Homer Simpson.

"Dude, that is not going to work," said Ned. "Crazy still has to pay."

"Hey. Hey. Hey."

"Stop it!" yelled Lynn. "You're disrupting people's lunch. They pay good money to eat here."

"Hey. Hey. Hey."

I looked at Leo and he held up his hands. "I don't know."

"Somebody grab him," I said.

Ned reached for Steve and he rolled away, getting to his feet like a guy who'd just been in a Dizzy Bat race, staggering around and bumping into people on his way to the door.

"Where do you think you're going?" Ned ran after him and tried to grab his arm, but Steve darted out the door, stumbling into the parking lot.

Ned moved to go after him, but Lynn said, "Let him go. I'll get Hugo to pay up."

The entire restaurant was on their feet and watched as Steve jittered around the lot, looking for his van. When he finally made it, it took six tries to get his key in the lock. Then he got in and peeled out of the lot, barely missing a Camry driving in.

"Wow," said Lynn. "I never thought he'd go that far."

"He tried lazy," said Ned, "but Libby didn't give up."

"Do you think he's okay?" I asked.

They and the rest of the regulars scoffed.

"He's fine," said Ned. "Just a new twist on an old loser."

I looked in the direction Steve had driven, not toward Hugo's house. "I don't know. That was really bizarre."

An older man at the bar said, "He once tried to avoid paying for snow removal by not answering the door for three months. I had to get the cops to go over and do a welfare check before he'd pay up."

"How'd he get Hugo to go along with that?" I asked.

"Steve was living on his own then," the man said. "What a cheapskate."

People started telling stories about Steve's laziness and cheapness. I wouldn't exactly call him a grifter. *Loser* was more apt. He'd agree to exchange labor like dog sitting. When it was his turn to dog sit, he'd be too busy. Stuff like that. No one thought he was a bad person exactly, just lazy. He did do what he agreed to, but it took persistence to get him to do it.

"This is going to get so many likes," said a woman from another booth.

"Did you get it on video?" I asked.

"I did, and you're okay," she said.

"Why wouldn't I be?"

"I just meant that you didn't do anything to cause that. Steve's famous freakout. I should TikTok the different segments. Viral, here I come."

I asked to see the video, and she got most of our exchange. I could make out some of my questions over the din in the restaurant, and it was interesting to see Steve's reactions after the fact.

Is he that good an actor?

"It looks real," I said.

The woman snorted. "Yeah, right. Steve Olsen wins an Oscar."

"So," said Ned. "Unless you're going to chase down that idiot, how about some lunch?"

"Love to, but I need it to go." I ordered a good amount for Eric and myself. Then I realized I needed some more help and added Tank to the order. A little feeding of a skinny newsman goes a long way.

Chapter Twelve

Tank unwrapped his brisket sandwich and groaned with happiness. "This is a real treat. I don't get over to that joint nearly often enough."

"I'm right there with you," said Eric. "My second lunch of the day. Don't tell Sylvia."

Eric had pulled pork, baked beans, and coleslaw. Tank had fried mushrooms and grilled corn on the cob. Lynn had an encyclopedic memory for repeat customers' favorites. I got my burnt ends without being asked.

After we were halfway through our sandwiches and having a little breather, Tank asked, "I assume this largesse comes with a price."

"I might need a little more help on the Blazevic case," I said, sliding over the container of homemade pickles that were Ned's favorite thing.

Tank took one and said, "Worth it. What's up? Have you got the lady's details?"

"Nothing that good," I said. "I want to know if you have anything on Steve Olsen."

Tank finished a pickle, wiped his hands on a napkin, and

then got on his computer. "Nothing springs to mind. Did he sell that trunk to Mika?"

"He did." I told them about my encounter with Steve, and the two of them were stunned.

"Maybe he had a stroke," said Eric.

"I didn't think of that," I said.

"Strokes don't make you spin on the floor," said Tank. "That guy's full of it."

"What did Leo say?" Eric asked, glancing around, but Leo hadn't come with me. He'd gone to see if he could hear anything at the Olsen house. I don't think he would normally have agreed to eavesdropping, but Steve's performance and disrespect helped me talk him into it.

"Nothing. He doesn't know what that was about, but he doesn't think Steve will tell me what was in the trunk."

"You could call in Larry," said Tank.

Eric chuckled. "Libby Forest and Larry Fischer, the dream team."

"You joke, but I've considered it," I said.

"In all seriousness, Lib, I don't think he'll tell you. Larry or no Larry," said Eric. "If he's willing to do that in public, it's a secret he's going to keep at all costs."

Tank nodded. "I'd still think about calling in Larry, but you're probably right. Scaring won't be enough, and you don't want Larry to actually beat him up."

"I don't, but what other recourse do I have?"

"Let's see," said Tank. "I'm not seeing anything on either Steve or Hugo. They've never been on our crime report. At least not since we got it searchable on the computer, but I don't see either of them committing a crime."

"Steve did something," said Eric. "Why else would he try to hide what was in the trunk?"

"Could be a lot of reasons," said Tank. "My best guess is

A TRUNK, A CANOE, AND ALL THE BARBECUE

monetary gain. He wants to sell whatever it was or he already has. It was probably questionable."

"Stolen goods," I said. "Jess thought there might be money from a bank robbery. That sounds nuts, though."

"I don't know," said Tank. "They found a safe on *Storage Wars* that was chock-full of money."

Eric nodded. "And there was the video collection. Fifty grand."

"Steve doesn't seem so stupid for buying the units now," I said.

"Most of the stuff is crap."

Tank stopped typing. "All I have on Steve and Hugo is nothing. They used to advertise with us when Hugo had a shop at the house, but that stopped years ago. Since then, nada."

"Your best bet is seeing what else was in the unit," said Eric.

"That's what I'm thinking, but how do I get Steve to tell me what it was? He's probably sold it off by now, anyway," I said.

"You said the storage guy had pictures," said Tank. "What did you see in there?"

"Lots of bins that were labeled, but I couldn't see the labels. The corner of the trunk and a canoe. Not very helpful, I'm afraid."

Tank waved his sandwich at me. "Have you got the pictures?"

"No, but I think Perry would give them to me if I asked. He was really sweet," I said.

"Ask him," said Eric. "I have an idea."

"What's your idea?" Tank asked.

"Let's see the pictures first."

I texted Perry, and he got back immediately with the

pictures he took for the auction. I sent them to Tank, and he put them up on his computer.

Tank leaned in. "I can make out...books on one bin. Maybe."

"We don't need a bin," said Eric.

"We don't?" I asked.

"Check out the canoe."

Tank and I looked carefully at the canoe. As far as I could tell, it was just a canoe. It didn't have a name on it or anything, just a sticker.

"What do you see that I don't?" I asked.

"See the sticker?"

"It's a Missouri sticker," I said. "How is that helpful?"

"It isn't, but that looks like a canoe that was part of a rental business. I can't make out the other end, but it looks like there's more info on there."

Tank smiled. "That's right. Rental businesses number their stock and have their business on their canoes."

I made a face. "But it's been in there for a long time. They must've gone out of business."

"Not necessarily," said Eric. "I have kayaks I bought off Black River Water Sports. They were beat up, and they sold them off so they could buy new ones."

"That canoe does look beat up," said Tank. "Besides, the business owners might still have their records."

"The question is whether or not Steve has sold it."

I smiled. "He hasn't. I saw it in one of his sheds at the house."

"All you have to do is get a look at that canoe," said Eric.

"Or ask Leo to look," said Tank.

"I'm for that," I said. "I don't think Steve would let me look at the outside of the shed, much less anything inside it."

Eric straightened up and said, "Leo? Dad? Are you busy?"

A second later, Leo popped up next to his son's chair. "Twice in one day. I feel popular."

"You were always popular," said Eric. "Did you hear anything at the Olsens'?"

Carol's chair appeared behind him and Leo sat down. "I'm afraid not. Steve doesn't tell his father anything. He checked on him, gave him his pills, and then said he was going to the mall."

"Nothing about lunch?" Tank asked. "It sounds like something you'd mention."

"He didn't say a thing about it."

"How did he look?" Eric asked.

"Pale and shaky." Leo got thoughtful. "I think he's scared."

"Of me?" I asked.

He shook his head and said, "I wouldn't think so. You didn't do anything to him, but he is scared. *Rattled* might be the best way to put it."

"Can you go back and look at the canoe they have in one of the sheds?" I asked and then explained why.

"I can try, but all the sheds were closed and had padlocks on them."

"Sounds like Steve is battening down the hatches," said Eric.

"I have to get a look at that canoe," I said.

"Let me go check and see if I can see anything inside." Leo popped out and we finished lunch while we waited.

He popped back and sat back in his chair. "Sorry. There's no light. I couldn't see anything."

"Was it still in there?" I asked.

"I didn't see it, but I think it must be," said Leo.

"I agree," said Eric. "He's not going to sell it in November."

Tank offered me and then Eric the last pickle. We passed,

and he took it himself. "He should've sold it during the summer."

"I wonder if he still has the bins," I said.

"Steve is gone right now, Lib," said Eric. "I doubt Hugo is paying attention. We could go over and break into the shed."

"Eric!" exclaimed Leo. "I taught you better than that."

His son was slightly abashed, but not much. "We wouldn't steal anything. Libby just needs a look."

Leo crossed his arms and eyed us. "That is a last resort."

"At least you agree that it's a resort," I said, smiling.

"Barely, and I think you'll find another way to get the information."

"If only the Blazevic kids could understand her," said Tank. "How many languages did you try?"

"Every one we could think of," I said, "including Slovene and Latvian."

"I'm surprised you thought of Slovene," said Eric.

"We didn't. Google did, but the kids said no." I pulled up the photo of Jelena's trunk. "Maybe listening isn't the thing."

"What do you mean?"

I held out the photo. "We have her trunk. We should find out where it was made. Then we'll know the language."

The men looked doubtful.

Eric took my phone and said, "It's not very distinctive."

"It's not to us," I said. "Haven't you seen the antiques roadshow? Those experts know where stuff came from on the slimmest of evidence."

"I always wonder if they're just guessing and presenting as fact," said Tank.

"Doubting Thomas," said Leo with a smile.

"It's my job. All facts must be triple-checked."

I threw away my trash and asked, "Where can I do my first check?"

"We've got Rothschild's Antiques on Main," said Eric. "Julie's known as a straight arrow."

"Better than Steve?" I asked.

"Steve's not known to lie about his stuff," said Eric. "His stuff is just crap."

"Julia's like Hugo was. Honest, but a saleswoman, for sure," said Tank.

I texted Mika and asked if it was possible to borrow Jelena's trunk for an appraisal. He was all for it and said he'd be right home to help me.

"Anybody want to come?" I asked, but the men had settled in and were talking football, so I was on my own. Leo was smiling, even though he was in Carol's chair. A win in my book.

I cleared out all of Jelena's toys, piling them neatly on the bed. Then Mika carried the trunk down the stairs and out the back to put it in the back of his extra-large SUV, the only vehicle that could possibly fit him.

"Where are we going?" he asked.

"Rothschild's Antiques," I said.

"Julie's place. Good. I like her." He drove us the few blocks to the shop, and I asked, "Is Julie's last name Rothschild?"

He laughed. "I asked the same thing. It's not. She picked the name because it's fancy."

"It is that," I said. "Is her stock fancy?"

"A bit of everything, but she specialized in painted antiques. Beautiful stuff. She had a lovely hand-painted trunk, but we were afraid Jelena would mess it up. What a mistake that was."

"You never know," I said. "Five ghosts could've come with that trunk."

Mika parked and clapped a heavy hand on my shoulder. "I didn't think of that. Thank you."

"No problem. I'm starting to understand that I have to expect the unexpected."

We got out and walked to the front door. Mika opened it for me and I walked into a gorgeous shop that looked like it belonged in a magazine. There were quite a few customers for a Monday afternoon, and I wanted to be one of them. We needed lamps, and Julie had amazing lamps from a variety of eras.

"Getting distracted?" Mika asked.

"Very," I said. "This place is wonderful."

"Wait until you see the prices."

I checked a tag on a Craftsman-style lamp. "Cha-ching."

"Another reason we didn't buy my baby girl's trunk here," whispered Mika. "There's Julie at the register."

We went over and waited behind a couple buying two bookcases and a low Victorian armchair with the original horsehair fabric. That's what Julie told the couple who were quite excited by the news, but I thought it was ghastly, all hairy and faded.

Once Julie had settled up with the couple and got a man I took for her husband to carry out the items, she turned to us with a smile. She was pretty in a way I'd always envied. Not a stitch of makeup with prematurely gray hair and a pair of dimples deeply etched into her cheeks. She couldn't have been much over thirty-five, but she had the full middle-aged mom uniform on. Riding boots, jeans, white blouse, and vest. I liked the look, but once Mariah saw a group of moms wearing it and called it Han Solo season, I could never wear the combo again.

"Mika. Hi. How are you?" Julie asked, making her dimples deeper.

"Very well," he said.

She turned to me and said, "You must be the infamous Libby Forest."

"Infamous?" I asked.

"Perhaps *infamous* is putting it too strongly," she said, extending her hand.

I shook it and asked, "Did you come to the Halloween Battle of the Bands or the haunted mortuary?"

"Neither. We were out of town at a show, but news travels fast among my competitors." Julie's smile grew. "I haven't laughed so hard in ages."

Mika looked at me, and I shrugged. "What are you talking about?"

"Steve Olsen, of course. The video is genius. I just love the expression on your face."

"What video?" Mika asked, and Julie showed me the video the woman at Dutzow Barbecue made. I never imagined it would reach people that quickly.

"It's hysterical," said Julie, wiping tears from her cheeks.

"What is happening to him?" Mika asked. "He needs medical attention."

Julie started laughing again. "You don't know Steve."

"He does that?"

Julie told a story about being in a show in Kansas City where Hugo had a nearby booth when he was still working. They sold a beautiful armoire, and to avoid having to load it, Steve dramatically faked a trip and fall to claim a twisted ankle. Hugo had to get a couple of kind shoppers to do it.

"This isn't that far out of character, then," I said.

"That is way over the top," said Julie. "What in the world were you asking him about? Does he owe you money? Must be a lot."

"I just wanted information."

"Really." She looked down at her phone. "He made a laughingstock of himself over information? What a weirdo."

"Actually, Julie, the information is why we are here," said Mika. "Could you do me a favor and look at a trunk for me?"

"I don't usually do evaluations for free, but since it's you and something to do with Steve, I'd be happy to," said Julie. "Where's the piece?"

"In my truck," said Mika. "Do you want to come out to see it?"

"Can't. I have to mind the store while Mark is loading up those pieces."

"I can bring it in."

"Would you? That would be helpful and warmer," said Julie.

Mika went to get the trunk, and Julie offered me hot cider. I accepted, and it was delicious steeped with cinnamon sticks and cloves. Julie answered a customer's question on a lamp and then asked me, "What's so special about this trunk?"

"I'm hoping you can tell us," I said.

"Mysterious."

"It is a bit."

I showed her the photo I had of the trunk and she asked, "Steve sold that?"

"He did at the Fond Memories Antique Mall," I said.

"Good solid outfit. I don't know why they let him stay," said Julie.

"He must have good stuff occasionally."

"I wouldn't have thought he'd have a trunk of that quality. How much did Mika pay? If you don't think he'd mind you saying, that is."

I told her, and she whistled. "That's a bargain. Too much of a bargain, to be honest."

"What do you mean?" I asked.

A TRUNK, A CANOE, AND ALL THE BARBECUE

A woman approached and said, "I'm interested in the hutch in the corner. Will you take four hundred for it?"

"Excuse me, Libby," said Julie. "I'll be right back."

Julie went off to haggle with the buyer, and I ran to open the door for Mika. He bought in Jelena's trunk without breaking a sweat and set it down next to the counter. A man immediately came over and asked if it was for sale. Mika said it was only being appraised.

"Too bad," said the man. "My grandmother had a similar one."

"What happened to it?"

The man sighed. "When she died, the relatives descended. By the time I got to the house, it was gone. I don't know who got it. No one will say."

"Families," I said.

"Not always the best." The man went over and joined a woman in looking at a trunk that wasn't as nice.

I elbowed Mika. "There's a market if you decide to sell."

"Jelena won't have it," said Mika. "It is her trunk and her lady. She's stubborn like my mother. Sandra isn't happy."

Julie returned and rang up the hutch. Then a couple came up with a pair of lamps that they wanted to pay half price for. Mika sat down behind the counter and I wandered around to see if it was anything like the mall in terms of ghosts.

It was, but they weren't so abundant. There was a maid dressed in a black ankle-length dress and starched white apron up on a ladder dusting a chandelier and singing a jolly song in an Irish lilt. Everything seemed so real, I wasn't sure if the ladder was there or not. As I passed, a lady in a tightly corseted dress with a bustle hurried over. I thought she was going to speak to me, but she looked up and said, "'Tis the season, Mary. Do get every speck."

"Yes, ma'am," said the maid, and then she smiled at me. "Hello, Libby."

The lady in the corset turned to me and said, "Fashions today. Such a shame. Liberty Sunshine, do stop wearing that paint. You do not need such garish applications."

My mouth fell open, and before I could answer, she hurried off, calling for William.

Mary wasn't looking at me, so I attempted to tap on the ladder and got a chill. "Mary?" I whispered, looking around. Even in St. Sebastian talking to yourself wasn't a good thing.

"Yes, Libby?" Mary looked down and stopped dusting.

I made a discreet wave for her to come down, but she shook her head. "I must finish or the missus will be ever so angry."

What in the world could I say to that? She was dusting a ghost chandelier. It was ghost dust, for crying out loud.

At a loss, I started looking for Mary's employer. I didn't find her, but I found a fat man wearing a porkpie hat and unbuckled trousers snoring on a fainting couch. I tried waking him up but only got another chill.

"I saw you looking at the chandelier," said Julie as she approached.

I glanced over at the man, who continued to snore. "What chandelier?"

She pointed at Mary and her chandelier, still working away. "That one. I thought Number Eight had all its original fixtures. Are you in need of lighting?"

"I'm not. I just wasn't sure…"

"If?"

"Nothing." I got up, and we walked back to the counter, where Mika was sipping a cider and Mark was selling the lamps. He nodded at us and swiped the credit card.

"Where's the trunk?" I asked.

"I had to move it into the back," said Mika.

Mark smiled. "People kept wanting to buy it."

I laughed, and we went into the office behind the counter.

Julie offered us seats. "I love this time of year. Buying like crazy."

"You have a great place for Christmas presents," I said.

"Presents, too, but everyone suddenly thinks their houses aren't nice enough for company and they have to spruce things up. I'm happy to help them." Julie squatted by the trunk. "This is a very nice piece. Excellent condition."

"Can you tell where it's from?" Mika asked.

"Hold on. Let me see." Julie began examining the trunk, going over every inch. She got a magnifying glass and looked closely at the joints and brass studs. Then she went through the inside with the same attention to detail.

"When you showed me the photo and told me the price, I thought it would be a reproduction," said Julie.

"It's not?"

"No. This piece is authentic. Are you interested in selling, Mika?" Julie asked.

"No. It is Jelena's, but we need to know the origins."

Julie tapped her magnifying glass in her palm. "Can you tell me why? I mean, I know who you are, Libby, and I know what you do. Is this piece..."

"Haunted?" I asked with a smile.

"Well...yes."

"Yes."

Julie blinked at me, still tapping the magnifying glass. "You really see ghosts?"

"I do."

She looked at Mika, and he said, "So do my children, but please don't tell anyone."

"I promise," said Julie.

"Can you tell us where the trunk is from?" I asked.

"I have a good idea," said Julie. "Do you mind if I get some second opinions to make sure?"

Mika agreed, and she sent off photos to her friends.

"Please tell me what's going on with this trunk. I'm a little freaked out."

Mika told her the story, and she started looking over the trunk again. "I can see why you need to know. What I don't see is why Steve won't tell you."

"That is an excellent question," I said. "I've got it back to a storage unit in Rolla, but no further."

"How did you do that?" Julie asked.

I told her and she said, "I might have to hire you. Provenance is so important. If only you could ask the old lady."

"We wish we could," said Mika.

Julie's phone started dinging, and she checked her messages. "Just as I thought. It's European. Western. Walnut. The brass studding is unusual, but it's obviously for both decoration and to make it sturdy for travel. The iron strapping is well done, and it also has a decorative flair. We're thinking about 1730."

"1730?" Mika gasped. "I had no idea it was so old."

Julie smiled. "It's not a showy piece like a Biedermeier. Of course, that's a later era."

"What about the fabric?" I asked.

"That was added later. I'd say it's Victorian and added around 1860."

"You can't say where in Europe it was made?"

She bent over and looked at the faded lions. "I can't really tell about these, but they could be Belgium or Scottish. Of course, lions are popular in heraldry, so it could be German too."

"We tried German with the children," said Mika, his usually cheerful face crestfallen.

"What do you mean, tried?" Julie asked.

"We played people speaking different languages to try and figure out what she was saying," I said.

"I love that approach," said Julie. "You tried French?"

"We did," said Mika.

"And everything else we can think of," I said.

"Do you think the kids could really identify the language?" Julie asked.

I nodded. "I think so. Jelena is very observant. She noticed all the details of the lady's clothing. Things you wouldn't think a child would pay attention to."

"Yes, she and Marko were very sure we didn't have the language," said Mika.

Julie got off the floor and sat down beside me, still looking at the trunk. "So you know what she's wearing?"

"Yes," said Mika. "We do."

"And it's not clothes from 1730?"

We laughed.

"No," I said. "It's pretty modern compared to that."

"How modern?" Julie asked.

I showed her Jess's drawing, and she marveled. "That is beautiful. I'd heard she did gorgeous work, but I had no idea. And this is her? The woman in your house?"

"That is her," said Mika. "Sandra is going out of her mind."

"We're going to figure it out," I said. "If I have to buy that canoe, I will."

"If he'll sell it," said Mika.

"Can I see that drawing again?" Julie asked.

I gave her my phone, and she asked if she could send it to a friend of hers that specialized in vintage clothing. "This sweater is a unique style. I want to see if I'm right about it."

She sent off the photo, and a few minutes later, her phone rang. She put it on speaker. "Hello, Evelyn. You're on speaker."

"Hello. I'm Evelyn. I specialize in vintage clothing and fabrics."

We said hello and Evelyn said, "The lady in your drawing

is wearing a Fair Isle sweater. It looks hand knitted to me, but it has lovely details. Do you know if the buttons are metal?"

"I believe they are," I said.

"And they are that shape? The diamond shape?"

"Yes," said Mika. "Is that important?"

"It is. Given the lady's sweater with its pattern, her skirt, and those buttons, I'd say your lady is Scottish," said Evelyn.

"Scottish!" Mika and I exclaimed.

"You're surprised?"

"Very," I said. "It's a long story, but we're told she doesn't speak English."

Evelyn laughed. "My grandmother was Scottish, and we had a hard time understanding her after living in the States for thirty years."

"What is it about the buttons?" Julie asked.

"The shape is typical of kilt jacket buttons," said Evelyn.

"But it's not a kilt," I said.

"My guess is that they were recycled and put on the sweater. Fair Isle is a common Scottish style, and she does appear to have a kilt on."

I looked at Jess's drawing. Of course, it was a kilt, but I'd just seen it as plaid because Scottish never occurred to me. Mika and I thanked Evelyn, and she hung up.

"Scottish works," said Julie. "I don't think it's originally Scottish, though. The lions may have been added later."

Mika ran his hands through his hair. "No wonder she's frustrated. She's speaking English to the kids."

"They just can't understand her," I said, standing up. "Thanks so much, Julie."

"Can I ask you a question before you go?"

"Sure."

Julie glanced around and said, "Do we have anyone?"

"Are you being haunted?" I asked.

"Yes."

"Well..."

"We are? Really? Who is it?" Julie dragged me out into the shop, past some startled shoppers. "Where are they?"

Mary had moved her ladder to another chandelier, and the fat man was still snoring on the fainting couch. I didn't see Mary's employer, but there was a dog curled up next to the fat man.

"Do you have a dog?" I asked.

"A dog? No."

"Actually, I think you do." I told her about Mary, who cheerfully waved at us, but only I could see her. The fat man refused to wake up, but the dog wagged when I whistled at him.

"And there's some lady bossing the maid around?" Julie asked.

"I don't see her, but she was here earlier," I said. "She wants the shop clean before the Christmas season."

"I don't know whether or not I should believe you."

"Totally up to you," I said.

"It is St. Seb," she said.

Mika and I smiled at her.

"Do you think Jess could come and draw them?"

I gave her Jess's number and assured her that Jess would fit it in. Ghosts were getting to be quite a big business for her. Now, if we could just figure out how to talk to our Scottish lady, we would be all set.

Chapter Thirteen

I heard the music before I got in the house. I didn't know which crazy person was playing "Macarena," but they sure liked it loud. I opened the door and got blasted, making me want to return to the quiet Blazevic house. I'd spent a good amount of time with the kids, trying to get them to understand a Scottish brogue. No dice. But they said the lady was thrilled when we put a map on Mika's laptop. She nodded and pointed at herself, tearing up. We should've thought of using a map before. It was so obvious, but it never occurred to me.

The lady kept taking us to her trunk. Jelena said she got upset when she pointed at it, but the little girl couldn't understand her. Marko thought maybe he heard her say the word girl a few times, but he said the lady spoke so fast, he wasn't sure. I needed to find a new way to communicate with her, but Sandra was starting their evening routine, and I couldn't get in the way of that. Kids need their routine, but from the sounds of it, there was nothing routine going on in our kitchen.

"What on earth?" I called out when I went through the arch and found Jess and the kids, including Taylor, Sam,

Ethan, and Keely, doing the Macarena. I had hoped to find homework in progress or perhaps someone making dinner, but the stove was cold and the dancing was hot. They were all laughing and collapsed against the island when the song ended.

"That is the best," said Taylor. "I never even heard of that dance."

"I can't believe you never heard of the Macarena," said Jess.

"It happened before we were born," said Ethan, who was texting. "My mom knows it and she thinks it's cool."

"Great idea, Grandma," said Henri.

"Grandma?" I asked.

"Over here, Libby."

I turned to the kitchen table, where my mother was standing with Poptart in her arms. She wore a knitted poncho in a rainbow of colors, stirrup pants (no, I'm not kidding), her favorite pair of Birkenstocks, and a huge smile.

"Surprise!" everyone yelled.

I dashed over and practically threw myself at my mother, instantly enveloped in her Revlon perfume, Charlie.

"How did you get here?" I asked.

"I got on a plane," she said, setting Poptart in his basket, purring loudly. "Are you really surprised?"

"Completely."

"Good." Mom turned to the kids and Jess. "We pulled it off."

Jess smiled. "You pulled it off, Bev. All I did was get you at the airport."

"An essential part of the plan," said Mom.

"So what's the Macarena all about?" I asked.

"The kids were telling me about the Christmas pageant they're doing with the littles," said Mom. "They wanted a dance number."

"And you suggested the Macarena?"

"I did." Beverly Forest was a teacher for forty years, and she knew kids. They needed something easy that the kids could remember, and everyone could do it, including the special needs kids.

"You hit the ground running," I said.

Mariah and the girls came over to my mom, crowding around her. "We already took her to the senior center and to The Grind."

I looked at the clock. "You've been busy."

"They had to take your soup," said Ethan. "My abuela was so excited. She loves turkey soup."

The senior center was thrilled to get the soup, and I'd made so much, they had plenty to send home with everyone with portions to spare.

"You liked the center?" I asked.

Mom nodded and took off her poncho. She had one of my dad's old flannel shirts on underneath it, and a pain went through my chest. I could see Dad in it, his blue eyes twinkling as he cracked one of his terrible jokes.

"Libby?" Mom asked.

"Huh?"

"You okay, dear?"

"Fine, Mom," I said, trying to refocus. "So you liked the senior center?"

"I did, but it needs some serious help."

"What do you mean?"

The group barraged me with the center's needs. Only two burners on the stove worked, the heating system needed repair, and a coat of paint wouldn't do any harm.

"The kid side is kinda sad," said Keely. "My little cousins don't really want to go anymore."

"There's a kid side to the senior center?" I asked.

Apparently, there was. Everyone called it the senior center,

A TRUNK, A CANOE, AND ALL THE BARBECUE

but it was really the community center. It had a hangout spot for kids and a daycare that was run by the seniors, but their funding had been cut.

"Don't worry, Mom," said Henri. "We're going to fix it."

"I guess we can paint," I said. "That's easy enough."

Max rolled his eyes. "That's not enough."

Everyone agreed on that, and they rolled into talking about the pageant. The boys had spent lunch and their free period at the elementary school organizing the pageant. They had auditions and an assembly to get the kids excited. It worked. Almost every kid in school signed up to take part.

"The parents are excited," said Max. "A bunch came to the assembly, and even a grandma was there."

"How many kids are there?" I asked.

"A lot," said Sam.

It was my turn to collapse onto the island. "How are we going to do this? We can't have that many people in the gym for one performance."

"We're not," said Henri. "It's at The Crown Theater downtown."

The Crown was a landmark. A local family built it in 1900 for plays and operas, but it'd been a movie theater for a long time and then they converted it back to stage work. I'd seen photos of it in the *Sentinel* when Tank had a piece on a bluegrass festival being held there right after Halloween. It was gorgeous inside. Someone had spent serious money restoring it.

"How are we going to pay for that?"

Max and Henri rolled their eyes.

"They comped it, Mom," said Max. "We're not crazy."

Taylor grinned. "My dad knows the owners. He called them. Tank's going to do another spread on the theater and give them free advertising to do it."

"How'd you swing that?" I asked.

"It's a community thing."

I had a sense that I was missing something, but I didn't get a chance to ask before the kids launched into the new pageant plan. I should've expected what was coming. My boys weren't traditional kids, and they couldn't just do *The Night Before Christmas* or something normal.

"So we start with 'Holiday' by Madonna," said Henri.

"What?" I asked.

"'Holiday.' Don't you know that song?" asked Mariah.

"Of course I know it, but it's not a Christmas song."

Keely laughed. "It is now."

Mom nodded. "It works."

"Um, okay." I winced. "What's next?"

So far, the kids had Madonna, and Whitney Houston's "How will I know." That was going to have a Santa theme, as in "how will I know I'm on the good list, not the naughty list."

"Tell her the best part," said Mom. "It's genius."

The genius idea was Janet Jackson's "Nasty."

"You can't be serious," I said.

"They changed it," said Jess.

"How in the world do you change that song to be appropriate for kids?"

"The teachers are going to sing it," said Sam. "The principal has an amazing voice."

"That doesn't answer my question," I said.

The kids gathered together and sang, "Oh, you nasty kids. Don't ever change. We love you even if your nasty gas ain't out of range."

I couldn't speak, and they went on. There were lines about nose picking and putting fish sticks in the lunchroom microwave.

Mom put an arm around my shoulders. "It's hilarious."

"It is, but the teachers aren't going to sing that," I said.

"They already agreed," said Max. "We pitched it today."

"You gave them the lyrics?"

"Mrs. Johns thought it was hilarious," said Mariah.

"Are you doing the show too?" I asked.

"We all are," said Taylor. "The Eggs need help."

The Eggs grinned at me and began firing on all cylinders. So many ideas. So much excitement. Somewhere in the barrage, I heard things about the community, but I wasn't clear on how the pageant would help St. Seb in general.

"The grand finale will be epic," said Max.

"So romantic," said Mom.

Jess nodded. "People will love it."

"Is it the Macarena?" I asked.

"We haven't figured out how to work that in," said Henri. "But we will."

"The grand finale is for you, Libby," said Mariah. "The *Love Actually* part."

"If people like the movie, they will probably like it," I said.

"No, it's more than just the sea creature nativity," said Jess.

"Like what?"

"We're having our own Hugh Grant kissing thing," said Ethan. "My mom is going to go crazy when I tell her."

"Hugh Grant thing?" I asked.

The kids nodded and told me that when Max and Henri pitched their nutty pageant plan, the elementary science teacher got super excited. His girlfriend was the art teacher, and *Love Actually* was her favorite movie. He'd been planning on proposing on Christmas Eve, but he thought doing the Hugh Grant kissing scene at the finale would be amazing.

"How are you going to do that?" I asked.

"We're going to lure Miss Wu backstage," said Mariah.

"Mr. Funke will be—"

"His name is Funke?" I asked.

Jess nodded. "It's his real name. He came out to meet me at the Horny Hotel."

"Weird."

Everyone laughed, and then Mariah finished telling me how Mr. Funke would hopefully kiss Miss Wu, then they'd drop the curtain like in the movie, and he'd propose.

"That *is* a grand finale," I said.

"Tickets are free, but maybe they shouldn't be," said Sam.

"We could charge a dollar," said Ethan. "That would be a lot of money."

"Money for what?" I asked.

"The senior center," said Mom. "It's a wonderful idea. They need the funding. I told the kids that you and Jess would be happy to participate."

I looked around at the kids, whose expressions ranged from incredibly excited (my boys) to nervous (Sam) to guilty (Mariah and Taylor).

"What am I doing?" I asked.

"We're having a raffle," said Henri. "Do you know what that is?"

"Yes, I've heard of raffles."

My son went on to explain raffles to me. I didn't realize my kids hadn't ever heard of raffles. They were kids of the electronic age. They knew Kickstarter and crowdfunding. My mom had pitched the idea to them and, like everything they did, they were all in. They'd already called Mrs. Johns and the elementary principal to get the green light.

"What are you raffling?" I asked as Mom excused herself to go to the bathroom.

The list was impressive, considering they'd had the idea for about two hours. Sylvia was donating two gift baskets from The Grind, McCann's was giving three whole hams and three turkeys to the cause. Tank included free advertising in the *Sentinel*. The vegan restaurant donated a romantic dinner for two. I know that doesn't sound great, but their food is amazing.

"That is impressive, but what's it got to do with us?" I asked.

"You're doing a free investigation," said Henri.

"That's crazy. You can't raffle a ghost investigation. People will think we're nuts."

"We bought a haunted mortuary," said Max. "People already think that."

"Who would buy a raffle ticket for that?"

"Lots of people," said Sam. "You've already solved a bunch of afterlife issues."

"Is that it?" I asked with a wince.

"I'm going to do two free portraits," said Jess.

"Of ghosts?"

"Of whatever they want."

Mom walked back in and asked, "What are we talking about?"

"Raffles," I said.

Max frowned. "I think we need more stuff."

Ethan nodded. "The center needs a lot. Paint's expensive, and they need new playmats and everything."

"What about Dad?" Henri asked, and my heart sank the way it did every time Derek's name was mentioned. He'd promised to come visit, but then, predictably, a case came up. The boys had gone up to see him, but it had only happened twice since we moved to St. Seb. The boys didn't seem to be upset, but how long could that last?

"Dad's busy," I said, glancing at Jess.

"Yes, Derek's always working," she said, and Mariah nodded. "Super busy."

"What do you have in mind?" Taylor asked, and I wanted to draw a line across my throat as a signal, but I doubted he'd understand.

"Let me think," said Henri. "There has to be something for him to donate."

"What's he do?" Keely asked.

"He's a lawyer," said Max.

"A great lawyer," said Henri. "He can do a case."

I held up my hands. "He can't do that."

"Why not?" Max asked. "People need lawyers to do stuff."

I outlined what cases cost in time and labor. I had all that knowledge tucked away from when I ran the practice years ago, but my figures didn't deter the boys.

"Okay. So not a case," said Max.

"Dad can do wills," said Henri.

"Great. Two wills."

"And maybe those other things."

"What things?" Max asked.

"Like when you hold certain assets for people," said Henri.

"A trust?" I asked.

"That's it. Dad can set up some trusts."

How can I stop this?

"Dad doesn't do that," I said. "It's not his thing."

"Yeah," said Mariah. "He's not that kind of lawyer."

"But any lawyer can—" Taylor broke off when Mariah gave his arm a smack. "Huh?"

"It's not a good idea," said Jess. "We'll think of something else."

Keely understood and said, "What about free dental exams, Taylor? Would your parents do that?"

"Oh, yeah. I'm sure they would."

"Uncle Larry will do a free yard cleanup," Keely said. "I'll call him."

"Well," said my mom, "I think Derek should help his boys."

"Mom," I hissed.

A TRUNK, A CANOE, AND ALL THE BARBECUE

"Derek is their father. He has an obligation to help the boys."

The boys high-fived and said they'd call Derek to ask him, or rather tell him. It would take a miracle to get Derek to help. My lawyer couldn't get him to answer the phone.

"You should just ask him on Thanksgiving," said Mom with a smile.

"Mom, I don't think he's coming," I said.

"He's coming," said Henri.

"He is?"

"Hello. It's Thanksgiving," said Max.

I wanted to ask if they'd asked their father, but the question got stuck in my throat. Jess saw my face and asked, "Taylor, what did you find out about Vic Delaney?"

"I almost forgot." Taylor ran over to his backpack that was in a pile on the floor and pulled out a folder. "I got stuff on my free period."

Poptart rose into an arch, screeched, and streaked out of the kitchen. Sam glanced around happily. "Grandpa?"

We waited for Leo to appear, but he didn't.

"Doesn't Tarty do that when Leo comes?" Keely asked.

"Usually," I said as a strange feeling came over me, a being watched kind of feeling.

"What's wrong?" Mom asked.

"Nothing. Cats are weird."

The kids all looked at each other, trying to gauge what my mom knew. The answer was simple. Not much.

"Poptart just does stuff," said Mariah.

"Leo's your ghost, right?" Mom asked.

"He is." Jess explained the problem with Poptart and Leo. Mom looked around. "So he's here right now?"

I shook my head. "He's not."

"Are you sure?" Mom asked with an odd expression on her face.

"We'd see him if he was."

Mom didn't reply, but I could tell she was suspicious. Then the kids distracted her with pageant details. Mom was a talented seamstress, and they started talking costumes.

"Can we see what you have?" I asked Taylor.

He brought the folder to the table, and we sat down to look at the short stack of printouts he'd gathered. The first was a birth certificate. Vic Delaney was born in 1895 in St. Louis. Taylor had all the relevant facts about the detective who investigated John K. Tunny III's death. Delaney served in WWI and then he was a cop. The very thorough Taylor found an advertisement in the St. Louis Post Dispatch for the Delaney Detective Agency. The address was downtown St. Louis.

"Any pictures?" I asked.

Taylor pulled out a photo of two police officers standing next to a building with broken windows, watching another two men pouring the contents of a barrel into the gutter. "This was in the paper. Delaney was part of some raid during prohibition."

Jess and I took a close look.

"Can you tell if it's him?" Jess asked.

"No. They're almost identical," I said. "The mustaches don't help either."

"This one's better." Taylor slid another photo over to us. The wedding photo looked like it'd been taken in the twenties. The bride and her bridesmaids were dressed in short, loose lace dresses and the men stood behind them, stiff with slicked-back hair and roses on their lapels.

"He's not the groom," I said. "Jess, what do you think about the one on the right?"

"I think that's him, but he seemed a lot older when we saw him."

"I thought he had clothes from the thirties," I said.

She nodded and squinted at the photo. "He did have that thirties vibe."

"I'm pretty sure that's the guy we saw in the Blazevic kitchen," I said. "What do you know about him?"

"Pretty much what I already told you," said Taylor.

"Was he Scottish?" Jess asked.

"I think Delaney's Irish."

I picked up the birth certificate. "Mary Reilly and John Delaney. Sounds pretty Irish."

"That doesn't mean he's not related to our old lady," said Jess.

I looked up. "You think that's why he's hanging around?"

"Don't you?"

"I thought it was because of Tunny. It was his case," I said.

"Could be," said Jess. "It just seems like why bother? We know ghosts get attached to people, objects, and places they loved. Some old case doesn't seem like a reason to hang around. He could be doing other things."

"Unfinished business," said Taylor. "The case he didn't solve."

"We're not looking into Tunny," said Jess. "So why's he's following us?"

"Good point," I said. "I guess we'll have to ask him."

Taylor looked at his phone. "I have to go. Mom's gonna kill me."

"Can we keep this stuff?" I asked.

"Sure. Tank wanted me to remind you that we want interviews when you solve this stuff."

"Not a problem," said Jess.

The kitchen cleared out, and our remaining three kids came to the table with my mom.

"What have you got there?" Mom asked.

I told her what we were working on, and she sat down to look at the photos. "Can I see your drawing, Jess?"

Jess got her pad and handed it to Mom.

"I think that's him," said Mom, and the kids agreed.

Max and Henri put their backpacks on the table and started unloading books.

"I called Dad," said Max as he opened a notebook.

I didn't say anything. The pit in my stomach prevented speech.

"Mom?" Henri asked. "What's wrong?"

"Nothing's wrong, ya dirtbags," said Mariah. "She's tired. She's been chasing ghosts all day."

"He's coming," said Henri.

"Coming?" I asked in a whisper.

"To Thanksgiving."

Why, Derek?

"Okay." I stood up. "What should we have for dinner?"

I was about to go into the kitchen and Mom said, "It's fine, Libby. Derek will help with the pageant. You'll see."

Mom's eyes were worried but also convinced. I'd kept most of what had happened from her. I couldn't bring myself to tell my mother that my husband had an affair with his paralegal, who liked to dress in cat ears and was half my age. She'd get so upset and want to talk about it. I didn't want to discuss it. There wasn't anything to say.

"It is fine, Mom," said Max. "You're not really getting divorced."

"Honey..."

"Dad doesn't want a divorce. He talks about you all the time," said Henri.

Mom hugged me. "See. This is just a phase. What does your dad say, boys?"

I would like to not be here anymore.

"I'm making dinner," I said.

Mom held me fast. "Hold on."

"He says how great Mom is and he misses her food," said Henri.

"Dad totally knows he screwed up," said Max. "He was really excited when I told him that you want him to come for Thanksgiving."

"Okay. Good. Carbonara? Do we want carbonara?" I went for the cabinet with the pasta and Mom followed. "Libby, you have to talk to Derek."

"There's no talking to Derek," I said.

"The boys are very attached, and they think this will pass."

"I know."

Mom hugged me and said, "You go work. I'll make dinner."

I wanted to stop this, but I couldn't think how. Derek said he'd come to Thanksgiving. He wouldn't show up, and the boys would realize it was over. On Thanksgiving. What a nightmare.

I left the kitchen in a daze and went into my office, where I retrieved my laptop to take it to the living room where Jess was building a fire.

"Are you okay?" Jess asked.

"He's not going to come," I said.

"He might."

I sat down next to Poptart on the sofa and opened my laptop. "What if he brings *her*?"

Jess gasped. "I didn't think of that. Does Bev know about *her*?"

"I couldn't bring myself to tell her."

She got a good blaze going and said, "There's nothing we can do."

"We can hunt him down and drag him to Thanksgiving," I said.

"Always an option, but let's think about Delaney and the

trunk. That's easier," said Jess. "There must be a connection between the two."

I googled Delaney and came up with nothing. "We'll have to ask him, but right now, I'm more concerned about the trunk. Do you think she wants it to go back to her family? She mentioned a girl."

"Marko thinks she said girl," said Jess. "Jelena didn't hear it."

"The accent must be really heavy."

"And they're so young."

"Maybe we can get her to tell us her name." I googled communication boards for the disabled. "We can get the kids to help us. She points at a letter. They tell us and so forth."

"She could tell us why she's upset about the trunk," said Jess with excitement.

"Can you imagine how long that would take, letter by letter, with the kids?"

"What choice do we have?"

"The canoe," I said. "If we can figure out where the trunk came from, we can find out what was in it."

Poptart started a low growl.

"Leo?" Jess asked hopefully.

The cat hissed and leapt off the sofa to slide across the hardwood and run out the door. There was a pop, and Leo stood by the fire.

"I keep hoping that will get better," he said.

"You freak him out," said Jess.

"And speaking of freaking him out, what was up with the kitchen?" I asked.

"The kitchen?"

"You not appearing."

Leo looked back and forth between the two of us. "What are you talking about?"

A TRUNK, A CANOE, AND ALL THE BARBECUE

We told him about Poptart freaking out, and the faint smell of cigarettes filled the living room.

"Don't be upset," I said. "Cats are crazy."

"Poptart never did that before, did he?" Leo asked Jess.

"Well, he used to zoom a lot."

"Zoom?"

"All the sudden, run around for no reason."

Leo nodded. "They do do that, but it's unusual here."

It was, but I didn't like the worried look on Leo's face. We hoped to cheer him up, not make him worry more.

"It's fine. Who can predict cats?" I asked. "Besides, we have more pressing matters."

"Like what?"

"I think we need to buy a canoe."

"In November?" Leo asked.

"Steve Olsen's canoe," I said.

He nodded. "I forgot about that. But don't you think it would be better to find a way to communicate with the lady?"

We told him what we found out, and the cigarette smoke dissipated completely. He was as surprised as we were to find out she was Scottish.

"The board idea is good, but very time consuming," he said.

I didn't say anything, and they looked at me.

"Libby?" Jess asked.

"I don't know," I said. "Something's going on with that trunk."

"Besides being haunted?"

"I just keep thinking about the way Jelena described her. At the trunk and so upset."

"Libby," said Leo, "we get attached to things just like the living."

I pulled an afghan over my legs. "I know, but it's weird, isn't it?"

"Very."

"She will tell us why she's upset," said Jess. "She wants to tell us."

"I still want the numbers off that canoe. It's the only way to track who owned the storage unit. Mika says he'll pay for it if that's the only way."

"Steve's not going to sell it to us."

"Or anyone associated with you," said Leo. "Tank might know someone."

"Julie could make an offer," I said.

Leo laughed. "It's an old canoe, not an antique."

Jess agreed. "He'd be suspicious."

"He's not some genius," I said.

"He doesn't have to be. Julie's in St. Seb," said Jess. "We can walk to her shop from our house."

I kicked my feet up on the coffee table. "Who do we know that could buy without Steve getting suspicious?"

"Me."

We turned and saw my mother standing in the doorway. Mom's usually ruddy complexion was pale, and her hands were clasped together. I jumped up and said, "Mom, I didn't know you were there."

She nodded, her eyes fixed on Leo.

"Mrs. Moss," said Leo. "It's a pleasure to meet you."

"Leo?" Mom asked.

I went over and guided my startled mother to the sofa. "Mom, this is Leo Pereyra. Leo, this is my mother, Beverly Moss."

Leo put his hand on his chest and said, "Please accept my condolences on the loss of your husband. I know from the children, as well as Jess and Libby, that he was a wonderful father and person."

Mom's eyes grew moist. "Thank you. It's my second holiday season without him."

"Sometimes that's worse than the first," said Leo.

She nodded, and Jess asked in a shaky voice, "Why?"

"Because it's becoming normal," said Leo.

"You know," said Mom.

"I do."

Mariah came in and looked around. "Everything okay?"

"It's fine," said Jess. "Just getting acquainted."

"Can you handle any more?"

"Any more what?"

Peg and Vern came in. Peg had her cake pedestal with what looked like a heavy-duty fruitcake on it.

"We heard you have a visitor," said Vern. "I hope we're not intruding."

"How did they hear that?" Jess whispered, and I shrugged before saying, "You're not intruding."

I introduced my mother to two more ghosts, and she got so pale, I considered checking her pulse, although I'd have no idea what to do with the information once I had it.

"Is that a fruitcake?" Jess asked.

"Yes, our special fruitcake. Steeped for ninety days."

Peg and Vern started chatting about the holidays and Mom kept looking at Leo, who signaled that they didn't see him, making Mom paler still.

"I know it's a Monday, but do you suppose we could curl up and watch Dr. Welby?" Peg asked. "If it isn't an intrusion?"

Jess turned to Mom. "We watch *Marcus Welby M.D.* together on Saturdays."

Some color came into Mom's cheeks. "I loved that show when I was…"

"Everyone loves that show," I said. "Let's turn it on."

We got Mom wrapped up in an afghan with a hot water bottle in her lap, and she watched two episodes of *Marcus Welby* with our dead neighbors and chatted about everything that happened in the early 1970s. Peg and Vern were old then and Mom was young, but they saw her as a contemporary and had a great time, talking TV shows and music until they had to go. Where? I have no idea, but they always had places to be.

After dinner and homework, I went up to bed, and it wasn't long before Mom knocked on my door. "Libby, dear?"

"Come in, Mom," I said.

Mom had her hot water bottle and two cups of Sleepytime tea. "Can I join you?"

"Sure." I flipped back the covers and Mom got in bed with me. That hadn't happened since I was in college. Like then, I poured out my heart and my mother listened. It was the best night.

Chapter Fourteen

It was not the best morning. Chaos reigned. Mom was up at the crack of dawn and I overslept. She didn't know I had to blast the boys out of bed, so they were late. I finally got them moving and stumbled into the kitchen that was filled with the smell of cinnamon and eggy goodness with a side of bacon.

"French toast," said Mom from the stove.

"It's so good," said Mariah at the kitchen table, typing away on something she probably should've finished days ago.

"You didn't have to do that, Mom," I said, going for the coffeepot.

"I have to make myself useful."

Jess walked in, fully dressed and clear-eyed. "Bev, that smells so good."

Mom gave her a stack of French toast and loaded her up with bacon. I said I'd wait until the coffee kicked in and then Mom picked up a recipe from the island next to a pile of Jess's art supplies. "Do the kids really like tuna casserole? Peg and Vern told me they love it."

"We do love it," said Mariah without looking up from her screen.

"How is that possible?" Mom asked.

"It's retro," I said. "And the recipe is good."

"This is it?" She handed me Peg and Vern's recipe.

"Yep."

"It has cheddar cheese in it."

"Yes, it does," said Jess with a grin.

"I'm amazed," said Mom.

"We all are."

"You know, if the kids like tuna casserole, I should make chicken ala king."

Jess threw up her hands. "Yes, please. I love your chicken ala king."

"Me, too, Mom," I said.

"What's chicken ala king?" Mariah asked, and Mom went over to tell her about the seventies stew served over toast.

Jess checked the time. "I'm going to the antique shop before class. Do you want to go?"

"I don't think so," I said. "I have to figure out how to get a look at that canoe. Maybe I can trick Steve into taking a picture of the numbers and sending it to me."

"Good luck with that," said Mom. "Nobody's that stupid."

I told her about the scene at Dutzow Barbecue and Mom said, "I take it back."

"I could get Larry to scare Steve into showing him the numbers."

"You shouldn't threaten people," said Mom. "I was serious about buying it. He doesn't know me. I can say I live in Florida and I'm here visiting."

"And you need to buy an old canoe in November because?" I asked.

"I'm on a fixed income and my son-in-law wants one for Christmas," said Mom with her eyes twinkling.

"That's not bad," said Jess.

"But you'd have to know about the canoe," I said.

"You'll think of something," said Mom. "Where are the boys?"

"Late," said Mariah, closing her laptop and gathering her books.

The boys dashed in and proclaimed that they were never late. Everyone else was just early. Mom gave them plates of French toast, but they were so late, they didn't have time for syrup and ate it rolled up like Swiss rolls with a piece of bacon in the center.

"That's a pretty neat idea," said Mom.

"It's us, Grandma," said Henri. "We're full of ideas."

Mom rolled her eyes. "You're full of something."

I got more coffee and went to get the *Sentinel*. In St. Seb, people still got their paper tossed on their doorstep every morning, and I kinda liked it. Coffee and the paper every morning. It reminded me of my dad.

When I got back in the kitchen, the boys were stealing my keys out of my purse.

"Hey," I said. "I need those."

"We have another meeting at the elementary school," said Max.

"How'd you get there yesterday?"

"Mr. Ford took us. He had to do something with their boiler," said Henri. "But he's not going today."

"Mrs. Johns is going to the meeting," said Max. "She'll take us. No biggie."

"How are we getting to school if Jess is teaching?" Henri asked.

Mariah put on her backpack. "Taylor's picking me up. He'll take you two too."

"Are you sure?" I asked. "I was going to throw on some clothes."

"No problem. He likes the dirtbags."

"Dirtbags?" Mom asked.

"I mean it affectionately," said Mariah. "But you two better hurry, Taylor will be here any second."

On cue, there was a honk in the front of the house. The boys panicked and raced around, grabbing stuff before dashing out through the arch.

"I forgot how exciting mornings with kids can be," said Mom.

"Don't the boys have English today?" Jess asked.

I looked over at the table where their English books were. "Yes, they do."

"I'll take them," said Jess.

"Don't worry about it. Eat." I grabbed the books and ran out to catch the boys at the front door, putting on their coats and halfway out the door.

"When do you have the elementary school today?" I asked. "I can probably take you."

"Nah," said Max. "It's a meeting with the parents. Somebody will take us."

The parents.

"Maybe I should go for backup," I said.

They looked at me with innocence filling their blue eyes.

"Backup for what?" Henri asked. "They love us."

"Well, you two are going off book."

"They love that," said Max. "Mrs. Johns will take us, or a parent."

"Or the grandma," said Henri, looking at me as he zipped up his backpack. "What's her name?"

"Who?" I asked.

"The grandma that was at the assembly yesterday."

"How would I know, Hen? I wasn't there."

"Jess knows her," said Max. "You two know all the same people."

Taylor honked and Mariah yelled, "Hurry up!"

"See ya, Mom," the boys said, and ran out the door.

What grandma?

I ran out onto the front porch and yelled as the boys jumped in Taylor's ancient Bronco. "How do you know Jess knows her?"

"She knows her," said Henri, and he dove in the truck just as Taylor started to back out. They waved at me and were gone in a squeal of tires.

Grandma? Peg? Was Peg at the assembly? Sure. Why not?

I went in and closed the door before going back to the kitchen where Mom insisted I eat an enormous plate of French toast at the island. I started digging in and then looked to my left. Jess's art supplies were there with her sketchbook open to the old lady's portrait.

"Was this here before?" I asked.

Mom put the skillet in the sink and said, "Yes. Jess showed it to me this morning." She came over, wiping her hands on a towel. "Isn't she talented? The lady looks like she could step off the page. I love the little details. The buttons on her sweater and the rings on her hand."

"This was out when the boys were eating?" I asked.

"Sure. Why?"

"Did they see it?"

"I don't know," said Mom. "Is it important?"

Jess walked in. "What's going on?"

I pointed at her portrait. "Did the boys see this?"

"My portrait?"

"Yes. This morning. Were the boys looking at it?"

Jess nodded. "They looked at it when they were eating. They thought it was cool. Why?"

"Hold on." I called Max, and he didn't answer. Heaven

forbid he actually answer a phone. I texted that I had to talk to him immediately. Then the boy called me.

"What happened?" Max asked in a panic. "Is it Grandma? It better not be Grandma."

"Grandma's fine," I said, and then I asked them about Jess's portrait. They confirmed that they'd been looking at it.

"Have you seen that lady before?"

"The grandma?" Max asked.

My chest went tight, and I could hardly choke out, "Yes. Have you seen her before?"

"We told you she was at the assembly. Super nice. Stayed right with her grandson."

"Who was the grandson?" I asked.

"I don't know."

"Describe him."

"Big kid, but he was in one of the younger classes." Max asked Henri, who got on the phone and described Marko perfectly.

"You both saw that lady with the kid?" I asked.

"Yeah," said Max. "What's up?"

"That's the lady we've been investigating."

"No way."

"Did you hear her say anything?" I asked.

"No," said Max. "She was just with the kid, talking to him. He looked kinda embarrassed, but I just thought she was being nice."

"I think she was." I told the boys not to tell anyone that Marko had a ghost at school with him and that I'd pick them up for the meeting. When I hung up, Mom stared at me with enormous eyes. "The ghost was at school?"

"That's not the big-ticket item, Mom," I said.

"The boys saw her?" Jess asked.

"Apparently so."

"Why them and not Mariah?"

"If I had to guess, they're closer to being kids than Mariah," I said.

"That's definitely true," said Mom. "They have very youthful spirits. Mariah's an old soul. I mean that in a good way, Jess."

Jess went over and hugged her. "I know, and you're right. Mariah is an old soul."

Mom held my best friend tight and then smiled at me. I'd say Mom was a second mother to Jess, but she really didn't have much of a first one.

"What do you want to do today, Mom?" I asked. "You can ghost hunt with me or—"

"Me." Jess told Mom her schedule, selling the fur trappers hard. They were hard to compete with. Mom was very interested in early American history, and the trappers experience was bound to be catnip to her.

"That all sounds very nice, but I'm going to buy a car," said Mom.

"What?"

"We need another car."

"Mom, we can't afford another car," I said.

"You can't, but I can," she said. "There are several cars that would suit me and the boys fine on a lot about ten blocks away."

"How do you know that?" Jess asked.

Mom pointed at the stack of old *Sentinel*s. "I did my homework. Now you should do yours, Libby."

"Huh?"

"Call the parents and have them give permission for you to see that little boy at school," said Mom. "No school worth its salt would let you talk to him without the parents' permission."

"Good call, Mom," I said. "I didn't think of that."

"That's what I'm here for."

"And for hugging," said Jess, looking more and more relaxed now that Mom was there.

"Naturally," said Mom. "I'd like to go to the car place first. Can someone drop me off?"

Jess squeezed her. "I can when I'm going to the antique shop."

"Perfect."

Mom opened the paper, and they discussed the merits of the different vehicles on the lot while I called Mika. Sandra had already taken the kids to school, and he was just walking out the door, but he was thrilled that the boys could see the lady. He'd call the school on the way to work and give permission. I had to promise to call him as soon as I knew something. Not a hard promise, since I would've done it anyway. I said goodbye and helped Jess pack up her stuff for a day of art.

"I've decided I'm going to the antique shop first," said Mom. "I'd like to see that maid."

"Fine with me," I said.

Jess slung her bag over her shoulder. "But what about you? I feel like you shouldn't go it alone."

"I won't be alone. I'll ask Leo to come."

"Where is he?" Mom asked.

We shrugged. Leo rarely told us where he was when he wasn't with us. I had a feeling he was nowhere, but I didn't like to pry.

"Do you call for him?" Mom asked. "How do you—"

Poptart arched and sped out of the kitchen.

"He's coming," I said.

Jess glanced around. "Unless it's like yesterday."

Leo popped in by the stove and smiled. "You called?"

Mom went and looked through the archway and then asked, "Does Poptart do that every time?"

"Yes," said Leo. "I tried all kinds of approaches, but he doesn't like me."

"Not possible," said Mom. "We'll think of something."

He smiled. "That would be nice."

"You take care of Libby and I will take care of Poptart," said Mom.

Leo put a hand on his chest. "Yes, ma'am."

Chapter Fifteen

I pulled up in front of the high school a couple of hours later and my boys ran down the front steps to fight over shotgun. Max lost because of Henri's smaller stature and ability to squirm in-between Max and the door.

They were both scowling as they buckled in, but then Max said, "Hey, what's that smell?"

"Cookies," I said.

The scowls vanished.

"I want cookies," said Henri.

"Imagine that." I gave them each two cookies, one sugar and one molasses before driving off campus. In the time I'd had that morning, I'd handled a couple new claims for Eric, made cookies, and put a chicken in the Crock-Pot to make stock. Peg and Vern thought the secret to Leo's mother's albondigas soup might be homemade stock. They'd never had the soup, having died before Leo came to St. Seb, but they had smelled it, and we trusted their judgment. Plus, Eric thought the soup had a chickeny flavor. Worth a shot. Leo was excited to try it, and I liked the enthusiasm. He was looking less and less mournful. He had a colorful pocket square in his suit that morning, and I took that as a good sign.

The boys finished their cookies and tried to get some more out of me between yawns.

"They're for the parents," I said.

Max grinned. "Are you trying to bribe them to go along with our plan?"

"Not bribe."

"I'm all for it," said Henri. "Get 'em doped up on sugar and they'll agree to anything."

"You make me sound nefarious," I said.

"Not nefarious," said Max. "Smart. Your cookies go a long way."

"I want them to know we're a nice family before you hit them with 'Nasty.'"

"They're gonna love it," said Henri. "And we finished the program last night."

"Did you finish your homework?" I asked.

After an enormous yawn, Max said, "We did. Leo got us through the math, and Peg helped with our papers."

"I didn't know she did that."

"Yeah, she usually comes over after you go to bed. Vern goes to sleep early," said Henri.

"You know he doesn't really go to sleep," I said.

The boys shrugged.

"That's what Peg says," said Max. "She's great with catching awkward sentences."

"How does she operate the computer?"

The boys chuckled and described their editing system. They printed the pages and went through them with Peg, doing their own red markups for her because she had arthritis.

"She doesn't think it's weird that she doesn't touch the pages?" I asked.

"Not so far," said Henri.

Maybe you shouldn't say it, but you have to.

"Guys, please don't tell your dad about this stuff," I said.

"We haven't yet," said Max. "It hasn't come up."

"Dad would be cool with it," said Henri. "He's not judgy and mean."

I turned into the elementary school parking lot. "I just don't want him to...think I'm not taking care of you properly."

"You're taking great care of us," said Max. "St. Seb is awesome."

"Dad might not think so," I said.

The boys blew that off, and I had a new worry. Derek could use the ghost thing against me. I couldn't really blame him. It was crazy. I *would* look crazy.

As soon as I parked, the boys jumped out and said hello to Leo, who'd appeared next to the car. Then they walked ahead, chattering about the pageant without a single worry weighing on them.

"Are you okay?" Leo asked.

"I think they're going to tell Derek about you," I said.

"It has to happen."

"Does it?"

"I'm part of their life now, and children shouldn't have to carry secrets."

I knew he was right in theory, and the old Derek would've been great about Leo and St. Seb. The new Derek was unpredictable, to say the least.

"I know," I said, dashing to catch up with the boys at the door.

A woman welcomed us in, and I couldn't help staring a little. She looked so much like Mrs. Johns from the high school, it was a little weird.

"Hello," she said. "I'm Mrs. Crystal, the principal."

"Libby Forest," I said. "Thanks for having us."

"It's a pleasure. The entire school is excited about the program. Mr. Blazevic called. You need to speak with his son, Marko?"

"Briefly." I could tell she wanted to ask if it was a ghost thing, but she just said, "I don't want to pull him out of class. Recess is after the meeting. Will that work?"

"Absolutely," I said. "Can I ask you a question?"

She smiled at me. "Am I related to Mrs. Johns?"

"Yes."

"She's my older sister."

I laughed. "You are the spitting image. If you said you weren't related, I'd have thought I was going crazy."

"We get that all the time. Our brother does too," said Mrs. Crystal.

"Is he a principal too?" I was half joking, but their brother was the assistant principal at the middle school.

"You're like a dynasty," I said.

She led us down the hall to a room marked Conference Room and said, "It's in our blood. Both our parents were principals."

"Mine were teachers," I said.

"I know. Max and Henri told us. It was part of their pitch."

I looked at the boys, who were grinning.

"Education's in our blood too," said Max.

"That's new," I said.

"Ya gotta use what you have," said Henri. "All avenues must be explored."

"Their father's a lawyer."

Mrs. Crystal smiled. "I can tell. Shall we?"

"Let's do it," I said, and we went in to find a group of fifteen parents representing kindergarten to fifth. The boys went to each parent, introduced themselves, and thanked them for coming. The parents were all surprised and immediately ready to listen to any plans the boys had. That's when I hit them with cookies.

With everyone happy and snacking, the boys set up their PowerPoint presentation. I don't know when they did that, but Leo was looking so proud, I was sure he had something to do with it.

"We're going to open the show with 'Holiday' by Madonna," said Henri.

That got looks of consternation, but they gave the lyrics and the concept for what the kids would do on stage, getting nods and smiles. They went through the entire lineup, including *Macarena*. I thought they'd met their Waterloo. A song with *seduce* in the lyrics was going to be a hard sell to little kids' parents, but I shouldn't have worried. Max and Henri rewrote the lyrics to make it about a naughty elf that keeps stealing treats.

"The special needs kids are going to lead it, and we want everyone up and dancing," said Max.

The parents weren't so sure about that, and Henri said, "The kids will like it if everyone joins them."

We all nodded.

"I don't know if we can get parents to dance," said Mrs. Crystal.

"Mom can do it," said Max.

I'd been sitting in the back, enjoying the show and thinking I was out of the line of fire. "Me?"

"If you and Jess do it, everyone will do it," said Henri.

"What makes you think that?"

"Dad said so."

What's he trying to do to me?

"Your father might be off the mark on this one," I said.

"Dad said you're cool and people always want to do what you do," said Max.

"You're confusing me with Dad."

"No way," said Henri, beaming at the parents. "It's in the bag. It'll be great."

The parents looked at me and I said, "I'll do it."

I got applause, especially from Leo and Mrs. Crystal. She came over and said, "I think they're right."

"I think they're nuts, but I'm really glad you like the 'Nasty' song idea."

"It's great," she said. "So funny."

The bell rang, and the parents filed out after thanking the boys for their efforts. Then Mrs. Crystal took us through the building and out the back past hordes of happy children going to the playground. We stepped off to the side, scanning the area. It didn't take long to spot Marko, since he was taller than all his friends.

"I see him," said Max. "Should we go get him?"

"Is she there?" Leo asked.

Henri nodded and said, "Yeah. She's by the fence."

"Who's by the fence?" Mrs. Crystal asked, her forehead wrinkling.

"It's okay, Mrs. Crystal," said Max. "She's just standing there. It's cool."

"Who are we talking about?"

I wasn't sure what to say. "You know we live at Number Eight, right?"

"I'd heard that," she said.

"So there are rumors about our house."

"Are you saying they're true?"

"It depends on the rumor, but they're mostly true."

The boys grinned at her.

"You don't need to worry. Mom will handle it," said Max. "It's what she and Jess do now."

"Handle ghosts?" Mrs. Crystal asked.

"In a word, yes," I said.

"Then there's one on our playground?"

We told her the situation, since Mika said we could, and she asked, "Is it just one?"

I glanced over at Leo, who smiled. "Two that I'm sure about."

"Why wouldn't you be sure?"

I explained how ghosts really looked. There were some kids on the playground that didn't look like they fit in with the current fashions, but Leo told me not to mention them. It would only upset the principal, and she had enough to absorb.

"Leo Pereyra is here," I said.

"Oh, my goodness," she said. "I love him. Is he really?"

A faint blush came up on Leo's cheeks. "Ask her why she likes me."

I did and, like many people in St. Seb, Leo's book *Departures at Eight* had gotten her through a rough time. Max started helping with the conversation between her and Leo, and I asked Henri to go over and get Marko. The boy was reluctant to leave his friends, but he came away with Henri, glancing over nervously. I tapped Max on the shoulder. "Is she coming with him?"

"No," he said. "She's staying at the fence."

"I wonder why."

Marko walked up and said, "Hi, Miss Libby. Is everything okay?"

"Everything's great," I said. "You know Mrs. Crystal, of course."

The boy got more nervous at the sight of his principal, but I quickly told him he wasn't in trouble.

"And these two boys are my boys, Max and Henri."

Marko smiled shyly at the big boys. "Hi."

"We're here because they can see *her*," I said.

"Really?"

"Yeah," said Max. "She's over by the fence right now."

Marko glanced back. "What's she doing?"

Henri gave him a playful punch on the shoulder. "Look at you testing us. She's knitting."

Marko grinned, and I could see the relief wash over him.

"So," Max asked, "how come she's here with you? Mom says she lives in your sister's room."

Marko told us that preschool was boring. He was a big kid and so much more interesting.

Henri didn't buy it. "Is that really it?"

Marko glanced back and said, "Don't do anything, but there's a boy that bullies me. She's stops him."

Mrs. Crystal gasped. "How does she do that?"

"When he says things to me, she makes him shiver." Marko smiled. "He hates it, but he thinks I'm doing it."

"Who is this bully?" Mrs. Crystal asked.

The boy shook his head. "I'm not tattling. She's taking care of it."

The principal looked at me and I said, "What can I tell you? Ghosts are useful."

"I don't even know what to say. Ghosts aren't a part of our training."

I laughed. "No kidding. Nobody's prepared for St. Seb." Then I turned to Marko. "Have you been able to understand her any better now that you know she's speaking English?"

He made a face. "It's not really the same as English."

"She just has an accent."

"A lot of accent."

"So you can't understand anything, then?" I asked.

He sucked in his lips, thought, and then said, "Maybe a little."

"Any words?"

"I think she was talking about a girl, but she started crying. I can't understand anything when she cries."

"Why is she crying?" Mrs. Crystal asked.

"We're trying to find out," I said. "Anything else, Marko?"

"I think I heard her asking for help," he said. "Jelena heard help, too."

"That's good. Can you get her to come over?"

The boy turned and ran across the playground and I watched him play it cool while trying not to let the other kids see him talking to thin air.

"Is she coming?" I asked the boys.

"Yes," they said.

Marko ran up and said, "They can see you."

He paused. "The boys, not the ladies."

"Hi," said Max.

"We're Henri and Max," said Henri. "This is our mom. You know her."

The boys started nodding and saying slow down.

"What's she saying?" I asked.

"Hold on, Mom," said Max. "She's really worked up."

Henri grabbed my arm. "Marko should go back to recess."

"Now?" I asked.

"Yeah. Right now."

Mrs. Crystal told Marko to go back to playing. He hesitated, but then ran off to his friends, who were watching.

"What's going on?" I asked.

"It's not good, Mom," said Max.

"Tell me."

It took a while, all of recess, to get the story. The lady's name was Elsie Boyd, and she came from Glasgow. The boys said it was incredibly hard to understand her, but they got that the trunk was a family piece and her father had given it to her for her wedding. Her husband died, and she came to America with a wealthy family as their nanny.

"Is there fabric in it?" Henri asked. "She keeps talking about the fabric."

"There is."

"Okay. Hold on," he said, not to me but to the empty space in front of him.

"Why did Marko have to leave?" I asked.

"Somebody put a dead girl in her trunk," said Max with a wince. "She's really upset about it."

Mrs. Crystal put her hands over her mouth, and Leo started pacing.

"No kidding," I said. "Whose body is it?"

"She doesn't know," said Henri.

"When did it happen?"

The boys asked questions and finally got that she didn't really know when it happened, but it was before the trunk was in the storage unit.

"Elsie," I said. "Who had your trunk?"

Henri told us that after she died, the family she worked for sold her trunk and a few people owned it. Like a lot of ghosts, she was sketchy on time. She wasn't clear on when she died or what year it was currently.

"Who put the body in the trunk?" I asked.

"She didn't see it happen. One day, there was a body in her trunk. Blood got on the fabric," said Max. "She wants you to clean it."

"No problem," I said. "We will totally clean your trunk."

"She's crying," said Henri.

"Why are you crying, Elsie?" I asked.

The boys looked at each other and then Max said, "She's just saying something like that poor girl over and over again."

I looked at Leo. "It's the fabric and the girl?"

"We have to find out who she is and what happened to the body," said Leo.

"How am I going to do that?"

"What?" Mrs. Crystal said.

"Find the body and the identity."

"Oh, that will be difficult if she doesn't know anything."

I thought it over. "Elsie, please stop crying if you can. We're going to figure this out for you. Was the body in the trunk when it was in the storage unit?"

"She doesn't know what a storage unit is," said Max.

I explained it and Elsie said yes.

"That just got easier," said Mrs. Crystal.

"Did it?" I asked, feeling overwhelmed. I never imagined we'd be dealing with an unknown body. At worst, I thought it was Elsie's body.

"Who had that storage unit?" she asked, and then looked horrified. "Please don't say Mr. Blazevic."

"No, he bought the trunk at an antique mall... Oh, of course," I said. "Steve bought the unit and dumped the body."

"Disgusting little weasel," said Leo.

"Gross," said Max.

"He should've called the police," said Henri.

"Selling the trunk would've been difficult if the police had it," I said. "Elsie, what happened to the body?"

The boys listened and then Max said, "She doesn't know. She came to the unit one day, and it was empty. It took her a while to find her trunk back."

"How in the world did you find it, Elsie?" Mrs. Crystal asked.

"She heard a guy talking about the unit, I guess, and followed him," said Henri. "It's kinda confusing."

"When she saw it again, it was empty," said Max. "She wants the girl to have a proper burial."

"Makes sense."

"Mom," said Henri. "We have to go back to school. We're going to miss our next classes."

I hated to leave when we were so close, but school was important. "Elsie, can you come with me? Jess can draw the girl. That will help us identify her."

"She's not going," said Henri.

"Why not?" I asked.

"She has to look after Marko so that kid doesn't hassle him."

Mrs. Crystal stepped up. "Elsie, who's bullying Marko?"

The boys pointed out a scrawny little boy who had a disdainful look on his face as he yelled something at a girl.

"I might've known," said the principal. "Elsie, I'm on it."

"She's still not going," said Henri. "She's his nanny."

Mrs. Crystal clasped her hands together. "I think I might cry."

She wasn't the only one.

Chapter Sixteen

When I arrived back at home, there was a BMW X1 parked in the driveway. It was at least ten years old, but looked to be in good shape. There were temp tags on it and a brand-new bumper sticker that advertised our Haunted Mortuary.

"Mom!" I called out as I came in and peeled off my coat.

"In the kitchen!"

I found my mother at the stove, making a grilled cheese with Kraft Singles. No cheddar for my mother. She was a classic.

"Want one?" she asked.

"Yes, please," I said, setting my phone on the island. My thumbs were tired from texting Mika. It would've been easier to call, but since he was at work, he couldn't do a call.

"Did you talk to her?" Mom asked, sliding a sandwich on a plate for me.

"In a manner of speaking," I said.

"All done? Mystery solved?"

I said nothing, and Mom looked up from her butter spreading. "No?"

I told her about the body and she had to sit down.

"When do I buy it?" Mom asked when she'd recovered from the shock of it.

"What?"

"The canoe."

Poptart screeched and ran out.

"We have got to do something about that," said Mom.

"I'm open to ideas," I said.

"I've got some, but—"

Leo popped in and startled her. "Oh, sorry, Bev. I thought you were expecting me."

"I was, but that is quick," Mom said.

"If there was a slow way, I'd do it," he said.

She smiled. "I know you would. Now have a seat and let's talk about this body situation."

Carol's chair appeared and Leo settled in, but he didn't look unhappy, just intense. Who could blame him? We had a body to find.

"I can buy that canoe and you'll know where it came from," said Mom.

Leo agreed that was our best shot unless there was paperwork in the storage unit and Steve knew who owned it. They tried to come up with ways to get Steve to cough up the information, and I ate my sandwich.

"Libby, this Steve is a money-grubbing weasel, right?" Mom asked.

"I'd say so."

"Offer to pay him if he won't do the right thing."

"He's not going to do the right thing," I said. "He had the chance, and he didn't take it. I don't think Steve is going to let us anywhere near that information."

"Why not? Money is money."

"He dumped the body. That's illegal, and I think they could see him as part of an ongoing conspiracy."

"Conspiracy?" Leo asked.

I looked back and forth between them, waiting for it to dawn on them that this wasn't an identity and location problem. It was a lot bigger.

"What?" Mom asked.

"She was murdered, Mom," I said.

"Oh, well, maybe not."

"Who put a girl's body in a trunk and storage unit for years if she died naturally?"

"When you put it that way."

"You're right, of course," said Leo. "I was thinking about Elsie and how to help her, but we have to find the girl and solve her murder."

I put my forehead on the island. "And the key is Steve."

"Maybe he can be reasoned with," said Mom.

I reminded her that the man spun around on the floor to avoid answering questions about the trunk. He sure wasn't going to tell me where he dumped a body.

"We'll just have to be smarter than him."

"That will not be difficult," said Leo. "The question is, can we be as devious?"

"I don't know if I'd call him devious," I said. "But he was thinking fast at the storage unit."

"What do you mean?" Mom asked.

"He got another customer to help him move the stuff and had to do some fast talking to keep him from emptying the trunk."

Mom asked to see the trunk, and I showed her a picture.

"That's a beautiful piece and heavy-duty. You'd need help, empty or not."

I made tea for us and her words kept bouncing around in my head.

Heavy-duty. Heavy-duty. Heavy-duty.

"Libby, what are you thinking?" Leo asked.

"That the trunk is really heavy."

"Yes, we know that."

"And Hugo is old. He couldn't help Steve with that trunk or the canoe or anything," I said.

A slow smile spread across Leo's face. "So who helped him?"

Mom blew on her tea and asked, "How is that helpful? Why would that guy help if Steve won't?"

"Maybe he saw the number on the canoe or something else," said Leo.

"I bet Steve didn't let him see the body," I said. "And if he didn't, he won't be so closed-mouthed."

"Very good," said Mom. "That makes sense. This is fun."

I got out my phone and called the Fond Memories Antique Mall. Unfortunately, Mr. Burgess answered, and I panicked, shoved the phone at Mom. "Ask for Dawn."

"Oh, oh. Okay." Mom got on the phone and apologized for the delay, citing her age and making her voice tremulous. Mom was not tremulous. What a ham. Maybe the boys got some of it from my side after all.

"Can I please speak to Dawn?" Mom asked. "Yes, I'm sure you can."

"Nice girl helped you," I whispered.

Mom nodded. "But Dawn is such a nice young lady and so helpful. I wanted to thank her." There was a pause. "What did I buy?"

"Um. Um. Um." I looked at Leo and he said, "Rocker?"

"A rocker. Very nice. I sit in it and knit. I make..."

"Scarves," I said.

"Scarves and hats. I'm going to knit a blanket for my grandson," Mom said with her eyes beginning to twinkle. "You'd love my grandson. He's such a lovely boy and so bright. He was on the honor roll last semester. Oh, yes he was. He had an A in Math. He had an A in Science. He had an A in Music."

Leo doubled over in laughter, and I had to clamp my hands over my mouth to hold in my laughter.

"Oh, there are other As too. He's such a smart boy. He had an A in English and he had a... Oh, yes, I would like to speak to Dawn. Thank you very much." Mom hit the mute button. "He's going to get her."

"You're a genius, Mom," I said, wiping the tears from my eyes.

"Thanks, Bev," said Leo. "I needed that."

"I'm so glad I came early. All we do in Florida is talk about politics and complain about our joints. This is much more entertaining."

"Hello?" Dawn's voice came out of the phone.

Mom unmuted and said, "Is this Dawn?"

"Yes, ma'am. Did I sell you a rocker?"

"Mom, speaker," I said.

Mom put the phone on speaker and I said, "Dawn, this is Libby Forest. My friend Jess and I talked to you about the trunk."

"Oh, yes." She sounded nervous.

"Is Mr. Burgess still there listening?" I asked.

"Yes. My boss is here," she said.

"Tell him that the old lady is talking about her grandson and knitting."

We got to hear Dawn saying the customer was yammering, and she offered him the phone. That made me nervous, but Dawn knew Mr. Burgess.

"He's gone," she said. "What's going on?"

I told her we were making headway and asked about anyone that helped Steve with his business, specifically moving items. Dawn said Steve never had help. He was all about getting her to help or Mr. Burgess.

A TRUNK, A CANOE, AND ALL THE BARBECUE

"You've never seen anyone with him?" I asked.

"His dad used to come, but not since he retired. Sorry. Did you find out where the trunk came from?"

"We did," I said.

"There's something weird going on with it, isn't there?"

"Definitely."

"I told my boyfriend about it and he figures you could store a body in that trunk. It was big enough," said Dawn. "Plus, there was that smell."

"I promise when we solve it, I will tell you everything."

Dawn thanked me and we hung up.

"What now?" Mom asked. "I'm ready."

"You've created a monster," said Leo, still chuckling, and I wondered if he still needed the soup. Mom was working wonders.

"She was always feisty," I said.

"I bet," he said, looking fondly at Mom. "The boys get it somewhere."

"Hey, I'm feisty too."

"Yes," he said. "You are very feisty."

They started laughing together, and I got to calling the only other people I knew to call.

"Dutzow Barbecue. Ned speaking."

"Ned. It's Libby."

I didn't get anything else out. Ned and Lynn were over the moon. Business was booming since Steve's freakout video went viral. They were sold out for the day already and closing up.

"This is amazing," he said. "I'm raking in the tips."

"I'm so glad," I said. "I never thought about that happening."

"Neither did we, but it's great coming into the holiday season. Things slow down. What can I help you with? Steve hasn't been back in. No surprise there."

"Does Steve have any buddies?" I asked.

"Drinking buddies?"

"More like moving buddies."

"Heh?"

I told him what I was after and he said there was a guy that helped out Steve from time to time, burning trash, moving furniture, and taking junk out to the Olsens' dump like appliances and old tires. His name was Bear Hotchkiss, and he lived in Dutzow.

"Do you think he'd talk with me?" I asked.

"Sure. He's a little different, but don't let that put you off," said Ned.

"Different how?" I was picturing Steve. I wasn't crazy about that guy.

"I think he's on the spectrum. Lives with his parents and does odd jobs around town. His real name is Andrew, but everyone calls him Bear because he's a sweetheart."

"Do you know him well?" I asked. "Could you maybe arrange a meeting?"

"Sure, but like I said, we're closing right now," said Ned. "How about tomorrow?"

"Perfect."

"This works. We need to move some wood, anyway. Bear usually helps with that. Can you come at around eleven?"

I told him I could and hung up.

"What are you going to ask Bear?" Mom asked with some worry.

"Just what he remembers." Then I smiled. "If Bear knows about the canoe, that's a way to get the word out."

"What word?" Leo asked.

"The word that Steve has a canoe. I was trying to figure out how we could make it reasonable that someone knows about it. Bear could tell someone. Perfect."

Mom wrinkled her nose. "You'll have to meet Bear and see how he feels before you rope him into anything."

"I'm not going to pull a fast one on Bear," I said. "Just Steve."

"That I'm good with."

Mom and Leo settled in for a chat about the stock. They both had strong opinions on straining. Colander or cheesecloth. I left them to it and went back to work on Eric's latest claims. It wasn't as exciting as communicating with the dead, but it paid the bills.

I was on the phone with Mika a few hours later when the kids got home. I followed the clamor into the kitchen where Mom was serving up her homemade biscuits dripping with store-bought strawberry jam. While I was working, she and Leo went to McCann's and picked canning supplies for fig jam. Leo had never had it, but he was all for cooking anything and everything. The island was now a canning station.

"How are we going to make dinner?" I asked as I looked over the mess.

"There's room," said Mom. "Chicken ala king isn't difficult."

"We should make fresh bread," said Leo.

The boys cheered and Mariah rolled her eyes, although she was a huge fan of the bread maker and used it the most.

"Where's Mom?" Mariah asked.

"Still at the Horney Hotel as of half an hour ago. She got hired to do an engagement portrait, and she's doing the rough sketch," I said.

Mariah picked up a second biscuit and asked, "Do you think she's working too much?"

"Too much?" Mom asked.

"Yeah. After Dad, she couldn't do anything, and now she's busy all the time."

Mom went over and put an arm around Mariah's shoulders. "We had a long talk about it. I think she's okay."

"Are you okay?" Mariah asked. "I know you're still sad about Libby's dad."

"I am still sad, but being here with all of you has lifted my spirits," said Mom. "I saw ghosts today."

The boys laughed.

"We see Leo every day," said Max.

"New ghosts." Mom told them about Julie's antique shop and the ghosts there. The little Irish maid, Mary, was very sweet and didn't quite get that she wasn't actually cleaning the chandeliers, but she seemed to love cleaning, so Mom figured she enjoyed the attempt. Her employer was Lily Cooper, and she had strong feelings about cleaning too. She just wasn't going to do it herself. As far as Mom could tell, they were at the shop because of the chandeliers, but she wasn't certain if they'd been in Lily's house or not.

"Was that guy still asleep on the fainting couch?" I asked.

"He was. Mary says he never wakes up."

"That's really weird," said Henri.

"We should wake him up," said Max. "We're loud."

"Yes, you are," I said. "Finish your snack. You've got a job to do."

The boys groaned and made a big fuss, but they weren't serious. They almost never were.

"We're going to the Blazevics' house to talk to Elsie again," I said.

"Am I going?" Jess walked in, carrying her supplies.

"I hope so, if you're not too tired."

She smiled and said, "I'm not tired at all. It was a fun day."

Jess showed us her work and the engagement sketch was wonderful, capturing the joy of a new life starting out.

"That's where the trappers are, right?" Mom asked.

"Yes, you'll have to meet them eventually," said Jess. "They are pretty funny."

"I like the sound of meeting—"

"No!" we all shouted.

Mom put her hand on her chest. "My goodness, are you trying to kill me?"

"You can't say their names," said Mariah.

"Why ever not?"

"They'll come, and they never want to leave," said Max.

Henri grabbed a can of Lysol. "We have to spray them."

"That's rude," Mom said.

"Trust me, Mom," I said. "It's necessary."

"I can't say their names at all?"

We all shook our heads.

"They're like Beetlejuice," said Jess. "Except it usually only takes one time."

"That's good to know," said Mom. "Are they rambunctious?"

"Very," I said. "Other ghosts don't usually like them."

"The smell is terrible," said Mariah. "Makes me want to barf."

The kids started discussing the worst smells of their lives, and the trappers won hands down. I could tell Mom didn't get it, but she soon would. The trappers showed up uninvited pretty often, and it was bound to happen soon.

"Jess," I said. "Mika says this is a good time to come over. The kids say she's there."

"Let me have a biscuit, and then I'm ready."

Mariah got started on her homework and the boys finished the biscuits off. Mom promised to make more, and I had to bribe them with the hope of the cookies I'd stashed away that morning to get them out the door.

"How long is this going to take?" Max asked.

"I have no idea," I said, getting into the passenger side of the Volvo.

"What are we doing?" Jess asked.

"We're drawing a dead girl."

"Cool," said Henri, perking up. "That's how we can find out who she is."

The boys and I buckled in, but Jess sat in the driver's seat, white-knuckling the steering wheel.

"You okay?"

"I'm just thinking about what she'll look like," said Jess.

"Do you want me to tell Mika we can't do it?"

She twisted the start knob. "No, we have to do this."

I wanted to deny it, but the best way to identify that poor girl was to find out what she looked like.

"You can do it, Jess," said Max, reaching over the seat to pat her shoulder. "You drew the trappers and they're gross."

"This is different," I said.

"Yeah, but you guys always say we have to help when we can," said Henri.

Jess backed out of the driveway. "We do say that."

The boys became The Eggs and did their sunny-side-up thing. All the great things about drawing a dead body. You wouldn't think they could make it sound good, but they did. Solving a crime. Closure for a family. Expanding her art repertoire, publicity for our afterlife business, and more.

"Alright. Alright," said Jess. "It'll be good and good for me."

"Now you've got it," said Henri. "I hope they have snacks."

"Yeah, I'm starving," said Max.

"You just ate," I said.

"That was hardly anything, Mom," said Henri.

"There are cookies, but you have to share with the kids."

A TRUNK, A CANOE, AND ALL THE BARBECUE

Jess parked in front, and the boys jumped out and ran up the stairs to the front door.

"They never do anything slow," said Jess.

"If only we could harness that energy," I said. "Imagine what we could get done."

Mika had opened the door and welcomed the boys inside by the time we lazy stragglers got up the stairs.

"Long day?" Mika asked.

"Not particularly," I said. "But those two exhaust me."

We walked into the living room, where Max and Henri were introducing themselves to Sandra and Jelena with boundless enthusiasm, making Sandra relax and Jelena come out from behind her mother's leg. Max scooped her up and asked if she was coming to the Christmas pageant. That got a happy yes, and he danced around with her, singing "Holiday."

"Mrs. Crystal wasn't kidding," said Mika.

I winced. "What did she say?"

Max dashed. "That we're the best and can be trusted."

Mika nodded. "Pretty much."

"Do you lift weights?" Max asked.

The enormous Croatian asked, "What do you think?"

"I think you do. Do you have a YouTube channel?"

That question stymied Mika. "No. Why?"

"You'd make bank. Tips and tricks. Dude, you're enormous," said Max, still dancing with Jelena.

"You can come to the gym with me," said Mika. "I will help you to learn techniques."

The Eggs were all in, and then Marko wanted to go.

"It's a miracle," Mika whispered to me.

"Big boys have big influence," I whispered back.

He turned to the boys and asked, "I heard you will be doing a raffle for the senior center."

The boys told them about the plan, and Mika offered two

hour-long massages. He was a certified massage therapist and a physical therapist, but I have to say a massage from Mika would probably be excruciating, bringing new meaning to deep tissue.

The boys added his massages to their growing list and got Mika and Sandra to agree to help with the rehab of the senior center. They didn't know what hit them. The Eggs had that way about them, just like the old Derek.

"Hey, Jelena, can we see your trunk?" I asked.

Jelena nodded and then asked, "Where's Mariah?"

"Home doing homework."

"Can she come over someday?"

"Of course," said Jess.

Sandra and Jess discussed future babysitting gigs as we all trooped upstairs. Jelena and Marko said Elsie was standing by the trunk. She wasn't crying. She was happy.

"It's been better," said Sandra. "The kids are sleeping through the night."

"That's great," I said, turning toward the trunk. "Elsie, we want to do some portraits for the investigation. Is that okay?"

"She said yes," said Henri.

"But she wants the kids to go," said Max.

"Why?" Marko asked. "I want to see the portraits."

"Me too," said Jelena.

Sandra tried to convince the kids that they didn't need to stay, but Jelena got stubborn and Marko angry. The kids knew something was up and were determined not to miss a thing.

"Well," I said. "I was going to save this for later, but..." I pulled a baggie out of my purse.

"Cookies!" Jelena exclaimed.

"In the kitchen," said Sandra.

The kids grabbed Max and Henri's hands and tried to pull them out of the bedroom.

"We have to stay," said Max.

"But can you make us something to drink?" Henri asked.

Jelena said she was very good at making cocoa, but we figured that wouldn't take long, so I suggested she call Mariah to ask her to babysit. That got the kids going, and I texted Mariah to ask her to keep the kids occupied.

Then we turned to the trunk and Jess asked, "Is Elsie still here?"

"Yeah, she's ready," said Henri. "What do you want to know?"

Jess pulled up a chair and opened her sketch pad. "Tell me what you saw the first time you saw her in the trunk."

The boys translated, and Jess got to work, but what the boys were saying was confusing. Sometimes the girl was visible and sometime she wasn't.

"Hold on," I said. "Why are you describing only her shoulder and cheek?"

It took a while, but we finally understood that when the body was first put in the trunk, it was empty. Sometime later, the man came back and filled the trunk with salt."

"He mummified her," said Max. "What a sick guy."

"It was probably to stop decomposition and to hide the smell," I said. "Elsie, tell the boys what she looked like before the salt, please."

Making it clear when in time we wanted to see her helped Elsie to focus, although the boys said she was crying a little at the memory. Jess worked almost frantically, and an image emerged from her pencils. The girl was curled up in the fetal position. She had blond hair and wore a sweatshirt, jeans, and one Nike tennis shoe. The clothing was a hard concept for Elsie. We ended up pointing at our own jeans to get an idea of the style. The girl's jeans were pale blue and had pleats. Elsie didn't understand sweatshirts, so we asked for some examples from Sandra and Elsie picked one, loose and an old style. It was a vibrant green, and it had something printed on the front, but Elsie didn't remember what it was, just that it was odd, but that could mean anything. The girl's shoe had a purple swish and a turquoise section at the ankle.

"The clothes sound like 1990," I said.

"Why 1990?" Max asked.

"That's when he got the storage unit," said Jess.

Mika walked over to the trunk and looked down into its depths. "Is she in there now?"

"No," said Henri. "Elsie says she's not."

"Have you seen the girl?" I asked. "I mean as a ghost."

Max nodded. "Yeah, she has." He hesitated. "At the other place."

"The storage unit?" Jess asked.

The boys listened.

"Yes," said Henri. "But mostly at the antique mall."

"What about here?" Mika asked, his muscles tense.

"Nope," said Max.

The story emerged slowly. Elsie was prone to crying, making her harder to understand. The girl had never spoken to Elsie and didn't seem to be aware of her. She had put off the terrible smells in Booth 51 and had climbed out of the trunk a few times, scaring a few shoppers who could see her, but Elsie didn't think the girl realized she scared them. She wanted to talk to them, but naturally, they ran away screaming.

We took a short break when Marko and Jelena brought up mugs of cocoa for everyone.

"It sounds like she was trying to tell people about what happened to her," I said.

"But she's not here now," said Max. "I wonder why she left."

"Would you stay with your murder trunk?" I asked.

The boys wrinkled their noses.

"No way," said Henri.

"If she wanted attention in the mall," said Mika, "why not try to get our attention?"

"We'll have to ask her," I said. "How's it going, Jess?"

Jess looked up and then showed us the finished drawing. Like all her work, it was incredibly lifelike. The girl was in the trunk, and I felt a terrible pang at what had happened to her. She was so young, barely older than Mariah. By the look on Jess's face, I knew she was thinking the same thing.

"She looks like she's asleep," said Max. "What killed her, Elsie?"

The girl's wound wasn't visible when she was in the trunk. Elsie only saw it when she was at the mall. There was a bloody section on the right side of her head, but Elsie didn't know what caused it.

"Jess," I said. "Do you think you could draw her out of the trunk?"

She looked up from some additional shading she was doing and said, "What do you mean?"

"Well, we can see her face and clothes. Elsie was great about describing her in the trunk. It would help to have her standing as if she's alive."

"That would be easier," said Henri.

"Easier for what?" Mika asked.

"We gotta look on those websites for missing people," said Max. "They're going to have pictures of her alive."

"Good thinking," I said. "We'll start with Rolla."

With the help of the boys, Jess drew the girl several times in both black and white as well as color. In one portrait she was smiling and whole, and in the other, she was injured and in pain. Looking at the last portrait, I could feel the pain. Mika couldn't look at it and asked Jess to put it out of sight.

"Sorry," said Jess. "I had to do the injury one first. That's what Elsie saw. Then I could make her whole and happy."

"Elsie," I said. "Take a look. Is this the girl? Anything that Jess should change?"

"No," said Max. "That's her."

"Okay. Great," I said. "Did you see the man who came to the storage unit?"

The boys said that Elsie had seen him many times, but she didn't know who he was.

"Did he bring anyone with him to the storage unit?"

Elsie had seen another man with the man that came and put the salt in the trunk. Two portraits came out of her description. An older man, about seventy, and a younger one in his forties. The one in his forties was the one who came to visit the trunk and poured the salt in. Unfortunately, his portrait could've been one of a million guys. He was thin with short brown hair, brown eyes, and wore button-down white shirts, sometimes with a suit and sometimes without. Jess struggled with his portrait. He was just so bland. There wasn't much to work with.

The older man was easier. He had a ring of snow-white hair, a heavily creased face, wore a plaid shirt and jeans. Elsie didn't remember the two men saying anything to each other, but she was so upset about the dead girl in her trunk, she might've missed it.

"Father and son?" Mika asked.

"Could be," I said.

"I guess that's it."

Jess closed her sketch pad and put away her pencils. "Time for dinner."

I turned back to the doorway and nearly jumped out of my skin. Vic Delaney was lounging against the doorframe like he could actually touch it. I must've yelped, because the boys said, "What? Did you see her?"

"No," I said. "Jess?"

Jess nodded. "I see him."

Mika balled up his fists. "Him? The murderer?"

"No. The detective."

Vic Delaney smiled at us and was gone.

Mika wasn't much comforted when we explained the situation. "How many are we going to get?" he asked.

There was no way we could answer that, but I said, "The detective has nothing to do with the trunk."

"How do you know that?"

"Because he died before 1990."

"Then why the heck is he here?" Mika asked. "Sandra is going to be very upset."

"Don't tell her," said Max. "You can't tell moms stuff like that."

"Hey," I said.

"It's true and you know it," said Henri. "You'd just get upset, and what are you gonna do?"

"Nothing," said Max.

Mika put his face in his huge hands for a moment and then said, "You must figure this out. I can't lie to my wife forever. I will have to tell her."

I put a hand on his rock-hard forearm and said, "We're getting there."

"Do I need to visit that Steve person and get answers?" Mika asked, and I saw how close the man was to the edge for the first time. This was wearing on him, very much.

"No," I said. "We have a way forward."

"You're sure?"

"You aren't getting charged with menacing or anything else," I said. "We will figure it out. Ready, Jess?"

Jess was still sitting in her chair, not moving.

"Do you see something?" Max asked.

"No. I just realized that Elsie knows where her trunk was," said Jess.

"We know," said Henri. "The antique mall and that flipping storage place."

She shook her head. "Before that. She said that the family

she worked for sold her trunk." She looked up at me. "Who did they sell it to?"

The boys slapped their foreheads. "Of course!"

They worked with Elsie, and like everything in life and death, it was more complicated than we hoped. Her trunk had gone through several hands in the years after her death and before the storage unit. Elsie wasn't particularly bothered by who owned it before. Her trunk was fine and well-cared for. It had blankets stored in it at one time and then someone used it to store video cassettes. She was fine with all that and wasn't with the trunk all the time.

"Where was the trunk before they put the girl into it?" I asked.

Elsie wasn't exactly sure, but she thought it had quilts in it, beautiful ones that would be heirloom quality from the way she described them.

"That doesn't sound like a forty-year-old-man's trunk," said Mika.

"No, it doesn't," I said. "Who was in the house, Elsie?"

After some serious thought, Elsie realized the old man Jess had drawn was around her trunk. He and an older woman used it. She described the house, but it was just a house, a typical tract home that could be practically anywhere in America. The old lady was very pretty, with long silver hair that she held back with tortoiseshell combs. Jess drew her with ease, and we all compared the portraits.

"It's a family," said Henri.

A family that committed and concealed a horrible crime.

"Not the mom," said Max. "She wasn't there. Elsie didn't see her at the storage unit either."

"She might be innocent, but the other two are guilty as sin," I said.

Sandra walked in. "Who's guilty as sin?"

We showed her the portraits, not the death one, and explained what we had.

"That's good, right?" Sandra asked. "You're getting somewhere."

"We are," said Jess, standing up. "I think we're done."

Sandra bit her lip and then asked, "Can you talk to her for me?"

"You can talk to her," I said. "She hears you."

The boys nodded and stood ready to translate.

"Um... Can she, I mean, can you stop being naked in the bathroom?" Sandra asked. "The kids don't need to see that."

The boys said Elsie was embarrassed about that, but said that she loved baths. She'd grown up without running water, and the luxury of a hot bath was something she still enjoyed. I suggested that the family keep the kids' bathroom door closed at all times and always knock before entering. That way, Elsie could vanish before the kids came in.

"Cool, Mom," said Max. "That works. She likes it."

We went downstairs and joined the kids where they were sitting at the kitchen table doing their homework while chatting with Mariah on an iPad. Even little Jelena had ABC sheets she had to do.

"Are you leaving?" she asked.

"We are. All done."

Jelena jumped off her chair. "I'm going to see Elsie. Bye, Mariah."

Mariah waved and logged off.

"Hold up," said Henri. "You gotta look at something."

"We're not showing them," said Mika.

"We should," said Max. "The nice one. They might've seen her."

Jess got out the nice portrait of the girl, and the kids looked hard before shaking their heads. They'd never seen her.

It was the same with the elderly couple and the man we presumed was the murderer.

"Can I go, Mama?" Jelena asked.

"Me too," said Marko.

Sandra said yes, and the kids dashed off to see their ghost and then their mother asked, "Why them?"

"Why can the kids see her and not us?" Jess asked.

"Yes." Sandra looked at my boys. "And why you? You're not little."

The boys grinned and Max said, "We're young at heart."

"Anyone can see that," said Mika. "But why kids? It would be so much easier to let adults see her."

"She loves children," I said.

"And they love her," said Jess. "I think that's who she was in life. More of a kid person than an adult person."

"Then..." Sandra trailed off.

"What?" I asked.

"She's not going away when it's solved."

Jess and I looked at each other.

"She's their nanny," I said. "She's not leaving."

"Their nanny?"

Jess explained how Elsie was looking after Marko on the playground, and Sandra flushed. "I have to call the school."

"No, my darling," said Mika. "You don't. Elsie has taken care of him."

"But we have to do something."

"If it helps, Mrs. Crystal knows, and she's going to deal with it," I said.

Sandra blew out a tense breath, and Mika gathered her up in his arms. "It's alright. It's going to be alright."

She peeked out at us from over a bulging forearm. "I think I see that now."

Now if only Jess and I could only convince Bear Hotchkiss to help us, *alright* would be a lot closer to being true.

Chapter Seventeen

Ned did not exaggerate. Dutzow Barbecue had a line around the building when we arrived at eleven the next day. Lots of people were getting to-go orders, and others had come with a bottle of wine from the local winery. It seemed like we should get in line, but we did have an appointment of sorts.

"Excuse us," I said, bypassing the line.

"Hey," said a man in a tracksuit. "No cutting."

"We have an appointment with the owner," said Jess.

"Oh. Sorry."

"No problem."

He wasn't the first to complain, and he certainly wasn't the last. We squeezed into a standing-room-only situation.

I waved at Ned, who was behind the bar, mixing two drinks at a time. He grinned at me and yelled, "One second!"

We nodded and wedged ourselves into a spot at the end of the bar.

"Jess. Libby."

I turned, and Lynn was in the kitchen waving us back.

"Thank goodness," said Jess as we entered the back. "I'm not claustrophobic, but that wasn't comfortable."

"I know," said Lynn, as she chopped meat with two cleavers at the same time. "The power of social media. We've always had great food. Now people know it."

She directed us to the staff room, where we sat down at a rickety table covered with coffee cups and to-go menus.

"I'm starving," said Jess.

"I wasn't, but I am now," I said. "We can't come here and not eat."

Ned walked in with a young man about twenty-five. He was taller than Ned, with wide shoulders and shaggy hair down past his chin.

"Hey there," said Ned. "This is Bear. Bear, this is Jess and Libby. The ladies I told you about."

Bear gave us a little wave and smiled from under his curtain of hair.

"Hi," I said, wondering if we should've brought the boys. They had such a way of connecting. "Do you mind talking to us a little?"

Bear nodded, and Ned got him to sit down before getting us all spiced cider.

"I like cider," said Bear.

"Their cider is the best," said Jess.

"I don't suppose you have some coffee," I said with a yawn. "We were up half the night."

"Sure thing," said Ned, and he went to get coffee. I needed it badly. I'd been sure that we'd find the girl's identity on a missing persons website. Easy peasy, but of course it wasn't. There were no missing girls in Rolla in 1989 through 1991 that matched her description. We branched out searching nearby counties and extending to the year all the way to 1995 with no luck.

A TRUNK, A CANOE, AND ALL THE BARBECUE

Ned put a warm cup in my hands and offered creamer, which I gladly took.

"Not going well?" he asked.

"It's going," I said.

"Do you need some fuel?" Ned asked. "We've got plenty of barbecue for the ladies that sparked this deluge of customers."

Bear got very bright-eyed at the word *plenty*.

"Love some," I said, turning to Bear. "What's your favorite thing on the menu?"

"Ribs and coleslaw."

"We haven't had the ribs yet," I said, and Bear brushed the hair out of his face and began telling us all about the ribs and sandwiches. Ned went and got us what he called a sampler, and you've never seen anyone happier than Bear in that moment. Christmas morning on a platter.

He helped us choose what we should try first, and then I began asking him about Steve. Bear was happy to tell us about helping Steve, and I was happy to hear that Steve paid him. I'd had my doubts about that.

"Did you ever move a trunk?" Jess asked after moaning over the ribs that were fantastic.

"I move lots of stuff," said Bear.

I got out my phone and showed him the trunk. He said he moved it out of Steve's van along with a canoe and a bunch of bins. They put all the stuff in a shed, but Bear had no memory of what was on the canoe or what was in the bins. They were closed, and he wasn't interested. He had another job to get to in town.

"I help at the grocery on canned-goods day," he said. "The boxes are heavy. That trunk was really heavy."

"I bet," I said.

Bear peeked at me and then said, "You look like Max and Henri."

My mouth dropped open, and Jess laughed. "She's their mom."

"They're funny," said Bear.

"How in the world do you know Max and Henri?" I asked.

Bear got out his phone and showed us the videos from the assemblies that had made my boys famous, or as Mariah would say, infamous. I told Bear how they were doing the Christmas pageant and he got very excited. He was so sweet, I would be happy to take him myself.

"You want to go?" Ned asked.

"Yes, I want to go," said Bear.

"Cool. My daughter is in it. You can come with us."

"Really, Ned?"

"Absolutely, buddy. I hear it's going to be great. It's all Ava can talk about."

They discussed Ava's part. Apparently, she was one of the bad kids in the "Nasty" skit and thrilled to be wiping her nose on her sleeves and coughing without covering her mouth.

"You should see her practicing," Ned said.

"When did she get the part?" I asked. "I didn't know we were that far in."

"Yesterday. Mrs. Crystal is going full steam ahead. Your boys made a good impression. They've never had so many volunteers."

"I'll help," said Bear.

"Bear's very handy," said Ned. "He helped us paint and build the new tables."

"We'll ask about how you can help with the show," said Jess.

"But right now we need a different kind of help," I said.

Bear's eyes got sharp. "Painting. I'm good at painting."

"You know, we might need some painting soon, but this is about solving a mystery."

A TRUNK, A CANOE, AND ALL THE BARBECUE

"A murder mystery?"

"How did you know?" Jess asked.

It turned out Bear was no stranger to mysteries. He and his parents were huge fans of all mysteries. Bear's favorites were *Monk* and *Psych*, but he watched everything and listened to an impressive number of audiobooks.

"You are just the person we need," I said.

"I am?"

"You are. You're going to have to keep secrets, though," said Jess.

"I don't like secrets too much," said Bear.

"It is a job," I said. "I'm afraid the job has to have secrets."

"A job. I will get paid?"

"Yes. We need help, just like Ned does when he's painting."

"Cool. I like to have new jobs."

We explained that we needed information to solve a murder, and that Steve had a vital clue, but he wouldn't help us. Bear listened intently and then asked, "You want me to get in the shed?"

"No," I said. "I want you to play along with a plan we have."

He nodded sagely. "You have to have a good plan."

I told him that his part was simple. He was to tell Steve that someone was looking to buy a used canoe. He met the man at Dutzow Barbecue and told him about Steve's canoe.

"I have to do it because Steve doesn't like you," Bear said.

Ned patted him on the shoulder. "And he likes you a lot."

"Will Steve get in trouble?"

"We won't lie to you, Bear," said Jess. "He might if he's done something wrong."

"He shouldn't have done it, then," said Bear.

"Absolutely," I said. "Will you help us?"

Bear said he would, and we gave him the name of the man who would buy the canoe.

"Now all that's left is to settle on your fee," I said.

"We pay fifteen an hour," said Ned.

Bear frowned. "It won't take that long."

"No, but it is a big favor. You will have to lie and convince Steve to sell the canoe," said Jess.

"How about thirty dollars?" Ned asked. "That's good, right?"

"I don't want it," said Bear.

My heart sank. I'd thought he was onboard, but the lying didn't look like it sat well with the young man.

"You won't do it?" I asked. "It's for a good cause."

Bear carefully wiped the barbecue sauce from his lips and folded the napkin neatly. "I want to give my mom something for Christmas."

Jess and I looked at Ned, and he shrugged. "What do you want to give her, buddy?"

"She wants to see your house," said Bear.

I was so surprised, my cup stopped halfway to my lips and stayed there.

"Our house?" Jess asked.

"You live in the haunted house. It said so on YouTube."

"We live in Number Eight in St. Sebastian. Your mom wants to see our house?"

"At Christmas on the tour," said Bear. "She said so. I heard her."

Ned poured him some more cider. "You're doing an open house for the historical society Christmas tour?"

"They asked us," I said.

"But you're not doing it?" Ned asked.

Jess and I grimaced. The historical society was all over us to do it and we weren't against it in theory, but it was a big deal. People decorated, like really decorated. The problem was simple. While our house might be Addams Family, our decorations were strictly Charlie Brown.

"We're not sure we can pull it off," I said.

Bear didn't meet my eyes. He never did, but he knew what he wanted. "That's what I charge."

"The Christmas open house?"

"Yes."

"Can you all just come over for dinner or something?" Jess asked. "We'd love to have your family over."

"Nope. She wants it like the old days," said Bear.

"The old days?"

I sighed. "Number Eight won best Christmas decorations nine years in a row."

"That's it," said Bear. "The old days."

"When Leo was alive," said Jess. "Well, everyone wants us to do it, and it is a good cause. Right, Bear?"

"Right."

We had a deal that was going to come back to haunt us, literally.

Clint Ford sat in Liz Doyle's room at the high school, munching on barbecue and occasionally groaning with pleasure. The English teacher that once tortured my boys with impossible essays was now a friend and having a salad, looking vaguely disgusted by Clint's copious amount of meat. She was a vegetarian, so it was understandable—her reaction, not the vegetarianism. I liked barbecue too much to give it up.

"Are you serious about this?" Liz asked.

"Completely," I said.

"He has to buy a canoe to solve this crime?"

Jess lifted the travel box of coffee that Ned had given us, and Clint held out his cup. "I don't have a problem with it."

"What are you going to do with a canoe?" Liz asked.

"Nothing. Not my canoe."

"Mr. Blazevic's buying it. We just need someone that Steve doesn't think is connected with us to do the face-to-face work," said Jess.

"And this will lead you to a killer?"

"It's a lead," I said. "Steve's not going to give us anything."

"You could go to the cops and tell them," said Liz.

Clint laughed, good and hearty. "I'd like to see that conversation. Hey, Chief Stratton, go search Hugo Olsen's property cause a ghost told some kids that there was a body in a trunk that his son sold. She'll get right on it."

Liz sniffed. "I suppose you can't get a warrant with that."

"I suppose not."

"And we don't need a warrant," I said. "We need the canoe."

"It might not lead anywhere," said Liz.

"All right, Miss Rain on our Parade," said Clint. "I think it can work, and what's the worst thing that can happen?"

"Mr. Blazevic's stuck with a useless canoe."

"We'll have to think of something else," I said. "That's the worst thing, but we'll deal with it."

"Let me see those sketches again."

Jess and Liz spread out the full complement, and Liz shook her head. "Poor girl. Are you absolutely sure that this happened?"

"As sure as we can be," said Jesse.

"Nothing on the websites?"

"Not so far."

"You should call now," said Liz.

"He can't until we get the go-ahead from Bear," I said.

She nodded and picked up the sketch of the girl smiling. "The sooner the better."

A TRUNK, A CANOE, AND ALL THE BARBECUE

"Why do you say that?" Clint asked. "It's been over thirty years since it happened."

Liz looked at the sketch. "Someone's been waiting thirty years for this. They shouldn't have to wait a minute longer."

My phone vibrated, and it was Bear. He sent me a selfie with a big thumbs-up. I sent back a thanks and showed everyone.

"That's means what?" Liz asked.

Clint got out his phone. "He did it."

"How do you know?"

"Bear went to school here. He took auto repair with me. Good kid. Sweet and thoughtful."

"Why didn't you say so?" Liz asked.

"I thought you knew."

"That changes everything."

"Does it?" Clint asked.

"Of course. You know Bear. The whole plan makes sense now."

Clint looked at us. "She thinks we don't know what we're doing. No meat for her."

"I don't eat meat."

"If you did, I wouldn't give it to you."

"I don't want it."

"Good. 'Cause you can't have any."

Jess and I started giggling from exhaustion and too much coffee. Liz took my cup right out of my hands and told me to get it together. I agreed that I should, but I still wanted more coffee.

"Call that Steve person and stop bothering me," said Liz.

"English teachers are the bossiest," said Clint.

"Science is the bossiest. Do this. Don't do that. Touch this. Not that."

They argued and finally got around to Clint calling Steve, who answered on the first ring. I held my breath, but Jess was completely relaxed and sketching Clint's smiling face as he pulled the wool over Steve's face.

"Hey, man, is this Steve Olsen?" Clint asked. "Great. I heard you got a canoe that you'd like to unload."

There was silence for a moment.

"I hear ya, but my old lady wants a canoe for Christmas. Don't that beat all? How's it look? Can I spruce it up with some paint or something? I'm not spending big bucks on a canoe that the woman will sit in one time max."

Silence.

"Yeah, well, Bear says it's got some dings, and I trust the kid. I'll give you half that."

They haggled for a little while and came to an agreement.

"You available tonight after work?" Clint asked.

He waited, and they agreed on six o'clock.

"I'll be there. Dutzow? What's the address?"

Steve gave the address, and Clint pretended to need it repeated. Then they hung up.

"You are shockingly good at that," said Liz.

"Why are you surprised that I can do things?" Clint asked.

"Because you got Ds in my classes."

"I took one class with you and got one D."

"One D is enough."

Clint looked at us and said with a grin, "I'm marked with the scarlet D forever."

"You're not even properly ashamed," I said, grinning back.

"I'm not. Who has time for that?"

"So who's your old lady?" Jess asked.

He kicked his feet up on Liz's desk. "I'm not married, but you got to spice it up, make it believable."

"That's believable?" Liz asked, smacking his feet off.

"Steve believed it, so yeah."

They began bickering, and the bell rang. We thanked Clint and left with smiles on our faces. For the cost of a little barbecue, we had a canoe buyer. I texted Bear a thumbs-up selfie of my own and got a lot of happiness in return. The guy loved it when a plan came together.

~

"You ladies do not disappoint," said Clint as he finished a third helping of my mom's chicken ala king. "That is good stuff."

Mom glowed under the praise. She'd thought she'd made too much, but she didn't realize that too much wasn't a thing at Number Eight.

"Any luck yet?" Clint asked me, and I searched through canoe rental companies. The plan had gone off without a hitch. Clint met Steve at Hugo's house and bought the canoe, no questions asked. I think Clint was a little disappointed not to have to use some of his persuasive techniques, but Steve couldn't have been less curious about him. On the upside, he did get a peek at some of the bins in the shed when Steve wasn't looking. Clint said they were filled with books, of all types. He saw physics textbooks, encyclopedias, science fiction, mysteries, biographies, and in no particular order. The thing was that all the books appeared to be library books.

That fascinated him and Jess. They decided our murderer had bibliomania and were busy trying to figure out how that fit into the whole murder thing while I tried to find a company with a particular sticker. On one side of the canoe was the Missouri sticker and a number. The other side had a sticker with a picture of a Native American. The kind of thing that wasn't remotely acceptable anymore. It looked like someone tried to scrape it off but couldn't get anywhere. And the thing was big. You couldn't cover it with another ordinary sticker. It'd have to be huge.

"Got it!" I threw up my hands.

The boys ran over from the island where they were doing math with Leo and looked.

"I don't see it," said Max.

"There it is," said Henri. "In the old photo."

"Onondaga River Rentals. What's *Onondaga* mean?"

Mariah came over and said, "Don't you remember going with me and my dad to the Onondaga cave?"

"Oh, yeah," said Henri. "That was cool."

"It's a tribe," said Jess.

"They should probably change their name," said Max.

"They have. Hence the new stickers," I said, picking up my phone. "Voice mail. They open at ten tomorrow."

"In the winter?" Clint asked.

"It said winter hours. They have a campground with cabins. Maybe people do that in the winter."

"Where are they at?"

I turned my screen toward him and he said, "I know Mike's. I didn't know they used to be Onondaga."

"You've floated with them?" Mom asked.

"A bunch of times, and we had our family reunion in the campground. Nice people. Are you going down there?" Clint asked.

"I guess so," I said.

"Use my name. The Snodgrass family knows me. Mike and I always have a few beers when we're there."

"Thanks."

Mom came over with the coffeepot. "More decaf?"

"You're spoiling me," said Clint, holding out his cup.

Poptart sauntered in through the archway, saw Leo, and streaked back out again.

"What is up with your cat?"

"He doesn't like ghosts," said Mariah. "We don't know what to do about it."

Clint looked over at the island where Leo was with Henri.

A TRUNK, A CANOE, AND ALL THE BARBECUE

He accepted that our ghost was tutoring without question. I totally appreciated that native St. Sebastians just shrugged and moved on, even when they couldn't see the ghost in question. "That's a problem."

"Yes, it is," said Leo, gazing through the archway. "I miss having pets."

"I have an idea," said Mom.

"What is it?" Jess asked.

"Let me work it out first. I'll let you know." Mom went and got a platter of her special iced oatmeal cookies. "Cookie, Clint?"

Clint took one, but he gave me a sidelong look. "Why do I get the feeling that you're buttering me up? Do you need another canoe bought? 'Cause I do work for food."

I explained about our deal with Bear and the Christmas open house.

"What's the problem?" Clint asked. "It's a great idea. I know Bear's mom. She loves Christmas, and everyone wants Number Eight to be decked out again."

"Decking is the issue," said Jess.

"Oh yeah?"

Mom held out the cookie platter again. "Would you consider assisting us in decorating? We could use a man to help with hauling trees and hanging lights."

"Hey," said the boys. "We're men."

"Remember the last time I tried to get you to do Christmas lights?" I asked.

They pretended not to remember, but I had photographic evidence. The Eggs decided we didn't need lights all over the house because they didn't feel like moving the ladder. So we had twenty strings of lights on one section of the house. It became a laziness meme.

"We won't do that again," said Henri.

"Ya darn skippy," said Clint. "I'll whip these goofballs into shape."

"What about me?" Leo asked, crestfallen.

"And Leo," I said.

"And Leo. His decorations were amazing. I wonder if Eric still has that stuff," said Clint.

"He does," said Leo.

Over decaf and a lot of cookies, we hatched a Christmas plan that would likely satisfy Bear and his mom.

Chapter Eighteen

I drove down the gravel drive to Mike's Campground, Cabins, and Canoe rental a little after eleven the next morning. I'd planned on getting there at ten, but Mom insisted on coming and had to work on the next version of Leo's soup so it could spend the day in the Crock-Pot. Jess was at the Horny Hotel doing a watercolor workshop and Leo was at Eric's, going through the family Christmas decor with him. I'd gotten a ton of paperwork on current claims while waiting, so I really shouldn't complain, but I was still grumpy. It was not a nice day for a drive down into the Ozarks. The sky loomed over us, dark and foreboding, and kept spitting sleet at us intermittently.

"We're here, Mom." I parked in front of a log cabin that was probably built in the seventies and had a wide porch with at least ten rockers on it. The sign told me I was in the right place, but there were no cars, and it seemed deserted.

Mom yawned and sat up. "That was a nice sleep."

"What is it with you and cars?" I asked.

"I like the rhythm." She looked out at the cabin. "Are you sure they're open?"

"Supposed to be." I took a breath and stepped out into the icy air.

I didn't get five feet before a tremendous yapping started.

"Dogs," said Mom.

"I hope they're kenneled," I said.

They were not. A pack of at least thirty hound dogs came bounding out from behind the cabin, barking and baying.

"Oh my goodness," said Mom.

"Oh crap!" I stepped in front of Mom and held out my hands. They didn't look like they were in attack mode, but you never know.

The hounds went straight for me. I braced for impact, but it didn't happen. They ran right through me, giving me such a cold jolt, I got brain freeze. I staggered to the right and spun around to warn Mom, only to find her in the center of the pack of ghost dogs jumping and trying to lick her.

Mom spun in a circle, waving her hands and belling out her long skirt. "What are they doing? Oh my goodness. Libby, what do I do?"

I was at a loss. I'd seen one ghost dog before, and all he did was wag. This was new territory. "Just keep walking, I guess. Maybe they'll lose interest."

Mom began walking awkwardly to me, jolting with each leap at her hands. "Ew, they stink. Did no one bathe these dogs?"

"They're hound dogs, Mom."

"Do you smell that?"

I smelled it, and it made me appreciate the self-cleaning Poptart. "They're hunting dogs. Nobody washes hunting dogs."

There was a loud snap behind me and I turned to see a man I recognized from the Mike's website. Mike Snodgrass himself. The man I needed to help us was watching like we were a couple of lunatics.

Mom got to me and I grabbed her arm as the hound dogs bounded around us. I felt like we were in a hound ocean and going down.

"Oh my goodness," said Mom.

"Quiet. He'll hear you," I whispered.

"He must know. They're his dogs."

I looked up at the man who had his phone out with a finger hovering it. Ready to call 911, no doubt. "Can I help you?" Mike asked.

"We're having a bit of a…senior moment," I said.

"What?" Mom gasped. "How dare you say that! I'm not crazy."

I hugged her and whispered in her ear. "Today you are."

Mike stared at us, and I waved at him as we waded through the sea of hound dogs toward the steps. "Sorry. We don't mean to bother you. I'm Libby Forest and this is my mother, Beverly Moss."

"Mike Snodgrass." Mike kept a beady eye on us and his phone at the ready.

Name drop time.

"We're friends of Clint Ford in St. Seb," I said. "He told us you might help with a case I'm working on."

Mike's broad shoulders relaxed. "You know Clint?"

"Yes. Wonderful guy. He works at my kids' school. That's how we met."

He tucked his phone in his back pocket. "What can I do for you?"

Mom and I stood at the foot of the stairs with the hound dogs still going crazy. It was hard to hear Mike over their racket. He may have said something else, but I wasn't sure.

"Do you breed dogs?" Mom yelled over the noise.

"Stop it," I hissed.

"Sorry."

Mike got nervous and said, "My dad did. Why do you ask?"

Mom held up her hands, and a hound tried to snatch her red mitten. "Ow. Oh, nothing. Nothing happened," she said.

"Are you two okay?"

"Fine," I said. "Can we come in and explain?"

"I did already invite you in," he said as if he was rethinking the invite.

"Thank goodness," Mom whispered.

We walked up the stairs, and to our relief, the hounds didn't follow. Mike opened the door for us and we went into a small lobby with furniture that looked like it came out of a dentist's office from my childhood. Mom was breathing hard and flushed. Mike offered her a seat and a bottle of water, which she gladly accepted.

"You said something about an investigation?" Mike asked.

I told him I was doing a favor for a friend and investigating a murder in 1990. Mike listened patiently and then asked, "What's that got to do with us?"

I showed him a picture of the canoe. "Was this your canoe?"

He looked and laughed. "That's a blast from the past. We got rid of those ages ago."

"Then it was yours?"

"Sure. We changed the name of the outfit and our symbol. Got to be sensitive. My grandfather wasn't happy, but it was the right thing to do. What has our old canoe got to do with a murder?"

"Nothing directly. But it's a clue to a man's identity. Do you have records of who you sold your canoes to?"

"We do, but this is a family business. We don't have some fancy record-keeping program."

"Whatever you have works for us," I said. "Could you please find that receipt if you have it?"

Mike thought it over and asked, "Who was murdered?"

"A college girl in 1990."

"Who?"

"We don't have her name," I said. "It's a long story, but you can call Clint if you're worried about me being on the up and up. I won't be offended."

He waved that away. "I believe you, but what college do you think she was at?"

"We think it was probably Rolla."

"Wow. My boys went there."

"Are they engineers?" I asked.

"Electrical. Graduated in 2010 and 2012, so they can't help you." Mike opened a door labeled Private. "Come on back. I don't know if we can find it, but let's give it a shot."

"Mom?"

Mom shook her head. "I'll stay here."

I followed Mike back into a cramped office stuffed with old equipment, computers of various vintages, and a desk littered with mail, mostly bills.

"As you can see, we're not the organizing types. My wife is trying to get through the mess and she could help, but she's at the hospital with her mom. Hip replacement."

"That's rough," I said. "I'm sorry to hear that."

"Thanks." Mike looked around. "Patty's been putting our old receipts in shoeboxes. My dad just threw them in drawers. A total mess. She said she had a lot of them sorted." He moved a deflated raft out of the way to reveal a stack of shoeboxes labeled in black marker. "Here we go."

"When did you start selling your old canoes?" I asked, squatting next to him.

"Well, not 1990. That's way too early."

"I didn't think so." I explained about the storage unit.

"Some dude just bought our canoe and stuck it in storage?"

"He may have used it. I don't know," I said.

"Let me think. We changed the name ten years ago, but we kept using the canoes. The one you have is a real geezer. Only a few had that huge sticker on them. I tried to get them off, but it was hopeless. I put the new sticker over the old ones, except for those huge ones."

"How many did you have of those?"

"Maybe five. Grandpa said the sticker was expensive. He couldn't afford many. Thank goodness. I had those five for sale, but we weren't in a huge hurry to sell them. Let me call Patty."

Mike called his wife. Patty thought they sold the last of the huge stickered canoes three years ago, so Mike pulled out that year's box and the five years prior. He put them on the desk and we went through every receipt, setting aside the canoe receipts. The bad news was that the number I had off the canoe was useless. They didn't use the number on the canoe. The good news was that Patty labeled the receipts "stupid sticker."

Eventually, we found all five. Three were sold to women and two to men.

"Do you remember these men at all?" I asked.

"Sorry. No. We sold them during the busy season. I'm lucky to remember my name, but I'm good with faces. If I see him, I might recognize him," said Mike. "Jerry Barnes sounds like a murderer. Let's google him."

I chuckled and asked, "What do you have against the Jerrys of the world."

"Jerry Lund used to beat me up in middle school. I still hate that guy," said Mike, going over to his desktop computer. "Jerry, the murderer, Barnes. Where are you?"

Google produced a million Jerry Barnes all over the world, and using filters didn't help much.

"Do you have Facebook?" I asked.

"Who doesn't?" Mike got into his account and started looking. "There he is."

Jerry Barnes was most definitely not our murderer. He was about thirty-five with a pretty wife and five kids.

"Darn," said Mike. "My money was on Jerry. Who's the other one?"

"Donald Schramm," I said.

"Sounds old enough. You don't get a lot of Donalds these days."

"Or Jerrys."

"Very true. Let me see." Mike paused and then said, "You said the girl went to Rolla?"

"We don't know. Just basing that on the location in Rolla."

Mike pointed at a name that Google had produced. Dr. Donald Schramm, Professor Emeritus at the university in Rolla.

"The murderer is a professor," I said.

"That's gonna be a scandal." He let out a long whistle.

Behind us, Mom squealed. "They're in. They're in."

Hound dogs filled the lobby, and Mom dashed past the door with the hounds in hot pursuit. "Oh my goodness. Oh my goodness. Oh my goodness."

"For goodness' sake, Mom! Sit down."

Mom dashed past the door. "I can't."

I put a hand over my eyes.

"Is she okay?" Mike asked.

"She's fine," I said. "What else have we got? A picture?"

"No picture. Sorry."

"I need a yearbook. Do your sons have any?"

"No. We didn't spring for that. College is expensive enough."

Mom went past the door again. "Oh my goodness. Oh my goodness. Oh my goodness."

Mike was looking at her like she was completely nuts, and she was from his point of view. "Does she have issues?"

"Looks like it," I said. "Mom, please. I'm almost done."

"I'm going out!" she yelled over the baying, and dashed out the door, followed by the hounds, who just ran through the wall.

"You're going to need help," said Mike.

"So much help," I said. "Do you think the university will let me look at their yearbooks?"

He smiled. "You don't need to go all the way over there. It's all online."

"Are you kidding?"

"Nope. My kids told me." Mike googled it and found the yearbooks easily.

"1990, please," I said, and he looked for that issue.

"You should check on your mom."

I went out to look and there was Mom in the car, surrounded by hound dogs. She waved and gave me a thumbs-up. At least they weren't in the car. That was something.

"I found it," said Mike, and I went back into the office.

"Let's see if he's pictured in the faculty section," I said.

Mike went through the pages and said, "There he is."

I stared at the photo, and a strange cold sensation went through me. Almost a ghost feeling, but more sickening than that.

"You okay?"

"It's him," I said.

"How do you know?"

I showed him Jess's sketch on my phone, and he whistled again. The hound dogs came charging into the lobby, and I could barely hear over their clamor.

"That guy doesn't look like he could kill a fly," said Mike, and I had to agree. Dr. Donald Schramm smiled shyly out of the small black-and-white photo. He was just as Elsie described him, but it was still a shock to see his face. None of it was a mistake. He was a real person in Rolla at the right time. I didn't know that I wanted it to be a mistake or a delusion on Elsie's part until I saw him there on the screen. That man put a girl's body in Elsie's trunk. It happened. It was all real.

"I can't believe it," I said.

"You're sure he killed a girl?" Mike asked.

"Very sure."

"How are you going to find out anything if you don't have a name?"

"We have a description."

"A witness?"

"Yes," I said, never having thought of Elsie as a witness before, but that's what she was. A witness. "I have a sketch of the girl."

I showed him the nice sketch, and he nodded. "Typical college girl. You don't know what was on her sweatshirt? They always have something printed on them."

"The witness didn't see what was printed on it, but it was green."

"Green? That's Rolla colors."

"Yeah, I know, but other schools too."

"Too bad the sketch isn't in color," said Mike.

"I have one in color." I flipped to the next photo of Jess's color version. We were less sure about that one, because she'd guessed the girl's eyes were blue, and that was enough to throw someone off if they recognized her. "Here it is."

"I bet that is Rolla," said Mike. "Yeah, I'm pretty sure."

"Why?"

He got up and dug around in a bin full of old clothes. "Check it out." He pulled out a vibrant green tee with St. Patrick's Day, 2010, and the university emblem on it. "St. Patty's day is a thing at Rolla. Huge party."

"That's the color," I said. "She was a student there."

"Did you look at those missing persons websites?" Mike asked. "They've got to have records of a girl like that going missing in a college town."

"I did, but there was no one that matched her description."

Mike sat back down and asked, "It happened during the school year?"

"We don't have an exact date, but we have when the storage unit was rented," I said.

"Do I want to know why that unit is so important?"

"Probably not."

"When was it rented?" Mike asked with his fingers over the keyboard.

"On March twenty-ninth in 1990," I said.

Mike leaned back. "I don't need to google it."

"What do you mean?"

"That's spring break."

My knees went weak, and I leaned on the desk. "I didn't think of that."

"Almost everyone goes home for spring break, Florida, or somewhere," said Mike.

"They didn't report her missing in Rolla because that's not where it happened," I said.

"Sorry."

"Sorry? For what? That's a huge help."

His mouth twisted. "I think that makes it harder. You don't have a place."

"Do you know anyone at the university, or do your sons?" I asked.

"No. They graduated a long time ago," said Mike, standing up. "Do you want to take the receipt with you?"

"Better not. If the police need it, I wouldn't want it to look like I might've done something to it. I'll just take a picture."

I took several shots and put my phone away.

"You think the police will come?" Mike asked.

"I hope so. That'll mean we figured it out."

He led the way back into the lobby that was filled with smelly hound dogs that were curled up on the floor and raised their heads eagerly when Mike walked in. He didn't see them and walked right through, which didn't seem to bother the dogs at all. It bothered me. They didn't get out of the way and my legs were numb by the time I got out the door.

Things didn't improve when I came up beside Mike, who was frowning at my car. Mom was out and standing at the open back door, making shooing motions at the empty air. There were no hound dogs there, but she was shooing like she was trying to get them in the car.

"What are you doing, Mom?" I called out.

"I had an idea," she said with a huge smile.

I turned to thank Mike again, but he said, "Hold on."

Mike went in the house, and I looked back at Mom.

"I did it," she said, and gave me another thumbs-up.

Please don't let Mom be losing it.

"Great!"

Mike came out and handed me a piece of paper. "They're very helpful. Reach out. You won't regret it."

He'd written down a bunch of elder care resources and dementia support groups.

"Thanks, Mike," I said. "I appreciate it."

"You're welcome. Let me know how your case turns out. I'd like to know before the cops show up."

I shook his hand and got in the car. Mom was smiling like a nut and I said, "That wasn't great, Mom."

"But I got a great idea," she said. "Do we have his identity?"

"We do."

"Look at us. Succeeding all over the place." She looked back into the back seat. "This is going to work."

I glanced back and saw nothing. The elder resources might come in handy after all.

"Tell me everything you found out," said Mom, but I only got halfway done before she was snoozing against the door, a smile on her face.

Chapter Nineteen

The sky got serious about the sleet about halfway home, and I had to have the defroster going full blast to keep it from building up on my windshield. Mom slept through the entire drive, and the minute I parked, she popped up, smiling.

"We're home," she said. "How nice."

"I'm making a fire," I said.

"That's a great idea. I'll make hot cocoa."

I got out, put up my hood, and went for the front door. Mom wasn't beside me. I turned around to find her at the car's back door, making kissing noises.

This can't be happening.

"Mom, what are you doing?"

"Trying to get him out," said Mom.

"Him?"

That was the moment a little grey and white cat came slinking out of the car. He sniffed around on the grass and Mom beamed at me. "See. Great idea."

"Are you crazy?" I asked.

"Poptart needs a companion. He'll calm down if he has a friend."

I couldn't say anything. The little cat kept sniffing, and Mom was smiling like she *was* crazy.

"Libby! What are you doing?" Jess came out of the house.

"Going nuts," I said.

"Oh my goodness, Bev!" Jess called out. "Who have you got there?"

"A surprise," said Mom.

Jess ran down the stairs, across the lawn, and scooped up the cat. "He's so sweet. What a cute little guy."

Mom gasped.

"Mom. You stole Mike's cat," I said.

"I thought he was dead," said Mom.

Jess looked at us in astonishment. "You thought he was dead?"

"All the hound dogs were dead."

Jess stared at Mom for a second before dashing back to the porch.

We followed her into the foyer and peeled off our icy coats.

"What is going on?" Jess said as she cuddled the cat.

"Mom stole the canoe guy's cat," I said.

Mom crossed her arms. "It's not stealing if they're dead."

"I don't know. It might be. The hound dogs are his."

"Mike can't see them. How's he going to know if one's missing?" Mom asked. "You can't steal a ghost."

"This cat isn't a ghost. It's an actual cat. What were you thinking?"

"I was thinking he was dead."

"Why do we want a dead cat?"

"It will help Poptart. He's scared of Leo. A cat would be more familiar. He'd get used to the idea."

Leo walked in from the ballroom and said, "Bev, that is the sweetest idea."

"See, Libby, it is a good plan," said Mom, taking off her poncho.

"It's not a good plan," I said. "Now I have to drive another three hours to take back this cat." I pulled out my phone and dialed.

This is going to be a fun conversation.

"Hi, Mike," I said. "It's Libby Forest."

Jess poked me. "Libby."

"Hold on."

"Libby."

"Hold on, please."

"No, Mike. Sorry. People are bugging me. I didn't solve it yet, but I'm afraid my mother stole your cat."

Mike started laughing, but I didn't join in. Another three hours. In sleet.

"You can keep him," said Mike. "He's the last of the litter."

"I don't think we want another cat," I said.

"Libby!" Jess shouted.

"Hold on, Mike. It's a crazy house here."

I looked at Jess and Mom, grinning at me. "What?"

Leo waved at me.

I'm so tired.

"What? What do you want?"

Jess held out the little cat toward Leo, and he didn't react. He just purred and looked at Leo.

"Holy cannoli," I said. "Hey, Mike?"

"Yes?"

"You sure we can keep your cat?"

"Very sure."

I thanked him and hung up.

"My plan worked," said Mom with a swish of her skirts as she went down the hall. "I'm making cocoa. You can tell me I'm a genius later."

"Is it genius if the plan was the opposite of what you were going for?" I asked.

"Who cares?" Jess asked. "He likes Leo."

"I'm so happy," said Leo.

Our ghost was glowing with happiness.

"I guess it is," I said. "So we've got a new cat. What should we call him?"

Leo's dark eyes were eager and the smell of his cologne strong. "We were going to get a cat when the boys were young."

I kicked off my boots and slipped on a pair of fuzzy slippers. "Why didn't you?"

"Carol was allergic," said Leo. "We found out when we went to the Humane Society. The boys were so disappointed."

Jess scratched the little cat's head. "Sounds like you were pretty disappointed yourself."

"I was. We had cats growing up, and I loved them. Dogs aren't really right for a mortuary, with the possibility of barking."

Mom called down the hall, "Are you hungry?"

"Yes. I'll be right there." I went to get my computer out of the office and met with everyone at the island. Leo had a ball of yarn. He was trailing it across the floor and the little cat was chasing it.

"We've named him," said Jess. "Unless you object."

"No, no," said Leo. "It's your cat. You name him whatever you like."

"Pesto," said Mom. "It's the name Leo's boys picked when they thought they could get a cat."

"That's adorable," I said.

"The boys thought of it because Carol wasn't wholly on board with getting a cat. She said it might be a pest."

I laughed as Pesto darted across the floor, pounced on Poptart's bed, and began kicking the stuffing out of one of his toys. "I'm sure Tarty's going to think it's appropriate. This guy's a kitten and not nearly so sleepy."

"Look," said Mom, pointing at the back stairs. Poptart's yellow eyes glowed in the darkness as he peered into the kitchen, listening to the fuss his new housemate was making.

"That's the closest he's ever come to me," said Leo.

"I'm waiting," said Mom.

"You are a genius," I said. "Now everyone help me figure out the girl's name and we won't be doing this next week during Thanksgiving."

Jess came over and looked at my screen. "Dr. Donald Schramm?"

"A doctor of mechanical engineering." I told her everything I'd found out, and she went to get her computer while Mom made us ham sandwiches and tater tots.

"We have to find out everything about him," said Mom. "If she wasn't in Rolla when he killed her, where would it have happened?"

"He would've lived in Rolla," said Leo. "But he might've had a summer place."

"A professor?"

"You never know. Could be family money." Leo rolled up his yarn, since Pesto was busy exploring all the nooks and crannies in the kitchen under the watchful eye of Poptart, who was making low growls on the stairs. "I'll go ask Tank."

I didn't get a chance to say anything before he popped off. "Jess, let's look through the yearbook. See if we can see her picture."

"She has to be there," said Mom. "Probably a freshman or sophomore."

"Oh, bummer," said Jess. "They only have the seniors."

"Lots of pictures, though," I said, and we began the search.

Looking through the 1990 yearbook didn't reveal any

clues, so we went back to 1989 and 1988. Nothing. I went ahead to 1991 in case I was wrong about the date and still nothing.

"Do you think the school knows something?" Mom asked. "She was a student."

"I'm sure they do, but I doubt they'll tell us," I said.

Jess nibbled her sandwich under Mom's strict gaze. She ate a lot more when Mom was watching. "What we need to know is who was enrolled in 1990 and didn't come back the next year."

"Would that come under the privacy laws?" Mom asked.

"Probably," I said. "What we need is someone who was there in 1990."

"It's a big school," said Jess. "Not everyone knows everyone."

I googled the enrollment. "It's not that big. Just over seven thousand students total."

"That's huge, Libby," said Mom.

"But think about it. We're talking a missing student. A girl that went on spring break and never came back. There must've been talk. Rumors."

"Do we know any engineers?" Jess asked.

"I can't think of any that went to Rolla."

Mom went over to Jess and said, "Please eat that sandwich, Jess. You're so thin."

"I've gained two pounds since you got here."

"My job is not done," said Mom. "Now, who do you know? Start calling people."

I ate my late lunch between calls to everyone we knew in St. Seb. Ned didn't know anyone who went to Rolla in 1990, and neither did Lynn, Liz, Clint, Larry, or anyone else. Sylvia said she'd ask around at The Grind.

"We could post on the town Facebook page," said Jess.

"There's a town Facebook page?" I asked.

"Of course. St. Seb Friends." She turned her computer to me and there it was, with posts about finding a dog sitter, recommendations for restaurants, and wine. All sorts of stuff.

"We're in there," said Jess. "The Halloween stuff was very well liked."

"Nice. Go ahead and post," I said.

"Okay. What should I say? Looking for someone who attended…" Jess trailed off, and the doorbell rang.

Leo popped back.

"It's Tank," he said with a grin as Pesto ran straight through his legs without hesitation.

"I'll get it." I jogged out to the front door and let Tank in. He had an enormous umbrella crusted with ice that he left on the porch.

"What a day," he said. "Global warming is freezing."

"Did you walk over here?" I asked.

"Heck, yeah. It's the holidays. I need all the exercise I can get."

I helped him off with his coat and hung it up. "It's not a crisis. You didn't have to rush over."

"You're on the verge of solving a crime from 1990. I want in on the action."

I brought him back to the kitchen, saying, "There's not much action, but there is cocoa."

Mom spun around at the stove. "Did someone request cocoa?"

Tank's mouth fell open briefly. My mother did have that effect on people with her questionable wardrobe and waist-length silver hair parted in the middle. Mom looked like she'd never quite gotten over the hippie thing, which, of course, she hadn't.

"Tank Tancredi. My mother, Beverly Moss."

"I didn't think there'd be another Libby," he said. "But here you are."

Mom glowed and proceeded to feed him a sandwich and a huge mug of cocoa.

"I'm coming over more often," said Tank.

"Tell them what you found," said Leo.

"Oh, right. I got distracted by cocoa." Tank pulled some papers out of his back pocket. "I didn't find anything on the girl. Rolla had a newspaper, but shut down last year. I'll make some calls and see who has the archives. My online sources had nothing from the Rolla paper, but I found some info on your murderer."

He pushed the papers over to me and Jess. Schramm was born in 1950 in North Carolina, making him forty in 1990 when he put a girl's body in the trunk. He did his undergrad work at North Carolina State and graduate degrees in Minnesota. In 1990, he was an assistant professor in Rolla. He'd retired ten years ago and was still alive, but in a nursing facility in Springfield.

"He never married," said Jess. "Thank goodness."

"The guy was pretty vanilla," said Tank. "I called in a favor, and he had no arrests ever in Missouri."

"How is that possible?" Mom asked as she topped off our cocoa.

"It happens," said Tank. "He just wasn't caught."

"There must be something in his background," said Jess.

I kept looking down at Tank's papers. Long career. A few awards. Not much else.

"Why Springfield?" I asked.

"Huh?"

I pushed a paper back to Tank. "He had a house in Rolla. He lived there for about thirty years. Why is he in a nursing facility in Springfield?"

Tank sipped his cocoa and said, "There was something. Can I use your computer?"

I handed it over, and Tank went to work. "Here it is."

"What?" I asked, coming over.

"The newsletter for the retirement home that he was living at before he transferred to the nursing facility. They did a short bio, and it says that he moved back to Springfield after his retirement."

"Back to Springfield?" Jess asked. "That sounds like he was from there, but he wasn't."

"Do you have access to papers in Springfield?" I asked.

"What are you looking for?" Tank asked.

"His parents."

Tank grinned and got to work. We sipped our cocoa and watched as the newspaperman dug around his websites and came up with the goods. "There's the father, Ernst Schramm. The obit says survived by two sons, Donald and John."

"Can you look at 1990?" I asked.

"Where?"

"Springfield."

"Why?" Mom asked. "Just his parents lived there."

"I don't think he killed her in Rolla. She was on spring break. It had to be close to her home."

"Yes," said Leo. "That makes sense. He had to kill her and stick her in a trunk. Then get her back to the storage facility."

"He had to have had help," said Jess. "His father?"

"It wouldn't be the first time a father covered his son's crime. That's what happened in the Kristin Smart case," said Tank.

"Can you see the headlines from back then?" I asked, my stomach in a knot.

Tank worked on it and then shook his head. "Not online. I can make a call. I know a guy."

The newsman wandered off, talking to a buddy that sounded like he was in Springfield.

"Are you as nervous as I am?" Mom asked.

Jess's phone buzzed, and she looked at the screen. "I wasn't."

"Who is it?" I asked.

"Mr. Carter." The color drained out of Jess's face.

"Who's Mr. Carter?" Mom asked.

"The lawyer handling the Hal situation," I said.

Mom crossed her arms. "Surely Jeff isn't keeping on with that nonsense."

"He is. Jess, what does he say?"

"He wants me to call him." She shook her head. "I can't. I just can't. If they allow the disinterment before Thanksgiving..."

"I'll call." I grabbed my phone, took a breath, and prayed for it to be okay. Mr. Carter's secretary got him on the phone immediately, and I smiled.

"That's it?" I asked him.

"That's it," said Mr. Carter. "The judge denied the order. Insufficient evidence."

Jess and Mom hugged, with Jess sobbing into her shoulder.

"More like no evidence," I said.

"Exactly. The judge saw it for what it was. A money grab."

"Can Jeff appeal?"

"He can, but it won't go anywhere," said Mr. Carter. "I've contacted the insurance company. They're doing a song and dance, but they're going to have to pay up."

I thanked him, and we all had a bit of a cry. Tank walked back in and stopped at the archway. "What did I miss?"

"They're going to have to pay the life insurance," I said.

"About time."

"Did you find anything?" Jess asked after she blew her nose.

"I did," said Tank. "Do you mind if I use your computer again? I need my email."

266

A TRUNK, A CANOE, AND ALL THE BARBECUE

I gestured to my laptop, and he logged in. "We have several stories on a missing college student in late March and early April."

He clicked on a link, and a newspaper page appeared on the screen.

"Oh my goodness," said Mom.

"It's her," said Jess.

There she was, almost exactly like Jess had drawn her. Christine Anglin. Nineteen. She was home on spring break in 1990 at her parents' home in Springfield. On the morning of March twenty-eight, her parents went to work and her younger sister was home sick from school with a bad cold. Christine was supposed to meet her high school friends at the mall at noon, but she left early, telling her sister she had something to do. She never made it to the mall and was never seen again. The police never located her Dodge Omni, and there weren't any leads. Christine Anglin simply vanished.

The suburb where the Anglin house was located got searched repeatedly by volunteers and the police. The family held vigils, but despite their efforts, Christine's story petered out. This was before the twenty-four-hour news cycle had taken hold. The disappearance of a pretty college student was a local matter. It wasn't even reported in the St. Louis or Kansas City papers.

The family offered a reward, but nothing came of it. This was a time before doorbell cameras, and security didn't include cameras on practically every corner. None of the leads went anywhere. There was a small article in the local paper on the year anniversary, but then nothing after that.

We all sat back with Christine's picture up on my computer. No one said anything. Pesto zoomed around our feet, chasing a piece of dried pasta he'd found, but other than that, the kitchen was silent until a timer went off.

"Oh," said Mom. "The soup."

She went to turn off the Crock-Pot and Jess said, "That poor family."

"I can't imagine," said Tank.

"Neither can I," said Leo.

"We have to find her," I said.

"The police will do that," said Leo.

I said nothing, and neither did Jess. This was our case. We wanted to finish it.

"The question is, where would Steve dump her?" asked Tank.

Leo looked down at Pesto as the little cat ran up and mewed at his feet. A ball of yarn appeared in his hand and he rolled it out, dangling a string for Pesto to jump at. He didn't seem to notice that he never got the string and was highly entertained.

"The choices are endless," said Leo.

"No, they're not," said Mom. "It has to be around St. Seb or that mall."

"Do you have any idea how much woods we have?" Tank asked. "Hundreds of acres."

"Not to mention the river," said Leo.

"I didn't think of that," said Jess. "Do desiccated bodies float?"

Tank googled it, but couldn't come up with an answer. "Even if you don't find the body, you have an answer for Mika and Sandra."

We heard the front door bang open and an icy breeze came into the kitchen along with shouts and complaints of the kids. Tank stood up and said he had to go. Taylor would be at the *Sentinel* soon, and if Tank wasn't there, the kid would start digging around and getting into things.

"You'll keep me up to date?" Tank asked.

"Yes," I said. "I guess you can start working on the story."

"Without a body, there's nothing we can report."

"Sorry," said Jess.

"Don't be sorry. I haven't given up hope. You two have an advantage, and I still think you'll figure it out." Tank crossed paths with the kids coming in with red cheeks and ice crystals in their hair.

"What are you figuring out?" Max asked as he and Henri dove for the remaining tater tots.

"Where the body is," Jess said.

"You don't have to find it if you've solved it," said Mariah. "The Blazevics don't have to have that."

"The family of the victim does," said Mom from where she was ladling the soup into a huge container.

"Have you solved it?" Henri said, looking at Christine's picture.

"We have," I said.

"Cool. You can tell the family."

"They'll think we're nuts or con artists," said Jess. "We need proof."

"At least tell the Blazevics," said Mariah. "So it can be over for them."

The boys looked at each other and grimaced.

"What?" I asked.

Before they could answer, Mariah asked, "Leo, are you okay?"

Everyone looked at Leo, who was on the other side of the island, holding out the ball of yarn and shaking it.

"Come see," he said with a smile.

The kids dashed over and went nuts over Pesto, passing him between the three of them to give kisses and scratches.

"Wait a minute," said Mariah. "He's not scared of you."

Leo dangled the yarn for Pesto and the little cat took a swipe at it. "No, he's not."

"Why not?" Max asked. "That's pretty weird. Tarty's scared to death."

My mom told them of her genius plan, leaving out that she thought Pesto was dead.

"So you just swiped their cat, Grandma?" Max asked.

"Well…"

I informed them of the actual plan and they loved it, although to their credit, they didn't think you should swipe someone's cat alive or dead.

"So he's not afraid because he was raised with dead hound dogs?" Henri asked.

"That's our best guess," I said.

"Where's Poptart?" Mariah asked.

"Hiding in the back stairs," said Leo. "But it's progress."

Leo and Mariah took Pesto to the stairs in an attempt to coax Poptart into the kitchen, and the boys went in search of more food. They had to settle on eating ham straight from the package, since the biscuits and cookies were gone.

"At least make a sandwich," Jess said.

"It's charcuterie," said Max with a grin. "We're in style."

"You're lazy," said Mariah.

"That too," said Henri with zero shame, just like me. None of us were big on shame.

Once they'd finished the ham, I asked, "What was that look?"

The boys avoided my gaze and went to root around the pantry.

"I'm waiting."

"What look?" Henri emerged with a box of raisins. He was clearly desperate.

"You two had a look when Mariah said it was over for the Blazevics," said Jess.

"We didn't have a look," said Max with a box of graham crackers and some peanut butter.

Mom pointed her ladle at them. "Tell the truth or no cocoa."

"We can make our own cocoa," said Henri.

"Yeah, right," said Mariah over her shoulder. "You'll try to get me to do it."

"That works," said Max.

"Not today." She came out of the stairway with Poptart in her arms. He was puffed up and hissing, but he didn't jump out of her arms. "I have stuff to do. Just tell them. It's a case. They need to get paid so they can buy you two greedy dirtbags more food."

The greedy dirtbags weren't insulted, but they were persuaded.

"Well," said Max, "we're not sure."

"About what?" Jess asked.

"We called Dad," said Henri.

Mom and Jess looked at me, but I held my interested expression with some serious effort.

"What about?" I asked.

My boys called their father because he dealt with people who lied all the time. They figured he might have some tips, and he did.

Mom put the lid on the soup container and asked, "Who's lying?"

"Elsie."

The boys hadn't wanted to say anything, but they suspected that when Elsie said Christine wasn't in the Blazevic house, she was lying to protect them. She certainly didn't want to upset Sandra. The boys were sure about that. Derek had given them some tells he'd observed over the years, and Elsie did most of them.

"Christine's in the house?" Jess asked. "That isn't good news."

"Does it change anything?" I asked.

"Of course it does," said Mom. "You have to bring that poor girl home."

Mom was right, but could we do it without holding Steve at gunpoint? For one thing, we didn't have a gun, and for another, we wouldn't know how to use it if we did.

"Hey, Grandma, is that Leo's soup?" Max asked. His attention could only be held for so long.

"It's for tomorrow," said Mom. "The flavors need time to marry."

Leo looked up from Pesto and said, "I think my mother let it sit overnight too. I forgot about that."

"Then we're on the right track."

I hope we can find some tracks of our own tomorrow.

Chapter Twenty

Jess eyed me over coffee the next morning but said very little as the kids ran around like a bunch of nuts, late again. That time because they'd been sure school would be closed on account of the sleet. It wasn't. Mom let them have her new car because it was four-wheel drive and had snow tires. They were thrilled after the arguments about who should drive were settled. Mariah won because she wouldn't get distracted by squirrels.

Once they were out of the house, I said, "So I have paperwork, Mom. Can you go to the store and get stuff for Pesto?"

Leo already had a list and had wanted to go shopping last night, but the weather stopped that idea in its tracks. There were accidents all over town. Tank spent the night at the paper because the roads were so slick. He didn't even want to try to get back to us. Taylor didn't make it to the *Sentinel* because he slid into a ditch. He was okay, but I had a claim for his Bronco.

"Do you think the roads are okay?" Mom asked.

"The radio said they're salted, and the schools didn't close," said Jess.

"There's a pet store next to McCann's," said Leo. He was

still wearing his mortician suit, but the tie was gone and the top buttons of his white shirt weren't buttoned. He had a mistletoe pocket square, and I took that as a good sign. The best sign was that he no longer felt the need to watch me work, and a comfy recliner had replaced Carol's chair. He was still mournful when Mom talked about having Eric and Darren over for dinner to try out the soup. The name Patrick hung in the air as the missing son, but there was nothing we could do about that.

"It's not far," said Jess. "You can take the Volvo. I have great tires."

"You don't need it?"

Jess said no, but I knew something was up and not just with me. Mom finished her breakfast while I noodled around with some claim stuff and Jess called Mr. Anders at the Horny Hotel to delay her morning class on account of the roads. She sounded totally reasonable, but that woman used cross-country skis to get to school after her car battery died.

Mom grabbed her purse and said goodbye to the cats. Pesto was in Poptart's bed and Poptart was on the stairs, still not totally over it. "Be back soon."

"Take your time," I said, looking very serious, sitting at the kitchen table in front of my laptop.

"I will. Work hard. I want to make a flan this afternoon."

Jess and I waited until we heard the front door close, and then we both said, "I have an idea."

We both waited and then said, "Steve is lazy."

We both broke down laughing until our sides hurt.

"I haven't had an ab workout like that in years," said Jess.

"Neither have I." I wiped my eyes and said, "You first."

"We've established that Steve is lazy," said Jess. "He's not going to work hard at it."

I poured us some more coffee and said, "My thoughts exactly."

"Bear helped him get the trunk out of the van and into the shed, but he didn't help him with it again."

"Steve must've dragged it," I said. "There were those fresh scrapes on the bottom. He must've somehow gotten it in the van alone with a ramp or something."

"But he couldn't have done it with Christine and the salt still inside," said Jess.

"What's the easiest thing to do?" I asked with a smile. "If you are super lazy and not particularly concerned about getting caught. After all, that body had obviously been in that abandoned storage unit for decades."

"The absolute easiest is the trash can," said Jess with a shiver.

"True, but I'm thinking about the dump that Bear mentioned."

"I forgot about that." Jess held her cup under her nose. "And Hugo might see her in the trash, or the pickup guys could spot her when they empty the can."

"Men have done that and gotten away with it," I said.

"Have they?"

"Derek told me about a case. They never found the body, but I'm thinking the dump makes the most sense. Nobody's going to go digging around back there."

Jess went and got our travel mugs. "Steve works at the antique mall on Fridays."

"It opens at nine." I went to my laptop and got on Google, zeroing in on Hugo's house. "What do you think? Does that spot at the back of the property look like a dump?"

"Hard to say, but nothing else does," said Jess. "Do we have time for The Grind?"

"I say we make time," I said. "We want Steve good and gone."

"We can avoid Hugo. No problem."

Jess held up her empty travel mug, and I picked up mine.

Clink.

~

I drove through Dutzow in my front-wheel-drive car, fishtailing and going as slow as possible. I wished we had either of the other cars, but I'd rather have Mom safe at the market. If she'd been home, she'd have come with us. There'd be no stopping her. Stomping around through the ice to a dump was a good way to break a hip, and we couldn't have that.

"Oh, look," said Jess, waving. "There's Bear."

Our helpful friend was throwing out salt in front of Dutzow Barbecue and waved back enthusiastically as we drove past. The rest of the tiny town was asleep with everything encased in icicles and looking like a scene out of *The Lion, the Witch, and the Wardrobe*, beautiful and foreboding.

I pulled off—or rather slid—off the road at Hugo Olsen's driveway with my front end bumping his mailbox.

"That didn't go the way I planned," I said.

"What does?" Jess pulled on her hat until it was over her eyebrows. "I don't think you really hit it."

"As long as Hugo doesn't see us coming."

We got out and peered down the driveway. There were tire tracks where someone had driven out and not back in. It'd be easier to walk down the drive, but there was a chance that Hugo would see us, so we walked through the woods off to the right, our boots crunching on the ice.

"I'm glad we sent Bev to the store," said Jess. "This is pure ice."

"I keep expecting to run into Mr. Tumnus," I said.

"Or Mr. and Mrs. Beaver."

We smiled and held onto each other. The house was off to our left through trees and underbrush, with smoke coming out of the chimney and a new wreath on the door. There were several sheds, all locked, or I would've considered getting in them to find more evidence against Schramm.

Instead, we shivered our way in a big loop to the back of the property where there was a drop-off. We were slipping so much, we had to go from tree to tree until we could see down over the edge. I had hold of a maple and Jess a birch. The dump was down in a gully and looked like it had been in use for a very long time. There were several old refrigerators, a washing machine, piles of brush and garbage, what looked like old Christmas trees, a couple of rusted-out charcoal grills, and one avocado-colored toilet.

"Nice," said Jess.

"People used to do this all the time," I said.

"They're still doin' it."

"Well, who's going to stop them?"

Jess grinned at me. "Probably us, if we're right."

"Ready?" I barely got that out and Jess was sliding down the hill. She made it about ten feet before she lost her balance and landed on her rump. I didn't make it that far, but I had more padding, so it probably didn't hurt as much.

I ended up sliding into Jess and ramming her against the toilet.

"Ew," she said. "Not the toilet."

"Remember when you passed out in the bathroom at CBGB?"

"Don't remind me," said Jess. "Now I feel grosser."

I laughed and hauled myself to my feet with the help of the closest fridge. "This can't be good for the environment," I said.

"I doubt Hugo's worried about that." Jess used the toilet to stand up. "Do you see anything...suspicious?"

"Not really, but he'd have covered her up."

"To the brush pile." Jess led the way around decades of the Olsen family's debris to a massive pile of brush and conifers.

We started yanking on limbs that looked easy to move, but the ice stuck everything together, and it was real work to make any headway.

"Look," said Jess.

"I see it."

Under a Christmas tree and what looked like some recently placed branches was a heavy-duty trash bag, the first we'd seen. It was lumpy and large, the kind you use for yard cleanup.

I took a breath, but Jess charged ahead, throwing aside branches and reaching the bag fast with her renewed energy.

"It's tied shut," she said.

"We have to look inside," I said, my stomach in knots. If Christine was in there, we couldn't unsee that. The sight of her poor body would replace Jess's drawing and the photo on my laptop. She'd become not a beautiful girl, but a horribly abused corpse. She'd be that forever. I didn't want her to be, but we had to know. Her family had to know.

Jess looked at me and said, "I'll do it."

"I can."

She didn't answer. She reached over and ripped open the bag.

I clapped my mittens over my mouth to quell the scream that wanted to come out of me. There in the rip was a leg in jeans with a desiccated foot sticking out of the end.

Jess stepped back, and I grabbed her.

"We found her," she whispered.

A loud snap erupted behind us.

"What the hell do you think you're doing?"

We turned, and Steve stood above us at the top of the hill with a shotgun.

I reached for my phone in my pocket.

"I'll shoot you." He pointed the weapon at me. We

weren't very close, but I had no idea how far the range of a shotgun was. I held up my hands.

"Fine," yelled Jess. "Shoot us!"

"Jess, what are you doing?" I whispered.

She put her hands on her hips and yelled, "You'll be arrested for double murder instead of..." She looked at me.

"Um... Unlawful disposing of a body!" I yelled. Was that right? I didn't know.

Steve smiled down at us. "No one will find you."

Jess snorted. "Oh yes, they will."

"They didn't find her."

I rolled my eyes. "Because Christine Anglin didn't tell anyone where she was going."

"Who?"

"Her." I pointed at the leg and he frowned.

"That's Christine Anglin," said Jess. "Her professor murdered her in 1990."

"That...doesn't change anything," said Steve.

"Of course it does," I said. "We solved the crime. Do you seriously think no one knows that? Get real."

"Who knows?" Steve yelled, looking around the dump.

"Our families, for starters!"

"Tank Tancredi at the *Sentinel*!" Jess yelled.

"His friends at the newspaper in Springfield!"

"Liz!"

Someone was moving behind the brush to Steve's right.

"Ned!" I yelled. "Lynn!"

Jess pointed at him. "Mika Blazevic!"

"You're lying!" Steve yelled. "Nobody knows. You're just going to disappear like her."

Bear emerged from the brush behind Steve, moving so slowly, he didn't make a sound. He had a thick branch in his hands and a look of absolute concentration on his face.

"What about Leo Pereyra?" I asked.

The barrel started shaking. "What about him?"

"You think he's not going to tell?" Jess asked.

"He...can't."

"Of course he can," I said. "He's a witness."

"I'll risk it." Steve steadied the barrel.

Jess looked to his left and pointed. "Go tell Eric!"

Steve jerked to his left, and Bear swung the branch. He cracked Steve on the side of the head and the shotgun went off, the blast echoing through the trees, the shot well away from us, hitting a fridge. Steve stood there for just a second before he collapsed, tumbling down the hill with the shotgun flying, rammed into the toilet, and lay still.

Jess went for the gun, falling repeatedly with me right behind, as always. She grabbed it and said, "Oh, thank goodness."

I looked up the hill at our rescuer. "I'd rather thank Bear."

"Okay?" Bear called down to us.

We gave him a thumbs-up, and he started sliding down the hill.

I looked over at Steve and said, "I have half a mind to bury him under rubbish and see how he likes it."

"He's not dead," said Jess.

"Doesn't bother me."

She laughed as Bear reached us. "How did you know?"

Bear grinned shyly and said, "Steve wasn't supposed to be home today, but he came back."

I hugged him. "And you figured we were in trouble."

He nodded. "I should call my dad."

"You do that," said Jess. "We'll call 911."

A siren sounded in the distance, saving us the trouble, and we climbed up the hill using whatever we could find for handholds. It wasn't elegant, but we made it to the top just as a deputy came slipping across the back lawn of Hugo's house, barely staying on his feet with his weapon drawn.

"It's okay!" I yelled.

"Libby?" Deputy Mosbach stopped and got his footing.

"And Jess," said Jess.

"And Bear," said Bear.

The deputy started coming toward us carefully and yelled, "What happened?"

"There's a body!" Bear yelled.

"A body?"

"They found it, and I hit Steve."

Deputy Mosbach got to us and said, "Hugo Olsen called in a gunshot. Did you shoot someone, Bear?"

Bear held up his hands. "No."

"What's with the shotgun down the back of your jacket?"

"It's Steve's," I said. "He was threatening to shoot us. Bear hit him and the gun went off."

The deputy looked down the hill and whistled. "He's dead?"

"No. Just knocked out," said Jess. "I saw him breathing."

"But you said there's a body."

We pointed at the bag and told him about Christine.

"And I thought today was going to be all fender benders." Deputy Mosbach called in for reinforcements and then shook his head. "The chief said you two were going to shake things up around here."

"Did she?" Jess asked. "Why?"

Steve started groaning, and the deputy looked down at him. "She said whoever bought Number Eight was bound to."

"It's a good thing," I said.

"But painful. I fell six times trying to get back here. You could've told us what was going on," said Deputy Mosbach.

"What's the fun in that?" Jess asked. "Come on, Bear. Let's see if Lynn will open up for us."

"She will," he said.

"You're just gonna leave me here with your mess," said Deputy Mosbach with a sigh.

"It's time for the professionals to take over," I said. "We'll bring hot cider if it helps."

"Bring a gallon. I think we're gonna be there a while."

He was right. They were.

Chapter Twenty-One

Hours later, we were still at the police station. Ned and Lynn had defrosted us and provided gallons of hot cider to the cops and forensic team that had to go through the Olsens' dump and sheds on the coldest day of the year. When Deputy Mosbach informed Hugo Olsen about why we were there, the old man had a heart attack on the spot. He and his son went to the hospital in the same ambulance. No one thought Steve's head injury required a trip to the hospital, but he made such a fuss, they sent him anyway.

If Steve thought staggering around and moaning would keep cuffs off him, he was wrong. Chief Stratton cuffed him to his gurney herself, looking like she'd have enjoyed spitting on him, but she restrained herself.

After enjoying the hospitality of Dutzow Barbecue for an hour or so, the chief allowed us to go back to St. Sebastian, where she interviewed us multiple times and came up with a plan for how she could explain yet another crime being solved by means that defied common sense. In the end, she decided simplicity was the best policy. Jess and I received an anonymous tip that led us to the Blazevics' trunk. No ghosts.

We sat in the police station's conference room, where the chief and her deputies arranged a timeline on a corkboard. Chief Stratton was a visual person. She had to see it, and I have to admit it was helpful to have it all up on the board. Not all the clues were up there yet, but the pathologist at the hospital had done a preliminary exam of Christine's body. He thought the cause of death was blunt-force trauma, but it was unusual in that it wasn't a pipe or bat. A pointed instrument had made a deep depression into Christine's skull. He described it as triangular, but he'd know more with a full autopsy. Christine would've died almost instantly, though.

Jess and I were there, trying to be wallpaper, when Christine's parents and sister arrived from Springfield and the chief delivered the news. They broke down crying and said that it was a relief. They'd feared the worst. I thought it was pretty terrible, but their minds had gone to places no parents should have to go.

The chief then introduced us. I'm not usually at a loss for words, but I found it hard to say anything. Luckily, my mom showed up with hot cocoa. She and Jess had no trouble talking. Bear's parents came and hugged their son so much, he began to blush and stammer. There was talk of an award for heroism for Bear, and we were all for that. I think Steve would've shot us. It's insane, but so is dumping a girl's body so you can make money on a trunk.

And Steve wasn't exactly a deep thinker. Once in the emergency room, he confessed to a pair of nurses that he'd done exactly what we'd thought. He bought the storage unit, had seen the body in the trunk, and decided to conceal it. Once he got the trunk home with the help of Mr. Thompson and Bear, he simply pulled the body out of the truck, put it in a bag, and hid it in the family dump. The cops found a pile of salt beside one shed, and Christine's purse was in the house. He'd spent her cash and sold her jewelry to another dealer at the antique mall. Steve tried to convince the nurses that what he'd done wasn't really a crime. The girl was long dead. That wasn't his fault. Why shouldn't he make a few bucks?

The nurses told him he was a shit stain on society and informed the deputy guarding Steve. It didn't hurt that one of the nurses recorded the confession on her phone, including when Steve asked her out. The recording was so clear that it was easy to hear her throwing up in her mouth.

His father, Hugo, knew exactly zero about the whole thing. His heart attack would keep him in the hospital for a few days, but he'd survive, although the deputies thought he wasn't keen on living through what his idiot son had done. The chief hadn't decided on the full charges for Steve, but she was starting with unlawful disposal of remains, larceny, and assault for holding us at gunpoint. The prosecutor didn't think larceny would hold up, since you can't steal from a corpse. That didn't go over well with Christine's family, or anyone else, for that matter.

"I will do everything I can to make it stick," said the young prosecutor, Mr. Robins.

Christine's mother nodded and said, "I know you will."

Her sister, Carrie, said, "I want to know when they will arrest the guy who murdered her. That's the important thing."

"It's all important, sweetheart," said Christine's dad.

"He murdered Christine and put her in that trunk." Carrie pointed at the trunk that Mika had brought over as soon as we called him. It sat at the end of the evidence table where different bags of evidence were laid out: Christine's purse, her jewelry the horrified dealer had brought in, and the salt. On the floor behind the table was the remaining stuff from the storage unit, including the canoe that Mika and gone over and picked up for us. I don't know if that was the weirdest bunch of evidence the St. Seb police had ever had, but it couldn't be far off.

Christine's mother cringed when her remaining daughter mentioned the trunk, and she avoided looking at it. Her husband and daughter had looked. I couldn't imagine the strength that took, but somehow Christine's father opened the lid and looked down into the space that had been his daughter's tomb. We all held our breath, but the man just looked and walked away. Carrie was so upset, she had to step into the foyer to compose herself.

"I'm so sorry," said Sandra from the other side of the room where she and Mika were going over their statement about buying the trunk.

"It's not your fault," said Christine's father. "It's no one's fault but his."

"When are they going to arrest him?" Carrie asked again as she walked back in.

"His condition makes it complicated," said Chief Stratton.

"He doesn't get off just because he has cancer."

The chief nodded and said, "I agree. The Springfield cops are working on it."

Carrie turned to Mr. Robins, who looked like he'd rather she didn't. "Will they arrest him? Don't they have to?"

"It's a judgment call when someone is in a delicate condition. That he's on a morphine pump and not completely coherent is a difficulty."

"I don't care if he's high as a kite," said Carrie. "I want—"

Chief Stratton's phone rang, and she said, "It's Springfield."

She took the call and then said, "I'm going to put you on speaker. We have the family here and they're eager for news."

A Springfield detective cleared his throat and gave us the news that Dr. Donald Schramm had woken up out of his morphine-induced slumber and, when confronted with the facts, had immediately confessed. Schramm said that he had fallen deeply in love with Christine during the fall semester when she was in his class, but he had done nothing about it. During the spring semester, he had offered to help her with her current class load after running into her, not so accidentally, in the library. She was struggling in her differential equations class and he offered to help. He wanted to tell her how he felt but wanted to do it away from school, so he told her he had notes from his own classes at his parents' house in Springfield. They made a plan for her to pick them up during spring break, but it had to be a secret, since a professor really shouldn't be giving a student so much help.

Christine went to the Schramm residence to pick up the notes on her way to the mall to meet her friends. When she was there, he told her he was in love with her and tried to kiss her. It freaked Christine out. She pulled away and fell, hitting her head on the corner of the brick fireplace surround. Schramm claimed he didn't push her.

The elder Schramm, his father, was home at the time and heard the noise. It was his idea to put Christine in his wife's trunk and hide the body, and that's what they did. Schramm's mother knew nothing about it. She was out shopping at the time and they told her they sold the trunk, making a huge profit, so she wasn't suspicious about it being gone.

The next day they made some excuse to the mother and took the trunk to Rolla, renting the storage space because Schramm didn't want to just dump her body somewhere. The body had begun to smell, so they covered her with salt, thinking that would inhibit decomposition. It did mostly, and Schramm made a point to say that he visited Christine regularly, thinking that was a good thing and made up for what he'd done in some bizarre way.

When the detective was done, Carrie asked when they would be arresting Schramm. He didn't have an answer. The prosecutor there was reviewing the case law and trying to decide what to do. Their jail didn't have facilities to handle someone in Schramm's condition, and they felt they needed more than a confession.

He hung up and Carrie said, "More than a confession? What's better than that?"

"They're searching his house, hoping to find something that backs it up," said Chief Stratton.

"He did it," said Carrie. "He said he did it."

Mr. Robins said, "He said it was an accident. They'll have to prove that it wasn't."

"How are they going to do that?" Mika asked.

"Look for some evidence of his obsession. A diary. Letters. Something that says he did it on purpose."

"He lured her to the house," I said. "Doesn't that show his intentions?"

Chief Stratton nodded. "It'd be enough for me."

"If they don't arrest him, it will never be over," said Mrs. Anglin. "It will be unsolved. I can't bear it."

She clung to her husband, and he said, "We have to be strong."

"I can't stand it. I can't."

"We'll get him," said Carrie with a strange glint in her eye.

Her phone rang again, and she said, "It's Springfield again."

The chief listened and then hung up. A search of Schramm's house had turned up Christine's missing shoe and multiple, unsent letters Schramm had written to the Anglins, saying he was sorry for hurting Christine. That was enough. They arrested him.

The Anglins held each other and wept. We watched their relief pour out of them, but then something caught my eye. My heart nearly stopped, and I grabbed Jess's arm.

"What?" Jess asked.

"Look," I whispered.

She turned and sucked in a breath. Christine, a beautiful

young Christine, was climbing out of the trunk. She was whole and clean, with no salt or blood on her. She smiled at us and said, "Thank you."

We nodded, unable to speak. She turned from us to look at her family with her hand on her chest, smiling and serene. Then she walked out the door. Jess and I looked to see where she went, but Christine was gone. We never saw her again.

"Oh my gosh," said Sandra, wavering in her seat.

"What's wrong?" Mika asked.

"Nothing. I...feel better."

The Anglin family looked at her with puzzled expressions.

Mrs. Anglin said, "I do too. I don't know why. Suddenly, I feel better."

Chief Stratton eyed us, but said, "He's been arrested. That changes everything."

It did change everything in more ways than they would ever know. A little while later, we told the chief and Mika what we'd seen.

"She was in the trunk all along," said Mika.

"At least some of the time. Elsie just didn't want to tell us that."

"The protective nanny," said Jess.

"What now?" I asked.

The chief said we could go, but to expect the Springfield cops to want to question us for themselves. Mom broke away from chatting with Bear and his parents to ask us if she could invite them to the house for dinner. We invited everyone, but only Bear's family wanted to leave the station. They headed out with Mom and we followed, not getting past the door.

Vic Delaney appeared the second the door closed behind Mom. He wore a heavy wool coat with a fur collar turned up to frame his face under a black fedora. "Nice job, ladies."

I crossed my arms. "Now you're talking to us?"

"Now's the time," he said. "Vic Delaney. It's a pleasure to meet you."

"We know who you are," said Jess, moving away from the door to the conference room so no one would see us talking into thin air.

"I know you know," he said.

"Why is now the time?" I asked.

"I wanted to see if you could do it."

"Solve the murder?"

"Yes."

"Why do you care?"

Delaney eyed us with amusement. "It was entertaining to start with, and then it took a turn. I want to hire you."

Jess and I looked at each other, then we both said, "You're dead."

The ghost spread his arms wide. "Clearly, I'm not done."

"You're trying to move on?" Jess asked.

"That is the goal. I've tried to get other living detectives to help, but they refused to see me. I'd given up hope until I got a load of you two in that kitchen."

"You didn't expect us to see you?" I asked.

"I didn't."

Jess wrinkled her nose. "I bet you didn't expect us to solve the crime either."

"I didn't. You are a couple of dames," said Delaney with a roguish grin.

"Well, these dames knocked it out of the park," I said.

"You did. Now I want to hire you."

"This is a business," said Jess. "How are you going to pay us?"

"I've got some berries stashed away," said Delaney.

"How are we supposed to get it?" I asked.

Delaney flipped up his sagging collar. "I got a kid. You solve it, I give him the skinny."

"You're holding out on your own kid?" Jess asked.

"You want the job or not?"

"Depends on what it is?" I asked. "Were you murdered?"

Delaney scoffed. "Do I look like a palooka to you?"

"That depends on what a palooka is," said Jess.

"I died in bed. You ain't got to worry about me. It's a case. I didn't solve it."

"John K. Tunny III?" I asked.

"I knew I picked the right pair of skirts."

"You know women don't like to be called dames or skirts anymore," said Jess.

"I'm wise to it, but it don't concern me. You want the job or not?"

Jess gave him our rate, and he whistled. "You dames are no better than a couple of shylocks."

"That's our rate. Take it or leave it," I said.

Delaney pulled out a pack of cigarettes and lit one with a beautiful silver lighter. "I got no choice." Then he looked back toward the conference room. "You two better blow. We'll talk business later."

Then he was gone, leaving a whisper of cigarette smoke, and a second later Chief Stratton came out. "What are you two doing?"

I smiled at her. "We don't really know yet."

"Why does that worry me?" she asked.

We laughed and assured her we wouldn't cause any problems if we could help it. The problem was we wouldn't be able to help it, but if we could solve a crime from back in 1990, why not 1941? We had a ghost on our side, after all.

Number Eight's driveway didn't have just the Hotchkiss family car in it. The kids were home, and Tank's truck was there alongside Eric's car. I hope my boss wasn't there to ask why I hadn't been knocking out the paperwork. I'd forgotten to tell him what had happened, but I thought finding a body and getting threatened with a shotgun was a pretty decent excuse as excuses go.

I parked on the street and we walked across the lawn, spying a load of boxes on the front porch.

"Are those Christmas decorations?" Jess asked.

"I think so."

The doors swung open and Mariah burst out, running down the well-salted stairs to fling herself into Jess's arms. "Why didn't you tell me?"

"I was going to, but you were at school, and I thought it could wait," said Jess.

"It couldn't wait," said Mariah. "It's a big deal."

The boys came out on the porch, giving me not hugs up but thumbs-up.

"Nice one, Mom," said Henri.

"Thanks, Mom," said Max.

I walked toward the stairs with Jess and Mariah. "Why are you thanking me?"

"Okay," they said. "Thanks, Jess."

What in the world?

"Why are you home?" I asked.

"They let us out early," said Mariah. "I think *someone* told them I was upset."

Jess stopped on the porch, paled, and asked, "Did Uncle Jeff call you? What did he say?"

Mariah wrinkled her nose. "Why would he call? Who's going to tell him?"

Jess and I looked at each other.

"What are we talking about?" I asked.

"You getting attacked in the woods after finding the body," said Henri. "You fought him off and—"

"Bear fought him off," said Max.

"Whatever. Mrs. Johns said we could leave early because you nearly died."

"I bet that wasn't her idea," I said.

"We may have planted the seeds," said Max with a grin. "Mariah is a sensitive soul."

"You dirtbags. I knew it." Mariah turned to Jess. "What were you talking about?"

Jess told us to go inside while she talked to Mariah and I hurried into the foyer, where our coat rack and hall tree were covered in coats.

"Where is everyone?"

"In the ballroom," said Henri.

Sylvia popped her head out of the ballroom door. "I'm showing the Hotchkisses around. I hope you don't mind. Leo asked us to come over."

"Not at all."

The boys went for the ballroom, but I snagged Henri's sleeve. "Why are the Christmas boxes out on the porch?"

"We thought we'd start checking the lights," said Henri. "Bear said he'd help."

"And Mr. Ford's coming for dinner too," said Max.

"He is?"

"Sure. He needs food, and he wants to ask you about the crime. He's totally into it."

Tank came out of the ballroom and said, "He's not the only one. Ready for an interview?"

"Ready for a snack," I said.

"That soup smells amazing," said Tank, and then he turned around. "Bear, you want to do the first interview?"

I didn't hear the answer. I was too busy sniffing. The soup smelled good, but also off somehow.

"Go ahead and help with the tour, guys," I told the boys. "Where's Grandma?"

"In the kitchen with Leo and Eric," said Max.

I went down the hall and the smell got stronger. What was that smell? I couldn't quite place it.

When I walked through the archway, I found Poptart and Pesto curled up in their beds. Poptart's fur was on end, but he wasn't hissing, which was a first, because Leo was at the stove with Mom, hovering over my enormous stockpot. Eric smiled at me as he leaned on the counter, holding a bowl of soup that was putting off a lot of steam.

"Hey, Libby. Nice job today," said Eric.

"Thanks," I said. "What's up with the soup?"

Mom turned around, her face all rosy and her glasses fogged from the steam. "We did it."

"What did you do?" I asked.

Leo turned, and I realized he wasn't wearing his mortician suit. He had on his favorite grandpa sweater and jeans.

"We found the secret to my mother's soup," he said.

"Guess what it is," said Mom.

"It's on the tip of my tongue," I said. "I just can't place that smell."

"Something you would never have put in the soup," said Eric. "Neither would Sylvia."

I drew a blank. There were plenty of things I wouldn't put in a soup, starting with fennel seeds and oysters. But neither of them was it.

Jess and Mariah walked in arm in arm and Mariah said, "It's all over, Libby. Dad's case is closed. I called Uncle Jeff and told him I don't want him saying anything else about Mom. If he does, I won't ever speak to him again."

"You're pretty tough," I said. "You know that?"

"I had to tell her everything," said Jess.

"You were right to."

"Uncle Jeff said he was sorry," said Mariah. "I'm not sure I believe him, but it's almost Thanksgiving, so I'm going to let it slide."

"An excellent policy when it comes to family," said Mom. "Ready for some soup? We got it right."

Mariah made a face. "Why did it have to be cilantro?"

"Cilantro," I said. "Of course."

Mom smiled at me. "Fresh cilantro in the meatballs and as a garnish."

"You're right. I never would've gotten it."

"Is that really what it needed, Leo?" Mariah asked.

"Yes. It's just like when my mother made it."

I was going to ask the two men most affected by Patrick's treachery how the soup made them feel, but I didn't need to.

Leo watched Eric take a spoonful. His shoulders dropped and Leo smiled. "Better, Son?"

"Better, Dad," said Eric.

"A family is only as happy as its unhappiest member." Mom smiled at me. Mariah and Jess hugged. We were better. All of us.

The End

Also by A.W. Hartoin

Historical Thriller

The Paris Package (Stella Bled Book One)

Strangers in Venice (Stella Bled Book Two)

One Child in Berlin (Stella Bled Book Three)

Dark Victory (Stella Bled Book Four)

A Quiet Little Place on Rue de Lille (Stella Bled Book Five)

Young Adult fantasy

Flare-up (Away From Whipplethorn Short)

A Fairy's Guide To Disaster (Away From Whipplethorn Book One)

Fierce Creatures (Away From Whipplethorn Book Two)

A Monster's Paradise (Away From Whipplethorn Book Three)

A Wicked Chill (Away From Whipplethorn Book Four)

To the Eternal (Away From Whipplethorn Book Five)

Mercy Watts Mysteries

Novels

A Good Man Gone (Mercy Watts Mysteries Book One)

Diver Down (A Mercy Watts Mystery Book Two)

Double Black Diamond (Mercy Watts Mysteries Book Three)

Drop Dead Red (Mercy Watts Mysteries Book Four)

In the Worst Way (Mercy Watts Mysteries Book Five)

The Wife of Riley (Mercy Watts Mysteries Book Six)

My Bad Grandad (Mercy Watts Mysteries Book Seven)

Brain Trust (Mercy Watts Mysteries Book Eight)

Down and Dirty (Mercy Watts Mysteries Book Nine)

Small Time Crime (Mercy Watts Mysteries Book Ten)

Bottle Blonde (Mercy Watts Mysteries Book Eleven)

Mean Evergreen (Mercy Watts Mysteries Book Twelve)

Silver Bells at Hotel Hell (Mercy Watts Mysteries Book Thirteen)

<u>Short stories</u>

Coke with a Twist

Touch and Go

Nowhere Fast

Dry Spell

A Sin and a Shame

Paranormal

It Started with a Whisper

About the Author

USA Today bestselling author A.W. Hartoin grew up in rural Missouri, but her grandmother lived in the Central West End area of St. Louis. The CWE fascinated her with its enormous houses, every one unique. She was sure there was a story behind each ornate door. Going to Grandma's house was a treat and an adventure. As the only grandchild around for many years, A.W. spent her visits exploring the many rooms with their many secrets. That's how Mercy Watts and the fairies of Whipplethorn came to be.

As an adult, A.W. Hartoin decided she needed a whole lot more life experience if she was going to write good characters so she joined the Air Force. It was the best education she could've hoped for. She met her husband and traveled the world, living in Alaska, Italy, and Germany before settling in Colorado for nearly eleven years. Now A.W. has returned to Germany and lives in picturesque Waldenbuch with her family and two spoiled cats, who absolutely believe they should be allowed to escape and roam the village freely.

Made in United States
North Haven, CT
26 August 2024

56585699R00189